KNOCK-OFF

It's an unsavory practice in the fashion industry, where imitation is the sincerest form of beating the competition.

KNOCK-OFF

It's murder, the kind that people in any business commit to undercut the competition—permanently.

KNOCK-OFF

It's the hot new police novel that brings Detective Joe Dante of *Midtown South* and *Sixth Precinct* to Fashion Avenue for the toughest case of his career.

Also by Christopher Newman
Published by Fawcett Books:

MIDTOWN SOUTH

SIXTH PRECINCT

MANANA MAN

KNOCK-OFF

Christopher Newman

FAWCETT GOLD MEDAL • NEW YORK

A Fawcett Gold Medal Book
Published by Ballantine Books
Copyright © 1989 by Christopher Newman

Library of Congress Catalog Card Number: 88-92213

ISBN 0-449-13294-3

Printed in Canada

First Edition: April 1989

For Tom Cayler and Clarice Marshall

ACKNOWLEDGMENTS

I would like to thank the following people for their generous assistance in my researching background for this book: Victoria Rastetter, fashion designer; Hank Dunning, fashion photographer; Glenda Price, merchandiser; Detectives Paul Patterson and Joe Firth of NYPD's Safe, Loft, and Truck Unit; Andrea Pincus, Sex Crimes Prosecution Unit of the Manhattan District Attorney's office; and my wife, Susan.

A fiend stands further back who dresses us
    In this grim fashion as you here behold,
        And as we circle all our wounds are healed
            So when the pain-racked round is done, again
            He wields his ax and gashes us afresh.

Dante's *Inferno*, XXVIII

ONE

The lock secured the two huge main doors of Close Apparel's corporate offices on the thirty-ninth floor. Murray Chopnik was pleased that the key moved effortlessly in the cylinder. This was a piece of cake, everything going as advertised. Street-level service ramp and the loading-bay access door. The service elevator locked open and standing at the ready behind him. Even the janitorial coveralls, stolen earlier from the basement, were a fairly decent fit. Murray liked the embroidered name tag identifying him as "Mack."

When the right-hand door gave with an all but imperceptible little snick, the tall, heavyset Texan moved forward with confidence. The same source that had provided the coveralls and keys had guaranteed that the place was all his, until the real janitorial crew reached the thirty-ninth floor at two-thirty A.M. It was still a couple minutes to two, and he had half an hour. The thick industrial carpeting muffled his steps and the wheels of the hand truck he pushed. He approached a huge, sweeping reception desk fronted by a half-wall barrier constructed of what looked like mahogany. The lights had been left on low, revealing the opulent appointments of corporate liquidity

1

in subdued tones. Murray parked the hand truck, circled the half wall, and spread his floor plan on the desk top.

A penlight provided sharper illumination as he determined the direction of his objectives. The design studio lay at the end of the hall running to his left. He was not concerned with any of the other facilities indicated on the blueprint: accounting, customer service, and the executive offices off to his right. Everything he was after was supposed to be sitting on a table in the design studio. This was going to be a quick in-and-out. All nice and neat. Penlight gripped in his teeth, he refolded the plan, retrieved the hand truck, and went to work.

The four cartons were on one of the design studio work surfaces. They were empty now, flaps folded back and recent contents hung on a nearby rack. The end panels were stamped with the logo of Janet Lake Casuals, a subsidiary line produced by the parent company. Its namesake was a hugely successful print model turned movie star, her face as familiar as Ford cars and Wonder bread. Murray quickly placed the boxes on the hand truck, eager to be done and out of there.

Peter Buckley was furious with those arrogant jackasses in Japan. They'd had all the Lake line knitwear specs for a week and still hadn't transmitted their detailed cost break outs. There was no way he could ask Jerry to approve production without them. That afternoon he'd called the Japanese company's New York rep and read him the riot act. The obsequious little fucker had been all apologies and promises. As soon as Peter hung up, he was going to get in touch with the home office and make sure that they transmitted before New York opened business the following morning. If they didn't, Buckley was in more hot water with future shipping schedules than he wanted even to think about. He'd elected to stay all night at the office, in order to receive and check the proposal.

At two o'clock the light on his console indicating FAX transmission still hadn't lit, and he was getting more impatient by the minute. To make matters worse, Jerry, bankrupt of further patience, had just stalked off announcing that he was grabbing a few things he'd left in his office and going home to bed. The Janet Lake line was Peter's baby but Jerry's plum and ultimate responsibility. He'd stuck his neck out to put the label together, fighting the objections of his wife and partner every step of the way. Close Apparel had never put anyone's name but Felicity's on a line. Bringing a luminary like Janet Lake on board may have made good business sense, but it was unprecedented. Felicity Close presided over her empire with jealous domination.

Peter's gnawing impatience drove him to pace the floor of his office. He was caught up on everything he might turn to for distraction. Lack of sleep was becoming a consideration. At just past two he filled a kettle from the hall water cooler and set it to boil on a maddeningly slow hot plate. To kill a little more time he dropped to the floor and cranked off another thirty push-ups. That made for two hundred and forty since midnight. Just as he started to catch his breath, the kettle finally boiled. He had pushed himself to his feet, reached for it, and begun pouring into a teapot when the goddamn FAX machine kicked in.

Chopnik was just leaving the design studio, pushing the hand truck before him, when he heard a curious noise emanating from an alcove down at the far end of the hall. A mechanical humming. Not loud, but sudden and persistent. His mind raced back over the blueprint topography. There were a number of rooms along here, including something called the pattern room. The machine noise was coming from a location directly opposite it. He couldn't recall what the designation was for the equipment in that alcove, and now advanced on it.

The apparatus in the alcove was perched on a pedestal. It looked something like either a teletype machine or some sort of computer printout station. At two-fifteen in the morning, the thing was humming merrily away, slowly spewing printout from its carriage. The rag trade wasn't Murray's regular beat. He didn't know whether to find this phenomenon curious or not, but the *real* janitorial staff was due on the floor in another fifteen minutes. He figured he'd wasted enough time staring at this contraption and started to push on toward reception.

Peter Buckley was moving with such singular purpose that he all but collided head-on with the big janitor's hand truck before pulling up in the nick of time. He hadn't heard anyone arrive on the floor and was surprised that the cleaning crew might actually be early. The maintenance and janitorial crews in this building were notorious for chronic ass dragging.

"Where are you going with those?" He indicated the four cartons stacked on the hand truck. "We don't throw them out; we save them."

The boxes were always saved. These had contained the Janet Lake summer-line salesmen's samples, which had arrived the previous morning. When the samples from the last season were removed from the showroom, they were packed away in these empty boxes and shipped back to the warehouse in Brooklyn. On the thirty-ninth floor of a midtown office tower, empty boxes were damn hard to come by. His assistant, Hillary, should have taped a note to these before racing off to catch that late-season skiing in Stowe.

Murray's mind raced. This joker had seen him and could make an identification. What the hell was he doing here anyway? These offices were supposed to be empty until two-thirty. The man confronting him was obviously accustomed to command. The fact that he was bare-chested and barefoot, dressed only in a pair of jeans, had not affected his attitude. This was his domain. On the other hand, Murray was experiencing the adrenaline-charged effects of the man's surprise appearance. It only took seconds to sort through his options, weigh them, and come

4

to the only conclusion. As he did so, he sized up his opponent.

Five ten, maybe. Nice, tightly muscled build on a spare frame. Twenty years younger than Murray. Thirty years old at the outside. But too light in the ass to make him a formidable adversary. Murray figured he had seventy-five pounds on him and a world of experience.

"Just doin' my job," he murmured, feigning to ignore this guy's demands and push on past. "Crew chief tells me someone called down for us to haul this shit outta here, I haul it out." They were shoulder to shoulder when Murray threw the forearm. His elbow caught the kid in the solar plexus, pushing a whoosh of air out of his lungs. The force of the blow threw him backward into the door of the pattern room. When it gave, he tumbled on inside.

As he agonized to get his wind back, the kid's face froze in a mask of outrage. To Chopnik's surprise, he recovered his balance quickly and got his feet planted firmly beneath him. In the room behind his adversary, Murray could see massive worktables and various sewing machines. Potential cover. Murray knew he was running out of time and had to get this over with quickly. He was plotting a means of getting the job done when the kid squared off and came at him.

From the way he moved, Murray guessed that he'd probably studied Akido, but it might also have been kung fu. He moved with athletic grace, knees bent slightly and his weight up on the balls of his feet. Instead of retreating and seeking cover, he was *attacking*. After closing the distance between them, the kid suddenly left the ground with a balletic leap and snaked a foot toward the side of Murray's head. But Murray's head wasn't there anymore. It had vanished from the spot where it was supposed to be. Still airborne and leg coming back from full extension, the guy was vulnerable. Murray drove his own heel into the exposed groin. All the man's systems went into shock; his body folded like a marionette cut loose from it's strings. The blood lust was upon Murray now. He snatched a heavy cast-iron object off a nearby table and brought it crashing down on the side of his opponent's skull. In a great profusion of gushing blood, the dying body began to convulse.

Chopnik's mind was racing. This wasn't a simple in-and-out job anymore. With a dead guy on the floor in here, the big finger was going to point right at the theft of four cartons and that was going to give rise to some dangerous speculation. He was going to have to make it look like he'd been after something else, and he was going to have to do it quickly.

The cartons were stamped with the logo of Janet Lake Casuals, and it occurred to him that this was as logical a place as any to start. His inside source had indicated that all the real nuts-and-bolts work was done in either this, the pattern room, or the design studio. Ignoring the mess on the floor, Murray now flipped on the overhead lights and took a quick look around. All along the far wall, a rack was hung with cardboard patternlike objects suspended from strings. The length of the rack was cut up into sections, each individually labeled. Murray hurried to the one designated Janet Lake, tore down an armload of these pattern things, bore them out into the hall, and stuffed them folded into the top of one of the four big cartons. Then he turned to push the hand truck back down the hall, retracing his steps to the design studio. He had three cartons to fill with everything he could find with the Janet Lake designation on it and less than ten minutes to work with.

Once he reached the design studio, he threw all caution to the wind, flipped the lights on, and started pawing frantically through the contents of the various file cabinets. When he came across the Janet Lake drawers, it became immediately apparent that the contents were arranged by season. It occurred to him that a thief who knew what he was doing would be after new stuff and not the designs for things already being discounted on remainder racks. Anything labeled summer or fall of the current year went into his cartons. He then emptied the wall rack of the recently arrived summer salesmen's samples just for good measure. With the clock ticking down to within minutes of two-thirty, he raced for the elevator bank, his adrenaline high starting to wear rough and raw at the edges.

TWO

It was not a night Joe Dante thought he might want to remember. In fact, it came toward the end of a month he was *sure* he didn't want to remember. Or the month before, and the month before *that*. There were problems in trying to live with romantic bankruptcy. Tonight the detective had attempted either to deal with or escape from those problems by getting drunk. He wasn't at all clear as to which path he'd set out upon, but the end result was clear enough. At five minutes to midnight, he was on his knees over the bowl in the bathroom. The puking seemed to do him some good. It stopped his head from spinning. Still, he slept fitfully. It was in the midst of this less than satisfactory slumber that the phone next to his pillow, the one designated for job business only, rang. As he clutched the receiver to his ear, a squinting glance at his clock radio made it out to be four-eighteen. The glorious precision of digital technology did nothing to comfort him.

"Yeah." It came out as a sort of gasp.

"Sorry, Joey." The gruff voice of Deputy Chief Gus Lieberman was apologetic in tone. Lieberman headed up the Manhattan South Detective Command, to which Joe was currently assigned. "We just got a real nasty one. I want you on hand to take a look. Rag trade designer with his head caved in on the premises of Close Apparel, Incorporated."

Even in his bleary state Dante recognized the name. Scantily clad, seductive women pushed it in magazine ads, TV spots, and on bus shelter broadsides all over the city.

"When?"

"Poor fucker's still warm. Nighttime janitorial crew stumbled over him about an hour and a quarter ago."

Joe got himself upright and was swinging his legs over the edge of the bed. He planted his feet for balance as his brain attempted a one and a half gainer, aborting midflip.

"Who's on the scene?" he asked.

"Regular night beat from the Borough Command Task Force. Whip from Midtown South. I've got a call in to a Sergeant Klein from Safe, Loft, and Truck. The intrigues of Fashion Avenue are part of his beat."

Dante was putting some muddled thoughts together.

"Do us a favor," he suggested. "See if you can get Rocky Conklin out of bed. It's a good bet the tabloids will want to sensationalize this one. Best to have a crackerjack ghoul working the carcass."

After giving him the precise location of the crime scene, Lieberman rang off. Dante took a deep breath and pushed himself to his feet. He recalled watching Paul Newman soak his head in ice water to counteract the effects of excess drink, first in *Harper* and then later in *The Sting*. It had looked pretty effective both times. Romantic bankruptcy or not, he knew he was going to have to stop doing this to himself.

The call from the Midtown South duty captain woke Felicity Close from solitary slumber at her Beekman Place town house. His news was shocking. Peter Buckley, the designer of their new Janet Lake sportswear line, had been murdered sometime after midnight on the premises of Close Apparel's midtown corporate headquarters.

Felicity was a diminutive, compact woman of forty-four years who was fabled in the trade for the energetic swath she cut. At this early predawn hour she felt at least ten years older as she surveyed her unseasonably tanned but haggard countenance in the bath mirror. Just dragging herself out of bed had taken untold effort. Charity fetes were becoming the death of her, with their rich foods and drink from caterers who'd never heard of calories or cholesterol. Charity fetes and the extraordinary effort of continual ebullience. These things took a toll she could read in the tiny lines in that face. Collagen injections only did so much. More plastic surgery was scheduled, a procedure slightly more complicated than the simple tit and tummy tucks she'd had done in Rio last fall.

She sighed, twisted on the tap, and splashed cold water on her face. It was time to kick good old Jerry out of bed.

Ensconced in his separate bedroom, Jerry Rabinowitz had heard the phone ring and chosen to ignore it. Then there came an anxious rapping at his door. He tried to ignore that as well. Jerry and Felicity shared a home and the responsibility of running a major corporation, but they were not lovers or even very good friends anymore. The pressure of life in the fast lane had combined with admittedly different appetites to push them into all but separate lives.

Jerry's tightly wound wife, wearing her perpetually intense "home face," entered his room and began to shake him violently.

"Jerry! Wake up! That was the police!"

He rolled slowly onto his back and rubbed his eyes. He would work the grogginess angle.

"What in the name of . . . ?"

"The *police*. A Captain Something-or-other from Midtown South. Peter Buckley's been murdered!"

He sat bolt upright. "Jesus! When? Where?"

"At the *offices*!"

Jerry looked stunned. Felicity fixed him with an impatient glare.

"I thought you two were there *together*, waiting for that transmission from Tokyo."

He shook his head and ran one open hand across his face.

"We were, but I bailed out a little after one o'clock. The fucking thing still hadn't arrived, and Peter offered to stay on. Jesus. It must have happened right after I left. Did they say what time?"

Felicity was still exhibiting a lot of impatience as she turned and headed for the door. "I didn't ask. But someone ransacked the design studio and pattern room. I'll be ready in ten minutes. Shake a leg."

Naked, Jerry started to climb out of bed. "Goddamn," he murmured. "We had three whole fall lines on the boards in there."

It was one of those late-March cold snaps that Joe Dante had learned to loathe. Even after forty years in this city, he couldn't get used to subfreezing mercury as late as Saint Paddy's Day or the first day of spring. Hell, baseball season was starting in two weeks, and he was out there on the sidewalk with a scarf wrapped around his neck and coat collar clutched up around his ears. He envied his car as he wandered down Perry Street to collect it. The Corvette was nestled in a nice, steam-heated garage.

En route, his drink-muddled brain and aching heart wrestled with why he and the woman he still loved hadn't been able to do anything in the last months but torture each other. That same brain had been trying to convince his heart, for the past six weeks, that it was over. Every time he thought he finally had his emotions pinned to the mat, they managed to wriggle loose and run amok. He drank in hopes of drowning them. His heart still ached. Right now, any spare imaginative energy he could muster was used to dream of coffee.

Dante parked among the city vehicles that crowded the street and sidewalk in front of a big glass-and-steel midtown office tower. Prominent were a host of blue-and-whites, but just as many of the cars were unmarked. There were also a forensics lab van and a meat wagon. Two uniforms monitored foot traffic into the crime scene from behind a barrier of yellow plastic tape. They stared stoically at the several news hounds who'd managed to tear themselves away from late-night poker games. Three more uniforms stood conversing inside the revolving glass doors. None of them looked as likely to freeze to death as their less fortunate brothers on the sidewalk outside. Dante ambled to the tape, threw a leg over and flashed his tin at one of the pair manning the barricades. The cop gestured him on, evidently grateful for any excuse to move his arms. The three boys inside gave his gold detective's shield a second look and directed him to an elevator bank leading to the thirty-ninth floor.

The doors of the elevator opened onto a lavishly appointed reception area, complete with a half acre of rosewood desk, a couple more acres of similar wood paneling, and monochromatic appointments done in hues from plum to dusty rose. Cops were huddled all about, conversing in subdued tones. The pop of a photographer's strobe came from down a wide hallway to the left. There was yet another knot of people blocking access to it as Dante started over.

"I understand, Captain. But my husband and I are concerned about the condition of our design studio. That's the heart and soul of our business back there."

The woman speaking these words delivered them as though she expected their weight and her presence behind them to clear any obstruction in her path. She was a handsome woman, in a petite, severe sort of way. The coat she sported was too slick-looking to be mink. Dante suspected sable, but he wasn't familiar enough with furs of the hundred-thousand-dollar variety to be sure.

At his approach the beseiged Captain Cullen, commander of uniformed patrol at Midtown South, glanced up.

"The deputy chief's down at the end of the hall, Joe. They're all waiting."

Dante nodded and swung around to confront the imperious little woman head-on.

"I take it you're Felicity Close, ma'am." There was sugar in the way he said it. "You're something of a legend in your own time, I guess. You and your husband here." He turned to make friendly eye contact with the man in snakeskin boots and a raccoon coat standing next to her. He, too, was slender and a bit on the short side at maybe five six. His hair was thin, balding on the top, and his most prominent feature was a pair of dark, penetrating eyes. Both Felicity Close and her husband were uncommonly tan for this time of year.

"And you are . . . ?" she asked.

"Detective Dante, ma'am. Manhattan South Borough Command's Special Task Force. Deputy Chief Lieberman's right-hand man." He let it hang there while the fur-bearing couple sized him up. Privately he didn't give a damn if they liked what they saw, but he wanted all the potentially helpful elements in a murder investigation to feel, at least to some extent, that they were all on the same side.

What they saw was a good-sized, competent-looking man in warm, casual street clothes. At six two and a hundred ninety-five pounds he outsized them both by quite a bit. His short, brush-cut sandy hair was rumpled, and his eyes were reddened by lack of sleep and the previous evening's excesses.

"Captain Cullen told me on the phone that our design studio has been ransacked," Felicity Close told him. "While we're horribly shocked at what's happened to Peter, we're also concerned about what might have been taken. It could have direct bearing on why the poor man was killed."

Dante digested this and moved to put her at ease. "That's an interesting point, ma'am. I'd like to pursue it. But right now, that's a crime scene back there. I'm going to have to ask you to be patient. The men in there are trained professionals. You'll have to trust us not to make matters any worse."

Jerry Rabinowitz, quiet up to this point but obviously steaming with pent-up irritation, blew.

"Those heavy-handed lummoxes don't know fuck-all about fashion design! We bill over a hundred million dollars with the lines on those boards."

Dante repressed his impatience and forced a mollifying smile. "Sorry, friend. One of your people got himself killed in there. Until I give it back to you, that's *my* domain now." He turned, nodded pleasantly to the lady, and strolled away down the hall.

Another knot of plainclothesmen was obstructing the door to a room on his right. He paused, prepared to poke his head in, when he spotted Gus Lieberman waving to him from a door at the end of the hall. Joe stood where he was as the deputy chief and medical examiner's pathologist, Rocky Conklin, approached.

"I hear you're the one suggested they drag me outta bed," Conklin greeted him. "I hope it's my shift when they finally drag *your* sorry ass onto a slab."

Joe grinned as widely as his condition would allow. "Don't give me any preferential treatment, Rock. The way I look at it, dead is dead."

Lieberman, a big bear of a man with thick, wavy gray hair and heavy jowls, cleared his throat. "You two clowns about finished?"

"Show me what you've got," Dante suggested.

Conklin pointed toward the door Joe had just passed. "Take a deep breath, big guy. This butcher wasn't interested in any of the finer cosmetic considerations. But like you say, dead is dead."

The crowd of detectives loitering outside the pattern room parted and let the three men pass. Lieberman pushed back a white plastic screen draped over the entrance, and Rocky led the way inside. The place was crowded with big worktables, rolls of paper, a rack crammed with hanging paper, and a series of contraptions that could have been sewing machines. Several lab technicians were methodically going over the room with fine-tooth combs. The senior of them was a shiny-bald guy named Bernie Horvath. The veteran lab man straightened to nod in greeting.

"This one must be hot, boys. They just got a *real* detective out of bed. Jesus, Joey, you look like hell."

Dante sighed, acknowledging him with a half lift of his right hand. "Thanks, Bernie. It's not enough beauty sleep."

The corpse was covered by another plastic sheet, the blue rubber body bag it would eventually wind up in lying zipped open alongside it. The contents of the dead man's wallet identified him as one Peter Buckley of Greenpoint, Brooklyn. Dante got his first look at him as Conklin lifted the sheet. The attitude caused by the convulsions of violent death was grotesquely unnatural. Blood soaked the gray industrial carpet around him. He was clad only in a pair of faded blue denim jeans, torso naked and feet bare. A good portion of his gray matter spilled from a gaping gash in the left side of his head.

Dante had already done all the puking he was going to do, but his stomach did a back flip just to remind him it was still on the job. "Weapon?" he asked. As he spoke, he stepped up and dropped to his haunches. A sight like this could do untold wonders for a hangover. The blow had crushed the whole side of the man's skull from temple to occipital lobe.

Horvath pointed toward a curious-looking metal object sealed in a clear plastic bag on the nearest table. "That gizmo. We're still waiting for word on what it is. Made of cast iron. Must weigh a good five or six pounds."

"How long's he been dead, Rock?"

Conklin gave him one of those little wiggles of the hand which suggested imprecision. "Two, three hours max. I'd put it sometime between one and three A.M. Definitely after midnight."

Dante's eyes travelled across the health-club musculature of the torso to the dead man's waist. He wore no belt. Dante also noticed that one of the several fly buttons was undone.

"Curious get-up for late-night work around the office, eh, pal?" he murmured. "What were we up to?" He glanced up at Gus. "Were the lights on or off when they found him?"

"Burning bright. Whole room just like this; the chunk of metal dropped at his feet. Everything else more or less neat. It's the design studio down the hall that's the mess. Somebody gave the contents of one filing cabinet a pretty good going-over."

Dante stood a little too quickly and winced. A wave of nausea swept over him, having more to do with last night's indiscretion than with the spectacle of gore at his feet.

"He's all yours, Rock. I'm interested in why his pants are all but down around his knees. Keep an eye peeled, huh?"

The pathologist assured him that he would and promised to get to the autopsy first thing. Gus led his crack crime hound out the door and down the hall.

"I guess I don't gotta mention that the broad and the concrete cowboy you conversed with on your way in are big news," the deputy chief muttered.

"Nice coats," Joe replied.

"Fuck their coats. They can make big trouble for us. That woman does charity work with every hotshot in the city. She eats dinner with his honor, the mayor."

Dante touched his elbow reassuringly. "Relax, boss. I'll handle them with kid gloves. You got any idea why the dead guy was here so late?"

"Something about an overdue transmission from the Orient. I'm hoping your kid-glove approach will help fill in some of the details."

The design studio floor looked like a tornado had swept across it. The lab boys were in here, too, just packing up after dusting and photographing the havoc. The evidence of their attentions lay on every surface in the form of light white powder. After Gus had stepped in behind him, Joe eased the door closed and glanced slowly around.

"Only the one cabinet broken into?"

"Just the one," Gus replied. "Contents emptied and strewn all over the floor."

Joe thought this over. "Perp was after something specific," he said at length.

Lieberman stood with his back leaning against the door. There was a gleam of interest in his eyes. He'd watched Dante sink his teeth into cases before. Joe's approach was not always orthodox, but his instincts often proved uncanny in their accuracy. Once those teeth were into something, Gus could trust him to hang on until he could shake something satisfactory out of it. Over the years they'd covered an awful lot of ground together. Joe had helped make him look so good to the brass-button crowd downtown that they'd recently made Gus one of their elite inner circle.

Fifteen years separated the two men. The deputy chief's once formidable linebacker's build had shifted its center of gravity downward under the weight of too many hero sandwiches and too much desk time. In contrast Dante fought the battle of encroaching middle age by staying in fighting trim. Both had the same penetrating eyes and no-nonsense approach to an investigation. Gus was now one of a handful considered to be in direct contention when the chief of detectives retired in August. The smart money had him getting the nod.

"You say that because he only dug into one cabinet?"

"Yep."

"You think the kid in there surprised him?"

Joe held up his hand and shook his head. "I ain't going *that* far. It's a bet. Even a pretty good one. But there's no sign of forced entry, right? That guy and the perp could have been in cahoots over something and had a falling out. It's way too early to speculate."

"You look like you crawled through hell last night."

"Somewhere in the vicinity."

Gus pushed himself away from the door as the lab techs

left, lugging their gear. He began pacing the floor as the two of them found themselves alone in there.

"Still Rosa?"

Dante had eased back from the mess on the floor and come to rest with one shoulder up against a blank wall.

"Yep."

Gus sighed. "You're gonna kill yourself over something you can't fix anyway."

Joe was staring at his feet and now shook his head slowly in resignation. "That's the problem, Gus. I *know* I can't fix it. I'm not sure I even want to. It's just my pride."

"So it's time to move on, Joey. Give it up. She's dating Bob Talbot pretty seriously now, and that oughta tell you something. That prissy, ass-sucking son of a bitch is an entirely different breed of cop."

Dante shoved himself away from the wall with a shrug of his shoulders. Hands plunged deep in his pockets, he wandered to the big sweep of glass at the far end of the room and stared out across midtown to the east. A faint pink glow from the sun was developing on the far horizon.

"Hunches?" Gus asked.

"Just some vague ones." In his haggard, down-spirited condition, Joe didn't look any more like a detective right then than he looked Italian. His grandparents hailed from a little village above the Alpine town of Bolzano, thirty miles from the Austrian frontier. He supposed a case could be made for his being a detective, too. There were the battle scars of eighteen years in the job, proving that he'd at least gone through the motions.

"I want to know why that guy in there is only half-dressed. I want to know why there's no sign of forced entry. I want to know what, if anything, was stolen from this file cabinet. I want to know how the perp got out of this building without being seen. There is, I assume, twenty-four-hour security in a dump like this."

A knock sounded at the door, and Gus moved to open it. The florid-faced Captain Cullen stood on the threshold with a second, slightly out of breath man.

"Sergeant Klein from Safe, Loft, and Truck, Gus. And the PC sent Captain Talbot to get the lowdown. He's in the reception area. Him and that new public information officer, Rosa Losada, are holding the company honcho's hands."

It came as no surprise that the commissioner would send an emissary to the scene of a murder involving a high-profile outfit like Close Apparel. Tony Mintoff was more politician than cop.

Lieberman stood aside and asked Sergeant Klein to enter. He shook the man's hand. "You made decent time," he observed.

"Coming off Staten Island at *this* hour? At seventy-five, I must've passed maybe two cars." Klein was of medium height, built like a fireplug, and sported a profusion of curly black hair. "It's actually a fuckin' pleasure, Chief. I don't fight too much rush hour traffic on my beat. Wanna let me in on what you've got?"

Gus introduced his own man. "Meet my Special Task Force team leader, Joe Dante. As long as we push this thing from Borough Command, he's your contact."

Dewey and Joe shook hands. Safe, Loft, and Truck dealt with safe crackings, truck hijacks, and garment industry break-ins like the one they were now investigating. Klein, the resident expert, began to nose around the room a bit.

"Design and manufacture data."

"How's that?" Dante asked. "This is all so much junk to us."

Klein stooped to retrieve a ring binder from a pile at his feet and began to paw through it with his big, short-fingered hands. "Spec sheets here." He flipped it over to glance at the spine notations. "Spring '87. Janet Lake Casuals. That's a relatively new line these people do. Big success. This shit here is all the precise manufacturing specs." He nudged open another binder with the toe of his shoe. "Lab dips. They specify the exact fabric dye color for each item in the line."

"It looks like the perp was after something specific," Dante ventured.

Dewey tossed the binder in his hands back onto the stack at his feet. "No doubt. I'd bet money against good odds that the binders for an entire future line ain't in with this other trash."

"That's what he was after? Why?"

Klein flashed him a smug little grin. "To knock off the entire fucking line, wholesale. Or to auction it off to the highest bidding douche bag who does that sorta thing on a regular basis. There's a rodent under every other rock in the rag trade."

Dante stood quietly for a moment, absorbing this. "Homicide," he said at length. "Are the stakes in this game high enough to justify it?"

Now Klein shrugged. "You gotta ask those two in the fur coats out there just how much revenue a line like this generates. Then you gotta consider that some coked-up freak'd dust a dude for a gram in this town."

"No evidence of forced entry," Joe said. "What does that tell you?"

"Same thing it tells you. That maybe there was an inside man. Could be the inside man is the dude in there with his brains on the floor. Get the goods and cut out an expensive accomplice. Look at it that way and maybe it adds up."

THREE

Murray Chopnik, now safely tucked away in his West 77th Street apartment, was working on his third big tumbler of straight bourbon. Throughout the drive uptown, wrestling the cartons upstairs, and ditching the stolen van, he became increasingly angry. Now home, he wasn't able to sleep. He knew he'd been set up, and he knew for his clever friends there was going to be hell to pay.

Outside his living room window the sun was coming up. He was bone weary and well on his way toward being drunk. His only solace at that moment was the payoff. The stuff was safely stacked on his dining room floor. The seeds of a fortune. Bumpy road or not, he was still in the driver's seat, and anyone who thought differently was sadly mistaken. Murray made his way in the world by learning early on how to take care of irritating problems, his own and other people's. Hell, growing up as a Jew in Midland, Texas, he'd cut his teeth on redneck hatred and left plenty of tough guys drinking dinner through straws along the way.

The image of that kid, convulsing there on the floor with his brains hanging out, came vividly to mind. He took another huge swallow of bourbon, his eyes squeezed shut, and then another, and then he drained the glass.

Lieberman led Klein to the pattern room for a quick look around before letting Felicity Close and her husband make an appraisal of damages from the company's point of view. As he walked beside the Safe, Loft, and Truck detective, Dante thought about the man with the raccoon coat, the snakeskin boots, and the handsome, intense wife.

He asked Dewey for a little background. "So tell me what you know about the happy couple."

Klein glanced over. "Felicity and Jerry? She's the chairman and he's the CEO. The company might be her namesake, but he's the real horsepower under the hood. They took it public in '82, but they still control the single biggest chunk of stock."

Dante was impressed. "You seem to know a lot about the players, even without a program."

"Only the superstars. You haven't been reading your *Women's Wear Daily*."

Joe chuckled. "That anything like the *Sporting News*?"

"Different addiction. Same general idea."

"Jerry said he billed a hundred million on what's on the *boards* in there. That kind of number real?"

"Close Apparel? All their lines for a single big season? Easy. We're talking major league here. If you count all the other pies they got their fingers in—cosmetics, accessories, lingerie, and a whole load of other shit—they gotta bill close to five hundred million a year worldwide."

"You learn all this from working Safe, Loft, and Truck?"

It was Klein's turn to chuckle. "Not likely. All I've learned in Safe, Loft, and Truck is how to drink too much coffee and eat too much fast food. My mom and pop were both garmentos. Mom made patterns for an outfit over on Broadway and 28th. Dad was a salesman. Hell, I grew up on Fashion Avenue."

They'd entered the pattern room, where they stood aside

as the corpse, zipped into the body bag and strapped to a stretcher, was wheeled out. When the plastic drape dropped back into place over the open doorway, only Dante, Klein, and Lieberman were in the room.

Compared to the mess in the design studio, this room was relatively neat, discounting the gore-soaked carpet near the door. Klein walked through, observing with eyes and hands. Eventually, he came to the pattern rack along the back wall and pulled up. His eyes traveled along it.

"I wondered."

"What?" Joe prodded.

"If the slopers were gonna be here. They ain't."

Confused, Dante stepped forward. "Give me another hint."

Dewey pointed to a section in the rack where the items hanging from it weren't so tightly packed as the rest. On the wall above the rack, boldly lettered signs indicated which particular Close Apparel line was hung below them. The sign above the section with gaps in it read: JANET LAKE.

"That rifled file cabinet in there. And all the shit dumped on the floor. Spec and design criteria for Janet Lake Casuals. A load of the slopers is missing, too."

"Slopers?"

"Designs change, season to season. The fit never does. They got permanent cardboard patterns that the new design patterns are cut around. Slopers. It's lookin' more and more like your perp was after the Janet Lake line."

As Joe and Gus tried to digest everything this rag trade encyclopedia revealed to them, Dewey elaborated. "Close Apparel is as hot as they come right now. Relatively new and in touch. Janet Lake is the hottest new thing they do. If a guy had the right connections, stealing this line, wholesale, could end up bein' real profitable."

"Hang on," Dante said. "Something isn't adding for me. It's a brand-new line. If some guy steals it "whole-sale," as you put it, I don't see the point. Wouldn't the company just have to design it all over again. Something entirely different?''

The sergeant shook his head emphatically. ''Not if *these* designs have already been put into production. The shit in that cabinet is *this* office's set of specs. The manufacturing facility's got it's own set. For a line due out next fall, they've definitely started on it already. Once that's happened, there's no turning back. These schedules are *tight*.''

For Dante it came suddenly clear. ''Timing. That's why the perp needed an insider.''

Klein made a gun out of his right hand and shot him with his index finger. ''Now you're zeroin' in. He'd need to *know* the crap'd been put into production . . . or the stuff he stole wouldn't be worth shit.''

''And the accomplice gets whacked once access is gained?'' Dante was speculating now.

''Maybe. It's sure a thought. You got a shitload of motives. Some kinda disagreement over how they split the take. Simple greed. Or maybe it was in the killer's plan all along.''

''And maybe the kid *did* surprise him, and the insider is someone else altogether.''

Klein walked away from the pattern rack, planted his hands on the edge of a worktable, and hoisted himself up to sit on it. He addressed Gus now.

''I see two avenues of approach, Chief. This guy and his team hunt around the inside here at Close. Me and my guys poke around in the trade for someone trying to swing a deal for the stolen shit.''

Lieberman turned to his team leader. ''That make sense to you, Joey?''

Dante shrugged. ''He and his guys know this turf. They've already got their ears out on the street. Me? I don't even know what to call the murder weapon yet.''

Klein's interest was piqued. ''Where is it?''

''They've already taken it to the lab,'' Gus told him. He looked around the room. ''But it wasn't any different than that." He pointed to a squat, cast iron object with a handle running back along an oblong body at forty-five degrees.

"A rabbit."

Joe and the deputy chief glanced at each other.

"A what?" Dante asked.

"A rabbit. Because it sorta looks like one. It's for punching holes to run the hanging strings through." He indicated the pattern rack, and sure enough, every pattern and sloper was suspended by a string tie.

"Another mystery solved." As Lieberman said it, he glanced at his watch. It was going on six o'clock. "I suppose the time has come to let the company bigwigs survey the havoc, huh?"

"Either confirm our suspicions or blow the little boat we just built right out of the water," Joe agreed. "Might as well bring them on."

Jerry Rabinowitz, an unlikely looking chief executive officer if Dante had ever seen one, was pacing the floor of the reception area like a caged hamster. If it were humanly possible, Joe was sure the man, who resembled a weasel in that ridiculous fur coat, would have had smoke pouring out of his ears. He whirled on the two detectives and their boss as they approached.

"I'm fed up with this bullshit! That's this company's lifeblood in there. Crime scene or no crime scene, I need to assess the damage."

Joe hardly paid attention to him. Rosa Losada and Captain Bob Talbot, both dressed in their spiffy big-building uniforms, were standing off to one side with Felicity Close. They looked like a matched pair, those two. Rosa was as radiantly beautiful as ever, even if that lustrous mane of black hair had been chopped into the contemporary style of anchorpersons on the evening news. *He* looked like a Park Avenue prince, true to his prep school and Ivy League pedigree. The Ken and Barbie of the downtown power base. Seeing them there aggravated the misery of Dante's nasty hangover.

Before anyone could react to Jerry's outburst, his wife reached out and caught him by the arm. Her expression was cool as she pinned him with it.

"The damage is done, Jerry. These men are just doing their jobs. Please."

Rabinowitz clamped his mouth shut so hard that his jaw muscles jumped.

"We were hoping you'd take a look at the design studio now," the deputy chief told them. "Your assessment of the damage is important to us. Detective Dante and Sergeant Klein will have questions. Please try to answer them as accurately as possible." He stood aside and held out a hand, indicating that the way was now clear.

Jerry broke away and hurried down the hall with Dewey Klein right on his heels. Dante hung back a bit to fall in step beside the Close woman. He noticed that she carried that tight little body elegantly. If she was suffering from lack of sleep, it showed only in a slight weariness etched around her eyes.

"We're sorry about the inconvenience, ma'am." He ventured it in a conversational tone. "It's a nasty hour, and I'm sure your husband isn't accustomed to being told what he can do in his own domain."

Felicity Close appraised the strapping, sandy-haired detective. The shirt he'd put on was rumpled. His eyes were more than a little bloodshot. Her look said that she was seeing it all.

"My husband is quite single-minded, Officer. He's upset. Peter Buckley was someone he worked very closely with. In fact, he was here with him most of the night, poor man."

That little tidbit got Joe's complete attention. Rosa, just a few paces behind him, might as well have been a million miles away.

"Come again? He was *here* with him tonight?"

"Most of it. There was some sort of a delay on a cost analysis from Japan. They had to have it in order to approve start-up on next fall's knitwear production."

"But Buckley stayed and your husband left?"

She shrugged. "Apparently. The transmission still hadn't come through by one o'clock, so Jerry went home. Or so I presume. That's what he says he did. I didn't hear him come in."

Dante found the revelation curious. The man's wife was putting him at the scene of a murder within a hair of when it might well have happened.

"Is that normal?"

"That I didn't hear him come in? We keep very different schedules."

"No, ma'am. That anyone would work so late."

"Oh. Quite normal, actually. We do a lot of manufacturing in the Orient. Communications with them can happen at the most god-awful hours. If there's a crisis, someone will generally stay on until it's resolved."

"And there was a crisis last night?"

At that query she smiled indulgently. "I'm afraid that is something you'll have to ask Jerry. It was something to do with the Janet Lake line. That's one of *his* pets."

They reached the door to the design studio and followed Rabinowitz and Dewey Klein inside. Beyond the big sweeping windows at the east end of the room, morning had broken across the frozen midtown cityscape. Steam from boilers in the bowels of great buildings adorned rooftops like whitened ostrich plumes. As he contemplated this scene, Dante found himself wanting it to be spring in the worst way. He also wanted to shove Bob Talbot out the nearest window, but none of them appeared to open. Rabinowitz was already on his knees, pawing frantically through the debris on the floor before the ransacked file cabinet.

"The sons of bitches have stolen my fall line! They've killed my most talented designer and taken the most wonderful work he's ever done!"

Dante turned from the view and spoke. "I understand you were with him for most of last night. Correct?"

Jerry shot a glance at his wife and then quickly nodded.

27

"That's right. We were waiting for a knitwear cost pro-posal from Tokyo. It still hadn't arrived by nearly one o'clock, so I called it a night."

Dante contemplated the man there on his knees. "The medical examiner's preliminary guess is that Peter Buckley was killed some time between midnight and three. When you left, Buckley was still alive, I presume?"

Rabinowitz shoved himself back on his haunches and shot to his feet. "And just what the hell is *that* supposed to mean? Of course he was still alive. I left him in his office, as alive as you and me."

"I'm not accusing you of anything, Mr. Rabinowitz. I'm just trying to get a fix on the time frame."

"I left right around one," Jerry insisted. "I'm not sure of the exact time. I decided to hit the road, and then we talked a few minutes about what was on the schedule for today. I left him very much alive, Officer."

"He was sound asleep at home when Captain Cullen called," Felicity offered helpfully.

Dante didn't mention that Cullen had called her some-time after four. Plenty of time between then and one, or even two, to fall asleep.

Dewey Klein took up the line of questioning.

"Can I assume that the stolen stuff—next fall, you said— is already in production?"

Jerry threw up his hands in exasperation. "*Hell*, yes. Why else steal it? Jesus Christ! If these guys are good, we could be talking about being cut out of as much as ten, fifteen million here. That line's performing like Secretariat in the stretch right now."

"How long to catalog all the damage? We'll need a list of everything that was taken."

"Days, maybe. Peter's assistant does all the filing and other paperwork. She left yesterday for a long ski weekend in Stowe."

"And if we managed to run her down?"

"Sooner. Less than a day, maybe. She's very familiar with all his current work." Jerry, the picture of outrage just moments ago, took a deep breath and sighed, his shoulders sagging. Tears sprang suddenly to his eyes, and he turned to rush from the room.

In another twenty minutes they decided to wrap it up. Dante told Dewey Klein and Felicity Close that he'd like to stop by and talk further with each of them sometime later in the day. Right then, all he really wanted to do was go home, grab a quick shower and change of clothes, feed his cat, and then get a little something into his own churning stomach. Before he left, he got the design assistant's name and called Communications, asking them to contact the state police in Vermont. There wasn't much else they could learn at the scene until Forensics finished running the bits and pieces through the lab.

Out on the sidewalk, as he headed for his car, Rosa rushed over to corner him.

"Joe? Can we talk a minute?"

He took a deep breath and let it out as he looked her over.

"Business or pleasure?"

She frowned in irritation. "I need something to feed those guys over there." Her head jerked in the direction of the gathered hounds of the Fourth Estate.

He smiled condescendingly. "You know the victim's name and where he died. You know who he worked for and how he was killed. You want something else from me?"

"*They* probably know all *that* by now. I'd like to have your *thoughts* on this thing."

He couldn't help but snort derisively. As he did so, Bob Talbot wandered over and extended a hand.

"Dante. Nasty one you've caught here."

Joe shook with him. "All murders are nasty, Bob. Dead is dead."

"I was just asking Joe for his thoughts on this one," Rosa interjected.

"And I was just about to tell Rosa that no street cop worth his salt speculates on a case before he's sunk his teeth into it. And once he *has* sunk his teeth into it, he doesn't speculate about it to anyone other than his commanding officer. You've been off the street too long."

Her nostrils flared and eyes flashed in a way he'd once been so enamored with. "Why can't you let it go, Joe?" she demanded.

"What? That a damn good street cop hung up her gum-soled shoes to head downtown and hang out with the likes of *this* window dummy? That her ambition's blinded her to the rudiments of investigation procedure? I didn't let anything go, bright eyes. You did."

It was Talbot's turn to get miffed. "Now hold on there a second, Detective!"

Joe grinned. "You got that last part right, Bob."

Rosa grabbed Talbot's arm to steer him away. "Forget about it, Bobby. He's just goading you. Let's go talk to the press."

Dante watched the pair of them walk away.

"Bobby?" he shouted after them. "I love it! I hope he fucks better than he shakes hands!"

FOUR

At this time of year, though the calendar said spring, the trees lining Perry Street were all still barren from winter. Dante lived his bachelor life in an obscenely cheap garden apartment here in the West Village. He'd rented the place eighteen years ago in what was then a neighborhood of dumps. The bright lights of Manhattan had beckoned seductively then to the rookie cop. He was a Brooklyn kid from the neighborhoods, eager to escape the ignorance-is-bliss mentality of his buddies. Manhattan was a brave new world on the other side of the East River. Most of them had either read something about it or seen it in movies.

He enjoyed the advantages of the old rent control law. It kept his rent well below the going market rate. Places like his, at what was now a very fashionable address, were renting for two grand a month. He paid a hundred and eighty-five. His block was one of the most beautiful in the entire borough, featuring federal and neoclassical architecture.

Copter the cat was glad to see him home so soon. He jumped up from the sofa as Joe pushed in through the front door. One of an exotic spotted breed called the Egyptian

Mau, the little guy was getting on toward ten now and had become one of the few stable fixtures in the detective's life. Joe stooped to scratch him between the ears and then headed for the kitchen to run some Kal Kan through the electric opener. The sound of tin going round in that machine invariably set Copter rubbing up against his legs. Shameless.

There was one message on his machine. He elected to ignore it until after he'd set coffee brewing, shaved, and showered. Once in a great while he forced himself to let real priorities prevail. When he finally got to it, the message turned out to be from his buddy Brian Brennan, who wondered if he'd survived the night. A sculptor with a blue-chip reputation, Brian and his rock-star girlfriend lived in the same ten-thousand-square-foot warehouse space where he worked. Diana was out of town, on tour in some place like Cleveland. The mice had played last night while the cat was away, and Joe's emotional state wound up getting him into it pretty deep. Evidence his carefree friend Brian, sounding too fucking chipper for a guy who'd been aboard the same sinking ship.

It was a curious friendship for a cop to have. Most of New York's Finest saw themselves as members of an exclusive society and tended to hang out only with other cops. Some time ago Joe saw how this life-style tended to narrow a man's perspective. In Brennan, he found a different, albeit screwball, outlook on life. After twenty years of slogging through the flotsam and jetsam of man's inhumanity to man, Dante had come to cherish the time he spent with the artist. His warehouse loft, with its studios for drawing and construction, represented safe haven from the city's social sewer.

After pouring himself a cup of coffee, Joe wedged the receiver of the living room phone between shoulder and ear, and punched in Brian's number.

"J. D.! How's your head?"

"Terrible. Gus dragged me out of bed at four to view a dead guy with him."

"When are you done for the day? I was thinking about a little hair-of-the-dog."

"Don't even *talk* about alcohol. I'm dying here. And I don't want any *part* of the dog, friend. I've learned my lesson for at least twenty-four hours."

"Forget the dog, then. I've got an ulterior motive for asking you over here. This commission for the L.A. Chamber of Commerce is going to end up being huge. There's some heavy shit I've got to move to make room for it."

Dante chuckled. "You're as transparent as Cling Wrap, buddy. It'll have to wait till five or six. I'm up to my ass trying to sort out this hatchet job I've caught."

"Whenever. By then I'll bet money you'll be wanting a beer."

Without waiting for his friend's reply, Brennan cut the connection. After pouring and drinking another cup of coffee, Dante slipped into his trench coat and hit the street. The two Alka-Seltzer tablets he'd downed after feeding the cat were starting to kick in as he strolled down Perry with his collar up against the cold. It was eight-thirty when he retrieved his car from a spot near a hydrant on Bleecker and drove toward Manhattan South Borough Command on East 20th Street. He wanted to get back up to Close Apparel and talk to the personnel director, but Gus wanted to huddle first and talk game plan.

The Borough Command offices were housed in a building that occupied most of the long block between Second and Third avenues, from 20th to 21st streets. Also contained in the same edifice were the Police Academy, Manhattan's Thirteenth Precinct, and a host of forensics laboratories. Dante swung by his cubicle Task Force office on the third floor to check for messages. Then he proceeded to his boss's more lavish digs, just down the hall.

Gus Lieberman's desk top was cluttered with messages. His tie was loosened, and his suit jacket was thrown over the back of his chair. He was standing, staring out at the morning bustle on the street below and drinking a cup of coffee. Deputy chiefs rated windows. Team leaders did not. Joe ambled across the carpeted floor, pulled up a chair, and collapsed into it. Team leaders didn't rate carpeted floors in their cubicle offices, either. He *did* have a few chairs.

Without turning away from his view, Gus pointed to the Mr. Coffee atop a bank of file cabinets.

"Help yourself. And while you're at it, talk to me."

Joe figured he'd had enough coffee for the time being and stayed where he was.

"I like everything about an inside-accomplice angle," he said. "Given the evidence we have, it seems to make the most sense. A couple of things bother me."

"Such as?"

"The fact that the victim was half-naked in the dead middle of winter. We're told that the kid was there waiting on something important that was overdue from the Orient. When I consider his state of undress and the fact that he had a legitimate reason for being there, I've got to consider that maybe he *was* surprised."

Gus turned to him then. "You think maybe the insider was someone else? They've got to have hundreds of people working for them up there. Your theory leaves it pretty wide open, then."

Dante shook his head. "Not really. Not if you think about what was stolen. The dead guy was designer of that line. How many more people could be connected to it directly, know the production schedule, know exactly where to look for all that shit, and just what to take? I'd say that narrows it down some."

Lieberman wandered to the Mr. Coffee and poured himself a fresh cup. "What *about* the dead guy's state of undress? You got any feelings on that one?"

Joe shrugged. "Girlfriend? Boyfriend? It sounds like he had more than enough time on his hands."

"The boss was there until one," Gus reminded him.

"And as soon as he left, the kid let his fingers do the

walking. There was still plenty of time to get laid *and* dead.''

"How do you want to run with this?"

Joe rubbed his eyes with the heels of his hands, yawned, and shook his head. "I want a shot at their personnel department. Poke around a little. Research the dead guy's background at the same time. Dewey Klein seems to know the scene pretty well. I think our best chance of finding the actual perp might be to let him run with the stolen goods. Check his sources for any rumors of someone trying to move them. I've heard of people knocking off a clothing line, but I haven't got idea one about how they'd work it."

"He's good," Gus assured him. "Busy as hell, too. Been a rash of truck hijacks the past couple months. Gang of wild-ass South Americans. Ain't enough to just take a guy's truck. They kill people, too."

Dante's hangover took a nasty turn for a second. "Tell me about Close Apparel," he said. "Those two we met this morning. What kind of trouble can they make for us?"

"Trouble enough. She's the image, and he's the fire in the boiler. I just got off the phone with an old buddy who recently retired from the trade. He says it's common knowledge that they have a marriage of convenience. He likes boys. Neither of them is likely to roll over and play understanding if this becomes some sort of scandal. They both got sharp teeth."

"I want Jumbo," Joe told him.

Beasley "Jumbo" Richardson was the last partner Dante had worked with on the squad level. They'd taken some lumps and worked well together. After Joe moved on to Borough Command, they remained friends.

"Unless he's got his hooks into something heavy, you can consider him yours," Gus told him. "Anyone else?"

His team leader shook his head. "Not right now. I wouldn't know what to do with anyone else until this thing gets revved up."

The deputy chief walked to his desk, picked a folded piece of paper up off the blotter, and reached it across.

"New sergeant's list came up this morning. Your name is second from the top."

Dante snapped his fingers. "Damn! I never could do square roots longhand."

"There weren't any on the test. I've chosen to overlook the fact that you're a wiseass. I've considered, instead, that I've got an unranked street cop running roughshod over the streets of this city with nothing more than my blessing as backup. It might look better if he were at least a sergeant. Better if he were a lieutenant, but miracles don't grow on trees."

Joe unfolded the piece of paper and scanned the wording of his promotion. "I guess this means I'll have to join the Sergeant's Benevolent Association, huh?"

"Comes with the territory, friend."

The hangover-hampered detective drew a dented blue Plymouth Fury from the motor pool and drove across town to the Market Diner on Eleventh Avenue and 43rd Street. He needed to get something solid in his stomach, and there was a counter waitress there who always had a paper for him. Rush hour traffic had died down a bit, but he still had to fight the usual midmorning Manhattan snarl. The growling in his gut eased with the poached eggs on corned beef hash he dumped down, but ill humor remained. Running into Rosa and Talbot together like that hadn't helped an already rotten disposition. It was all but impossible for him to erase his mental image of the two of them together.

In an effort to exorcise his own demons, Joe concentrated his thoughts on the couple at the helm of Close Apparel. Neither of them had exhibited what he might call compassion at the passing of a valued colleague. She'd been more in control of herself than he was, but that could be chalked up to temperament. The company's design assets appeared to be their primary concern in the wake of a brutal murder. Joe found that just a little cold.

There wasn't any doubt in his mind that the numbers Jerry Rabinowitz threw around had some grounding in reality. Corporate bigwigs liked to exaggerate the financial health of their organizations, either up or down, depending on the circumstances, but Jerry had been being dramatic, not crying poor. Slight exaggeration or not, the offices of Close Apparel occupied three full floors at a very high-rent address. He'd checked the building directory on the way out, and the Close listings were lengthy: Close Cosmetics, Close Cuts, Felicity Formals, Felicity Lingerie, Janet Lake Casuals, and Close Encounters Evening Apparel.

At the company's 39th Street location, Joe rode a whisper-quiet elevator up to thirty-eight and asked directions from the button-cute blonde at reception. She was sporting the late-night club look, but didn't act as bored as most of them did. He followed her precise directions along three halls to a big waiting area outside personnel. The receptionist there was a lot less button-cute. She presided over three rows of school-type desks, three deep. Half a dozen listless job applicants were busy scribbling on forms as she scowled at them. Joe approached.

"Sergeant Dante." He was using it for the first time and it sounded pretty good.

The woman examined the gold shield he extended toward her.

"Ms. Cooper, the personnel director, was told to expect me some time after ten," he told her.

The scowler nodded, picked up the phone, and punched a button. After a pause she announced him, paused again, then told him to go right down. Last door on the left. Corner office.

Ms. Cooper appeared to be considerably friendlier than her watchdog. She rose behind a massive Formica desk as the detective knocked on the frame of her open door.

"Come in, Sergeant. Please." She was about five foot six, with soft brown hair cut in a very corporate, elongated pageboy. Nice soft, ovalish face, and a trim figure clad in an expensive suit. When they shook hands, her grip was firm.

As he sat down, she said, "We're all very distraught about Peter. What a horrible thing."

Dante wasn't eager to reminisce about what a swell guy the deceased had been. He'd seen too many dead people to feel any inclination toward getting to know and love them.

"We're going to do everything we can to find the person or persons who did it to him, ma'am. You might be able to help."

"You wanted to see Peter's personnel file."

"For starters. I might also need to get back to you for information on other personnel. I'd like you to keep any requests confidential."

A slight frown knit her brow. "I'm pretty much my own boss, Sergeant."

He moved to put her at ease. "It's just the 'pretty much' that we sometimes worry about. Confidential means just that. This is a murder investigation."

She reached into a basket on the corner of her desk and extracted a manila folder. Her fingers worked around the protruding tab, pulling it open. They were nice fingers, long, with beautifully manicured nails. Joe took the file from them as she handed it across.

He placed the file on the front edge of her desk and scanned it. There was the standard initial application, representing a move from previous design employment with another big-name firm. Buckley had attended Parsons School of Design. He was born and attended schools in Fort Wayne, Indiana. He was twenty-nine years old. Six feet, and a hundred sixty-five pounds. Brown hair and eyes. There was nothing in there about the Kirk Douglas dimple Dante had noticed in the middle of his chin. Indeed, the file was altogether short on both pertinent and impertinent information. There was an initial hiring report and a series of subsequent six-month evaluations. Buckley was twenty-five when he came aboard at Close. He'd worked as a sort of junior designer for the Close Cuts line of sportswear. Three records of promotion documented his rise to his most recent status as top design dog for the new Janet Lake Casuals label. His current salary was ninety-five thousand, plus bonuses ranging anywhere from fifteen to twenty-five thousand, depending upon the year. Not at all bad for a kid still shy of thirty. Current address on East 66th Street. Joe squinted at that one.

"The ID in the man's wallet had him residing in Greenpoint, Brooklyn." He held up the latest address card. "This puts him on the corner of 66th and Park."

Cooper took the card from him, glanced over it, and then tapped it against her desk top. "I remember when he came in and filled it out. He wanted this year's W-2 sent to the new address. It struck me . . . because of this." She pointed to the apartment designation. The listing had him residing in penthouse B. "I remember thinking at the time that a Park Avenue penthouse had to cost a fortune."

"I was just thinking the same thing," Dante murmured.

Felicity Close almost bumped into Dante as he walked through reception on the thirty-eighth floor heading for the elevators. She stopped abruptly, and he could see on her face the weariness that generally follows a sleepless night.

"Detective. Did you get the message I left for you at your office?"

Joe shook his head. "Which message was that?"

"Could we go upstairs? There's something I found after you left this morning. I think you might want to see it."

Joe followed Felicity up to thirty-nine and through a pair of rosewood doors.

"My office is full of people doing the windows," she apologized, pushing open the door to a spacious conference room and standing aside. "The document I want to show you is in my desk. If you'll take a seat, I'll be right back with it."

With that, she disappeared down the hall, leaving Dante to observe the austere yet obviously expensive layout. A

wall of floor-to-ceiling glass, deep-pile carpet, and acres
of rosewood. A massive rosewood table was surrounded
by leather upholstered armchairs. He pulled one up, sat in
it, and found it to be as comfortable as it looked. A minute
later the chairwoman returned carrying a folder, pulled out
a chair of her own, and adjusted it to face him.

She was the sort of woman he might term handsome,
without meaning that she was particularly easy to look at.
There was something hard about her face. The hardness
was accentuated by the glitter of her intense brown eyes
and the way she carried herself. Even though she behaved
pleasantly enough toward him, everything about her
seemed contrived. The cut of her skirt and jacket was designed specifically to hide her shortness, accentuating, instead, a wasp-thin waist, decent curves, and a long torso.
She wore three inch sling-back heels. Her hair was cut in
a style that resembled the pelt of a small, fur-bearing animal. An otter, perhaps.

"What's that?" he asked, nodding toward the document
she extracted from the folder.

"I don't know exactly." She handed the thing to him.
A contract, by the look of it. "The thief was definitely
after our Janet Lake line, so I decided to look over the
stuff in our Janet Lake files. Not the design files, but the
business documents. I'm not sure what I was looking for.
I thought that I might come up with a name for you. A
supplier or maybe a dismissed employee. Instead, I found
that."

The stapled sheaf of papers named Janet Lake as the
party of the first part in some sort of agreement. Dante
thumbed quickly through them without being able to determine immediately what they pertained to.

"What exactly is it?"

"The licensing agreement between Janet Lake and Close
Apparel. It sets forth the terms under which we are al-
lowed to use her name. You'll notice on the last page that
Peter Buckley signed for the party of the first part and that

my husband, Jerry, signed for the party of the second. Neither signed for Close Apparel. Look for yourself.''

Joe flipped to the last page and saw that it was just as she reported it to be. ''I think I see part of what you're getting at,'' he said. ''But why Buckley? Here.'' He pointed to the designer's name in the first-party spot.

''Janet was out of the country at the time, Officer. Peter is her brother. There was the potential for some real conflict of interest, but Jerry and I went round and round about that, and he won out. That isn't what's bothering me now. *This* is. It's not the document our counsel prepared, and it's not the document I approved.''

Dante placed the contract on the table at his elbow and leaned forward. ''I'm listening.''

''It doesn't name the corporation as party of the second part. It lists something called Janet Lake Casuals Incorporated, instead. My husband, Jerry, is listed as the president of that company. Until this morning I'd never heard of it. At face value that paper means that the company I control half of doesn't own a stitch of Janet Lake. In the past two years we've built that line into a sixty-million-dollar-a-year subsidiary. *Our* sales force. *Our* manufacturing facilities. *Our* promotion department.''

It was certainly an interesting revelation, but Dante couldn't see where it led in his murder investigation.

''What you're talking about here is fraud, ma'am. That's something you should take up with the District Attorney's office. . . .''

Her weariness appeared to overtake her as she sat back heavily in her chair. ''Officer. What if my husband and Peter Buckley were in something shady together? I've been racking my brain . . .''

She sat forward abruptly, snatched the contract from the table, and waved it, anger flashing in her eyes. ''We built this company *together*, Detective! Equal partners. He's gone his way, and I've gone mine, but we've *respected* each other. Now Jerry's spat in my face. This is an outrage. I've got no idea who's at the bottom of your murder,

41

but the *theft* was timed just as this line went into production. The potential for profit, to a thief with the right connections, is enormous! I've just been stabbed in the back, and I'm not about to sit here and ignore it.''

As Dante left Close Apparel a few minutes later and climbed back behind the wheel of his Plymouth, he wondered how many worms were lurking in the can Felicity Close had just handed him. It made his head hurt to think about it. He now had to consider the possibility that Jerry Rabinowitz had engineered the break-in, and that Peter Buckley had been in on it with him. He had knowledge of all the particulars, and he had access. The *why* was something else again. Maybe Dewey Klein could help him with that one. Maybe the dead guy's apartment would turn up something. A penthouse on Park Avenue. And he wanted to locate and question Buckley's sister, the famous model–actress, Janet Lake. Whether she was out of the country or not at the time the contract was signed, it was possible *she* knew what her brother had signed. Worms. A whole can of them.

He needed another pair of eyes and ears if he wanted to ask all the right questions from this point. The copy Felicity had made of the contract was in his pocket. Now all he needed was Jumbo.

It was pushing into late morning, and it wouldn't be until after lunch that he could get a bench warrant authorizing a search of Buckley's place. Dewey Klein's unit, headquartered in the old Fourteenth Precinct house on 30th Street, was close by. He could call Jumbo from there and suggest they get started over lunch. At the same time he would lay this latest development on the resident rag trade expert and see if he could shed some light on possible motive. There was even the off-chance that Safe, Loft, and Truck might have decent coffee.

FIVE

Dante thanked himself for staying in decent shape as he climbed the stairs to the fifth floor of the old precinct house. No one was going to stumble across Safe, Loft, and Truck by accident. The place itself was dog-eared at best. Institutional green paint. Faded linoleum tile. Beat-up wooden tables and plastic dinette chairs. No high-visibility glamour for these guys.

A lanky red-haired Irishman paused, a doughnut on the way to his mouth, as Joe wandered in through the open door.

"I'm looking for Dewey Klein."

The guy bit a chunk off the doughnut, chewed twice, and bellowed, "Dewey! Company!" His pronunciation, wrapped in soggy dough, was not clipped.

Klein stuck his head out a cubicle doorway and, recognizing his visitor, waved him in. "Just got in from a hijack in the Bronx. Never a dull fucking moment around here. Bear with me a second?"

Dante asked to be pointed toward a phone. He called Gus to request his bench warrant and then caught up with Jumbo Richardson at the Sixth Precinct. Lieberman had had to put him on hold for a few minutes and then announced that he could pick up the warrant from Judge Lorenz at Criminal Court, any time after two. Jumbo was free for lunch at one. They agreed to meet at a Chinese place around the corner from the station house on Hudson Street.

Klein looked at least as tired as Joe felt when they settled in across a desk in the unit commander's office.

"Another hijack, huh?"

Dewey rolled his eyes and took a big gulp from the coffee mug in his right fist. "It used to be that the mob had it all wrapped up, nice and neat. Now that they've abandoned a lot of the old rackets, we got us a bunch of trigger-happy Ecuadorians taking their place. Waste of time for these assholes to cut a driver loose when they can shoot him. You want coffee?"

"How is it?"

"Better than most."

In the job, that was saying something. Dante got himself a Styrofoam cupful and was surprised to discover just how palatable it was.

"Word on the grapevine is that you made sergeant this morning," Klein said. "Congratulations. Sort of a surprise to me that it took this long. You've been a legend on the grapevine for some time."

"I'm what downtown calls a hardhead."

Klein chuckled. "Most of them ain't had an original thought since they crapped their first diaper. You and Lieberman seem to get along pretty good."

Joe took a deep breath, let it out slowly, and nodded. "If it weren't for Gus, I'd be pounding a beat on Staten Island. He's fetched my fat out of the fire more times than I want to remember."

Dewey leaned back, poured himself a little more coffee, stirred some half-and-half into it with a plastic spoon, and placed the mug before him on his blotter. "Don't give Gus *all* the credit. The way I hear it, you've scratched his back, too. Hell, the son of a bitch is gonna be the next C of D, and it ain't because of his smooth bedside manner. He's the only brass-button bozo in this city who could find his own dick in the dark.'' The fresh cup of coffee was conveyed to his lips. ''So what's up?''

Joe slid the photocopied contract from his breast pocket and tossed it across the desk. ''That, for starters. This morning Felicity Close took it on herself to review the Janet Lake files and ran across it. Claims it isn't the same document she approved. She thinks her husband might be trying some sort of end run on her. She and Jerry are husband and wife on paper only. Jerry isn't into girls.''

Klein glanced at the pages of the contract, paused to scrutinize the signature sheet, and then set the thing back down.

''Everybody in the rag trade knows about that marriage.'' He tapped the contract. ''This is kind of interesting.''

''She seemed to think it was *real* interesting. I guess I need you to tell me why. Right now, I feel like I've been asked to bob for apples in a bucket of mud.''

''Siphon scheme. That's what it's suggesting to her anyway. He controls design, manufacture, and distribution. He has access to order and reorder information. If he has somebody who can knock this crap off to his exact specifications, he could approach a few high-volume jobbers with a price that undercuts the Close Apparel numbers. That line's a hot ticket right now. Jobbers have a lot of confidence in it. Big retailers have the same confidence. Some'll risk taking bootlegged stock for seriously lower cash. Increases their margin of profit. If the numbers are right, on a line like that, it increases them immensely.''

Dante was scrambling to keep up with this deluge of information.

''Hang on a sec,'' he begged, holding up a hand. ''Jobbers. What are they?''

''Wholesalers. Supply boutiques that the companies don't want to ship to direct. Jobbers are big in this business.''

''So wouldn't Rabinowitz be cutting his own throat? Undercutting his own company like that?''

Klein shook his head emphatically. "The money from the bootlegged goods goes into his pocket, direct. Not into the corporation's. A corporation's got overhead. The margin of profit is nowhere near the same. He also doesn't have to share a nickel with his old lady. Some jobbers will make deals for cash, under the table. He won't pay a penny of tax on that."

Joe let it hang in the silence of the room for a moment. "He was there last night. He claims he left at one but can't prove it. How do *you* read that?"

Klein shrugged. "Same as you. Jerry Rabinowitz is up to something. It might or might not have to do with his designer's murder. Could be a dead end, but at least it's a direction."

Joe grinned. "I was *hoping* you'd read it that way."

Dante dropped two more Alka-Seltzer tablets into the tall glass of water the waiter had just poured him. Beasley "Jumbo" Richardson, a huge black man and Joe's erstwhile partner, looked on.

"When you gonna learn, Joey? First the girl fucks you over, and then you proceed to fuck yourself over. There's some bad arithmetic in there somewhere."

Dante scowled at him. "I didn't have you flown in so you could bust my balls about my personal life, big guy. You decided what you want to eat?"

Jumbo pushed the menu aside. "I'm just here to keep you company, dude. I been workin' a month now on whittlin' down my fat ass. Lost twenty-six pounds. I'll just drink water."

"Jesus." Joe stared at his friend in open surprise. "Twenty-six? That's terrific."

Jumbo nodded sadly. He was a man of nearly six feet who had recently been flirting with three hundred pounds.

"Agnes was really on my case for the way I been brutalizin' the bathroom scale. Got the fuckin' doctor on her side."

Impressed, Dante scrutinized Jumbo's appearance more

closely and noticed the looseness around the collar of his shirt and the way his jacket hung.

"So where do you stand right now?"

"Two seventy-three. I'm headed for two and a half and then reassessin'." He shrugged. "Who knows, dude, I may go for even less. First two weeks were hell, but I ain't even hungry all the time no more."

Joe ordered light, not wanting to make his friend suffer too much. The Alka-Seltzer started to kick in, giving him hope.

"So who's the team on this thing?" Jumbo asked.

"As of right now, you and me. Gus has a guy named Klein from Safe, Loft, and Truck running their own thing parallel to ours. The guy's good, sharp, and he knows the rag trade inside out."

"Just like old times," the fat man mused. "How about you sketch it for me?"

Dante offered a survey of everything he'd seen and learned. He wound up with what he intended to do next.

"I want to lean on Rabinowitz, of course. I'm hoping we can turn up something in the dead guy's apartment. The autopsy might show us something we missed at the scene. And then there's this Janet Lake. Rabinowitz is playing games with his contractual agreements. It makes me wonder if maybe she isn't in on it."

Jumbo sat with his hands wrapped around his empty water glass. The waiter arrived, set Joe's lunch of sliced Hunan pork and special fried rice on the table, and returned with a pitcher to pour them both refills.

"I take it you ain't interested in assemblin' the typical Task Force team, huh?"

"Not right away." Joe tasted the pork. "Not until we've had a chance to shake the bushes a bit. We're dealing with a handful of bona fide celebrities. The media's gonna have this one under a microscope. The fewer waves we make, the better."

Jumbo supposed that this made sense. "So where to from here?"

"The morgue. Rocky's doing this one for me, personally. Then we pick up the search warrant for the dead guy's apartment. You all clear down here?"

With a flick of his hand the black man waved away any concern about his schedule. "Slow as molasses in January. All the bad guys gone south for the winter."

Joe laughed out loud at that one. "We could wish, big guy. We could wish."

Sleep had finally come, but when Murray Chopnik struggled out of bed at one-fifteen to answer the door, he felt anything but rested. The whiskey he'd consumed toward putting himself out was nothing more than a stale taste in his mouth and a burning in his stomach now. The door buzzer sounded an insistent, second time.

Face reddened and eyes wide with agitation, Roger Brill dispensed with salutation and pushed past as soon as Murray opened the door to him. He was of medium height and roguishly handsome in that chiseled, tanned, Palm Beach-boy sort of way. His drawn, haggard condition was not displaying those features in the most flattering manner.

"What the fuck *happened*?" he demanded. "Jesus. It's been all over the news."

At six feet four and close to two hundred and thirty pounds, Murray literally loomed over his unexpected visitor. His eyes narrowed, and the veins bulged in his neck and forehead as he slammed the door, threw the bolt, and whirled.

"What *happened*? There was someone *there*, Roger. He walked right in on me. Saw what I was doing and got it in his pretty-boy pea brain that he was gonna stop me. Came after me like Bruce fuckin' Lee. What the hell was I s'posed to do?"

Brill shook his head, confusion etched in his expression.

"I don't *get* it. There wasn't supposed to be anyone in there. That's why we picked last night. The shit was supposed to be just sitting on the table." He stopped and turned to quickly scan the room. "Christ, you got them, didn't you?"

Murray jerked his head toward the dining room. "In there. I got every fuckin' thing . . . but I had to kill some son of a bitch in the process. You realize what that means, Roger boy?"

Brill pushed on into the room, approached the bar, and poured himself a stiff Wild Turkey, straight. The stuff burned going down and left him with a fierce glow in the pit of his stomach.

"She's got us both implicated in murder now. We've lost the upper hand."

Murray nodded savagely. Then he joined the other man at the bar.

"It's just the kinda opening she's been lookin' to wedge herself into. For two years we had her by the short hairs. Now she's got *us* by the balls."

Brill poured himself another and started to raise it to his lips. Then he reconsidered and set it down instead. He took a deep breath and pushed it out, hard.

"Are you still going to see the man?"

Murray walked away and collapsed into his recliner. He kicked it back and lay there staring at the ceiling.

"There's big money in them boxes, Roger boy, and a lot more on the way. This doesn't really change all that much. The bitch has enough on me to make her an equal partner now. We didn't anticipate that, but there still oughta be plenty for all of us."

Brill shook his head. "She's gone along up to now because we've had her by the short hairs. The rules of the whole game just changed."

Still staring at the ceiling, Murray waved a hand in dismissal. "*Fuck* the rules. She could maybe go to the federal attorney and cut a deal now, but even if she did, her precious career would be shot to hell. You know her better'n I do. You gotta know she's still gonna play. If we gotta pretend like she's got the upper hand now, we play it that way."

* * *

Dante eased the Fury to the curb in front of the medical examiner's office, set the brake, and flipped the official police business card onto the dash. The morgue was situated here, in the midst of the giant University Hospital–Bellevue complex that ran half a dozen blocks along First Avenue in the Twenties and Thirties. Public identification of the dead was mostly done via video monitor now. There was a reception area on the street level, and only authorized personnel were permitted to ride the elevator down to the basement. Joe and Jumbo showed tin to the attendant and climbed aboard.

They found Rocky Conklin in his office. The pathologist, tall and pale, with bushy eyebrows and bushier forearms, had one of his ever-present Honduran cigars lit. His feet were up on his desk.

"Hey!" he bellowed, as he jerked the cigar from his mouth and swung upright. "Laurel and Hardy ride again! What're you two doing here?"

Jumbo grimaced. "Certain ex-partner of mine had me roped in to solve his latest homicide for him. Can't rely on all beauty and no brains in this business."

Conklin nodded sagely, setting his cigar to rest in an ashtray fashioned from the top of a human skull. This guy was the ME office's dean of good taste.

"Pull up chairs. You're gonna love what I got to tell you about Peter Buckley."

They sat as the resident ghoul shuffled through a stack of notes, pulled several from the pile, and mulled over them.

"Male Caucasian. Age, twenty-nine. No surprises there, huh? Cause of death: a single severe blow to the head. Massive skull fracture. Time of death, approximately two-thirty A.M. Corpse was fresh, and we were able to get a good read on that one." He paused to pick up his cigar, puff furiously on it, and then set it back in the tray. "Now here's where it gets interesting. You asked me to keep an eye peeled, cowboy. I didn't let you down, and guess what I found."

Dante grunted. "Don't tell me. Peanuts, popcorn, and a prize."

"Semen in the esophagus and stomach. Lots of it, when you consider that sort of thing is relative. Very recently ingested. From the minimal effect that the stomach acid had on it, I'd say it wasn't there more than an hour, hour and a half before death." There was deep satisfaction in his tone.

Dante adjusted himself in his chair. With an ankle thrown over one knee, he tugged idly at his sock. "I guess that explains the state of near undress."

"It'd be my bet," Rocky agreed.

"So who crushed his skull?" Jumbo asked. "His special friend or some third party?"

Joe rubbed his face with his open hand. "My investigation's already turned up the fact that Buckley's boss, Jerry Rabinowitz, is homosexual. Rabinowitz was on the scene last night, late. He *claims* to have left at one o'clock but can't really prove it. That might be his semen, and that would put him there a lot later, but can *we* prove it?'

Conklin picked his cigar up and eased back in his chair. "You bet."

The detectives gave him their undivided attention.

"It's the latest in our bag of forensic medical tricks. A new process called the DNA print. If we can get a protein sample from two sources—in this case, the semen and a suspect—we can match the DNA structure if both samples come from the same person. Lucky for us there's protein in almost every human product: blood, tissue, hair, feces, semen, and even dried sweat."

Dante regarded the pathologist thoughtfully. "You're talking like this is foolproof."

"Virtually. DNA structure is as randomly different as a man's fingerprints. If we get a match, it's definitely the same guy. It's holding up in court."

"And if it's Jerry's semen, we can put him on the scene within an hour and a half of the murder. That'd be one o'clock, at the earliest. I tend to doubt it was *wham, bam,* and run."

Conklin nodded. "If it's this Jerry's."

SIX

"So why aren't we haulin' this joker's ass in?" Jumbo wanted to know.

They were back in the Plymouth, headed downtown toward the State Superior Court building on Centre Street. Even in the bright, full sun of midafternoon, the day was bone chilling and blustery. None of the pedestrians whose faces they glimpsed looked too happy about it. A stiff, sharp wind cut across the island from out of the northwest, something the colorful TV weather folk liked to call a Canadian Clipper or Arctic Express.

From behind the wheel Dante watched the traffic ahead. "I want all my ducks in a row. Scraping a little skin and getting a DNA match doesn't mean the man's our murderer. It just means he lied about when he left."

"How about that contract. Sounds like there's somethin' fishy goin' on there."

"No doubt. But I want to dig a little for the what and the why. Be able to ask intelligent questions. Really lean on him. I'm hoping either tossing the dead guy's apartment or an interview with Janet Lake might turn something up that we can use. Gus has people trying to run down the model for us."

It took them another forty-five minutes to pick up Judge Lorenz's bench warrant and get uptown to Peter Buckley's apartment building on the corner of East 66th Street and Park Avenue. It was one of those big, lavish addresses with lots of polished brass, a sidewalk awning, and uniformed staff. The doorman summoned the super, a heavyset, good-natured Irishman. The guy barely glanced at their piece of paper.

"Show it to his sister, gents. Her kid's still at school, so she's alone up there, I think. Saw her walk in just half an hour ago."

"Sister?" Joe asked. "She lives here, too?"

The super chuckled. "It's her place, Sergeant. Peter came on board around Christmas. Plenty of room up there for everyone, believe me. Shame about him. He seemed like a nice kid."

After the man lifted the house phone to let Janet Lake know that they were on their way up, Joe and Jumbo boarded a waiting elevator and had the operator run them up to the penthouse floor. When they got off, a red-eyed blonde stood waiting for them in the vestibule, one shoulder propping open her front door.

There was no mistaking that striking face and stunning physique. Dante reckoned that she had to be pushing forty by now, with her last *Sports Illustrated* swimsuit spread back in the late seventies somewhere. She'd done some film work since then, received with surprisingly good reviews. Mostly supporting stuff, but getting meatier all the time. Janet Lake. The namesake of their stolen clothing line.

They extracted IDs and presented them. She hardly gave them a look, indicating with a jerk of her head that they should enter. After closing the door behind them, she turned, hands behind her back as she learned against it.

"Why would anyone want to kill him?"

All three stood in a lobby-sized foyer, one side of which opened into a vast living room. Halls headed off the foyer in two other directions.

"I'm sorry," Joe offered. "Because of the nature of the break-in, we've been trying to locate you. This comes as a surprise. No one told us he lived here with you."

She pushed herself away from the door and preceded them into the living room. "Not many of them knew. Jerry does, and Hillary, Peter's assistant. Peter is . . . was a very private person."

As she spoke, Dante was working to dredge up everything he knew about her. She had a reputation of the society-page sort. Once married to a famous financier when she was still pretty young. The divorce had gotten a lot of ink. There was a custody battle the guy had lost because he'd beat her up. Sensational tabloid stuff.

The living room must have been fifty feet long and more than half that wide. Windows stretching along the entire west wall overlooked a broad terrace, the buildings of Madison and Fifth avenues and Central Park. The furniture was contemporary and obviously expensive: soft leather sofas and chairs, tables of gleaming chrome and white marble, two matching Persians that had to be fifteen by twenty feet each. She sat on one sofa and indicated another across the way. They took seats on it.

"We're trying to follow up a curious lead we've stumbled across," Joe started in. "It involves the way Janet Lake Casuals was structured and both you and your brother's involvement in the operation. What can you tell us?"

From where she sat, the model contemplated him. "It's complicated. The way Peter and Jerry explained it to me, there are problems inside Close Apparel. Three years ago Felicity overextended and got the company in a tight spot. That's when Jerry took over complete control of the business end. He knew that I was Peter's sister, and he approached him to put together a line of casual sportswear that could generate a positive cash flow quickly. Our agreement was that Peter got complete design control and that I would consult with him. If Felicity had known about that arrangement, she never would have stood for it. Jerry worked it around her because the company's cash flow situation was that desperate."

Dante had watched her carefully as she spoke. Her line was either very well rehearsed or the truth. He remembered that tough critics had given her good marks as an actress, and he wasn't ready to swallow her story whole.

"This cash flow problem," he said slowly. "Did you ever learn the nature of it?"

She shrugged as though it were totally unimportant. "It wasn't any secret, Officer. Management expands too quickly, getting ahead of financial growth. Overambitious projections. Results fall short of the mark. A product you're betting on breaks a leg in the backstretch. Overnight, your glamourous, flashy house of paper and glass is suddenly hurting for cash. It's not unique to Close Apparel." She didn't mince words. "But I don't see what any of this has got to do with Peter. Somebody walks in there and butchers him, and you're worried about cash flow?"

It was not a question Joe chose to answer.

"While we talk, would you mind if Detective Richardson had a look at your brother's room?"

She bristled. "Of course I mind. What the hell is this? My brother wasn't a criminal; the person who murdered him is."

Jumbo stood. "We came here with a warrant, ma'am. We aren't sayin' anyone is anything. We're conducting an investigation. Period. Sergeant Dante was just doin' you the courtesy of asking the way. I'll find it myself."

She gestured weakly in the direction of the foyer, the fire suddenly gone out of her. "First hall, third door on the left. The bathroom is his as well."

Once Jumbo had disappeared to poke through the dead man's effects, Dante sat forward a little in his seat and spoke softly.

"I realize this has to be tough for you."

"You don't have any fucking idea, mister."

He sat immobile for a moment, letting the bitterness wash over and past him.

"I've been scraping messes like your brother's body off floors for twenty years," he said. "I think I have an idea."

Now the woman seemed to focus for the first time on the person sitting across from her in her living room.

"I'm sorry, Officer. This whole thing's got me more than a little freaked out. I just got back from the morgue about twenty minutes before you showed up. It was horrible. They showed me his face on a television screen."

Dante figured that they must have just missed each other at the medical examiner's. "There's nothing pleasant about an experience like that," he said. "TV or no TV. I don't suppose there's anything pleasant in talking with me about it, either. For us, there are a couple of things that aren't adding up. Apparently there is some discrepancy in the contract you signed with Close Apparel. Felicity Close tells us that it isn't the one she approved."

The actress frowned. "This is going to sound crazy, but I never saw the thing. I was in Costa Rica shooting a film. My lawyer and I talked terms over the phone a couple of times. He sent one draft down for me to look over, and when I approved, Peter signed as secretary-treasurer of the receiving corporation we'd set up."

Dante's eyebrows went up at that one. "Wasn't that a conflict of interest on his part?"

"It was one hell of a leg up for his career. Have you ever looked at his stuff? My brother was a design genius. I *wear* that stuff, and not because it has my name on it. It's gorgeous."

Dante eased back in his seat again to regard her. "The results of our preliminary investigation at the scene suggest that the killer stole everything needed to knock off your next fall line."

Janet stiffened. "He did *what*?"

"The whole show. It was like he had a shopping list. And Jerry Rabinowitz was with your brother for at least part of the evening. He says he left at one o'clock, but we have evidence that suggests otherwise. Can you tell us anything about a personal relationship between them?''

It was like he'd slapped her in the face. ''What's Jerry suspected of doing, Officer?'' The question came out sharp. ''*Buggering* my brother to death?''

Dante was cool. ''I didn't say he was suspected of doing anything, ma'am.''

''Then what *are* you saying?''

''That a homicide's been committed and that when people get dead and I'm asked to investigate, I'll dig through anybody's dirty laundry I feel justified in digging through. Anyone who has a problem with that can call the commissioner. When something smells fishy, I'm gonna dig until I find either the truth or a dead fish.''

She bit the fleshy part of her right index finger, trying to fight back sudden tears and failing. By all appearances she'd done an awful lot of crying that day.

''It wasn't really secret,'' she started in slowly. ''I think they really loved each other. Not just because of the physical attraction but because they respected each other. Peter never had any head for business, but Jerry was a wizard at it. And Peter did best what Jerry admired most in the world. He designed beautiful commercial clothes.''

''Did *you* know they were going to be there last night?''

She stopped crying altogether, and her eyes narrowed. ''I knew that Peter would be working late, yes. My daughter gave a ballet recital last night. Her uncle promised to be there, but he cancelled at the last minute. Something about an overdue transmission from Japan. It wasn't at all unusual. He worked like a crazy man at that job.''

Jumbo reentered the room. ''The dude lived like a Trappist,'' he announced. ''There ain't a scrap of anything worthwhile in there. Not even an appointment book.''

''He kept one at the office,'' Janet told them. ''And he had a memory for detail that was frightening.''

* * *

It was almost time to call it a day as the two detectives emerged from the building and onto the street. Jumbo held out his hand as they approached the car.

"Give me the keys, dude. It's been hours since your last Alka-Seltzer, and you look like you're startin' to fade on me."

Joe had nearly forgotten about his hangover. His head was buzzing with the crosscurrents of conflicting information and wild supposition. Early-on speculation. Gut feelings. He climbed in on the passenger side and buckled up as Jumbo pulled into traffic and headed them back to Borough Command.

"So what do you think?" the big man asked. "You figure she's bullshittin' us?"

Joe shook his head wearily. "If she's shitting us, given what just happened to her brother, she's colder than anyone I want to know . . . and an awfully good liar."

"Most murderers are colder than anyone we want to hang around with. But you got a point. She looked to be takin' the dude's death pretty hard. How about all the other shit? The contract."

"She didn't have much time to rehearse a story. She said something about giving her brother's career a boost and Felicity Close getting the company into financial trouble. I suggested a slight conflict of interest, and she didn't seem to think much of it."

They rode down Park Avenue, around the Helmsley Building and Grand Central Station. With rush hour upon them, traffic was starting to pile up toward the Midtown Tunnel to Queens.

"Your ducks any closer to bein' in a row?" Jumbo eventually asked. "Time's awastin'. I think we oughta drag this Jerry's ass in and do a little recreational leaning on it."

No, Joe didn't think his ducks were any more in a row than they'd been at lunch, but he figured the fat man was right. Jerry Rabinowitz was the only ace they were holding now.

"Tomorrow morning. When I get back to my office, I'll

give him a call and ask him to come in for a chat. What, ten o'clock?''

Beasley thought that sounded fine to him. They crawled along at a snail's pace and talked about less pressing matters. The big man had recently bought himself a two-family house in the Fort Green section of Brooklyn. He wanted to be closer to the station house in Manhattan and closer to the better public high schools. Both of his kids were bound for college whether they wanted to go or not. So far, they seemed to want to go, and the schools of East New York weren't providing an atmosphere conducive to study and good grades. He and his wife had both grown up there and stayed on long past the time when they could afford much better. Jumbo had contended for years that the kids out there needed role models other than pimps and pushers. Now he was tired. He wanted a backyard and a chance to stop and smell the flowers.

There was a message on Joe's desk asking him to contact Gus Lieberman, ASAP. He punched in the boss cop's number down the hall and got him on the first ring.

''Joey. Any progress?''

''Too early to tell, Gus. Nothing that feels like it, but you never know.''

''Vermont state troopers tracked down the design assistant. She'll be on a late plane, landing at LaGuardia at nine-twenty. I didn't figure there was much chance of your being awake then, so I asked her to meet you at the scene. Ten tomorrow morning.''

Joe told him that was okay and broke the connection to dial Rabinowitz's offices at Close. He was informed by reception that Mr. Rabinowitz had left for the day. The home number Felicity had given him was answered by the maid. Jerry was summoned and Joe told him about Vermont's locating Hillary Fox. He agreed to be at Close Apparel the following morning at the appointed hour. Dante could detect no suspicion or trepidation in his phone manner.

* * *

It was seven o'clock before Joe had finished helping his buddy Brennan move heavy objects around his loft to clear space for the sculptor's latest commissioned work. He'd limited himself to one beer, taken a rain check on the offer of dinner, and stumbled off dreaming of sleep. The hangover was gone now. It had given way to an exhaustion that went to the bone.

He dropped the Corvette in front of his garage and hiked the three blocks up Perry Street to his building. As he paused to bend and unlatch the low wrought iron gate, Rosa called his name. He turned and watched her climb out of her Toyota Celica and cross the street toward him. There'd been a time when that sight could force his heart to skip beats. Tonight it forced his stomach into a poorly executed back flip.

"What's up?" he asked, trying to sound nonchalant.

"I've been waiting across the street for two hours."

With a frown he pushed the little gate open and proceeded along the short flagstone path to the front door of his building. As he searched his coat pockets for his keys, he spoke over his left shoulder.

"I didn't realize I was on a schedule."

"We have to talk, Joe."

"About what? Your current poor taste in men?"

"About us, you self-righteous son of a bitch!"

When he turned around to face her, he saw anger flashing in those big, dark eyes. Anger didn't make her any less beautiful. He might not like her current hairstyle, but that face was the sort that launches ships and pushes desperate men into drinking poison. He softened just a hair.

"You want to come in or carry on this conversation out here in the ass-freezing cold?"

He pushed his way inside, and she followed. His apartment was a spacious one-bedroom that occupied the entire street-level floor. Ten-foot ceilings gave the mostly open spaces a cavernous feeling. In the back, his bedroom opened on the garden through iron-gated French doors. A bath and kitchen lay between the bedroom and where they now stood, in the middle of a book- and art-lined living room.

Rosa still loved this apartment, still got good, comfortable feelings from a place she'd abandoned at a time of confusion and stress. And maybe it was because this place wasn't like any cop's home she'd ever known. One of Dante's passions was reading psychology. His shelves were crammed with it and a host of other works from criminology to pathology. A lot of the art was original, on loan from Brian Brennan, who no longer had room to hang all his acquisitions. An exquisite bronze nude, posed for by Brian's rock-star girlfriend Diana, graced the mantel. Rosa peeled off her coat, tossed it over the back of a wing chair, and took a seat on the sofa.

"Make yourself at home," Dante suggested. "You want something to drink? I think I do."

She shook her head. "You don't really look like you need it, either."

"Need it?" he asked with a snort. "I'm running on empty here. You say we've gotta talk, and all I can think of is sleep." He stepped to his liquor cabinet, pulled down a tumbler, and poured himself two fingers of Black Bush Irish whiskey.

"I don't think you know what kind of trouble Bobby can make for you," she said straight out. "I think you'd better back off."

He'd taken a sip of the smooth, amber liquid in his glass and was savoring the way it glided down his throat.

"What the fuck do you see in that guy anyway?"

"That's my business, Joe. Mine isn't yours anymore."

"Don't you think you're pushing this ambition of yours a little hard? As lady cops go, you're the job's shining star right now. You may want the PC's job some day, and Talbot's got his ear right now, but the man is a buttsucking *prick*. You've changed since we first met, but you haven't gotten any dumber. You've gotta see through that facade."

Her nostrils flared as she struggled to maintain control. Rosa prided herself on how well she could keep her cool.

Dante was still on his feet, facing her. "What are you doing, Rosa? Besides being the best-looking woman in the department, you also used to be a crackerjack street cop. Maybe you can't remember back more than a couple years, but you proved it to me. You even saved my life, and I can count the people who've done that on one hand."

"But I'm the child of brutally murdered parents and have never learned to trust the same sort of intimate bond I had with them, right? I've heard all this bullshit before, Joe."

"From who?" he asked. "Me? Your fucking shrink told you that. Why do you keep insisting it's bullshit? Hell, I *lived* with it. Back at the beginning, even you were willing to admit there might be something you had to deal with. Then you closed up and copped out."

"It takes two, Joe. You fucked around, same as me."

"Your rules. And I never did until you moved out and changed the name of the game."

She stabbed a finger in the air at him. "I was *suffocating* here. You wanted me to marry you, quit the job, move to some fucking suburb, and have brats. The Italian macho-man's wet dream. I didn't want to have anything to do with it."

Dante shrugged, and his face softened in a wan smile.

"Dreams change, babe. Just like the times. That used to be my parent's dream, too. And their parents before them. I'm forty years old and like to think I've maybe grown up a little. But I still dream about love. Commitment. On *some* crazy level."

She softened a little as well. "And I wish you luck with it. There's a lot about you that I still haven't gotten out of my heart, but that doesn't mean I want to let the rest back in. You think I'm an emotional basket case. I guess maybe I am. I like Bobby because he's a lot like me."

Dante downed the rest of his whiskey and carried the glass toward the kitchen. His back was to her as he spoke.

"Thanks for the advice about your boyfriend and how miserable he can make my life for me. I'm tired, Rosa. You know the way out."

In the kitchen he ran water into his glass, set it in the dish drainer, and fed the cat. Somewhere in there he heard the front door close.

SEVEN

The squad room of the Manhattan South Detective Command Task Force wasn't much different from those on the precinct level. The building itself and some of the furnishings were newer than most, but the clutter and bad coffee were the same. When reporting for duty, Dante always brought a Thermique jug of fresh home-brewed coffee. This morning he was sitting at his desk, drinking some and munching on a doughnut when Jumbo wandered in.

"Morning, hotshot. You look a little better today."

Dante grunted, pushed an empty Styrofoam cup at him, and filled it from his private stock. "The wonders of a full night's sleep. I hope you're serious about that diet, big fella. There ain't a single one of your jelly-filled calorie bombs in the whole bag."

Beasley waved him off. "Not a thing for me, thanks. Any new developments?"

"Rosa stopped by to warn me that Bob Talbot's set to make my professional life miserable."

Jumbo chuckled. "Got me shakin' in *my* shoes. You?"

Dante held out an unsteady hand. "We're due up at

65

Close Apparel in forty minutes. You ready to put the screws to this joker?''

"Just let me at 'im.''

Hillary Fox was an athletic, bouncy redhead of middle stature, complete with freckles across the bridge of her button nose. She paced the carpet of the reception area anxiously as Dante and Jumbo entered the Close Apparel thirty-ninth floor offices. Her boss sat at the reception desk with his snakeskin boots up on the rosewood short wall, crossed at the ankles. Yesterday's agitation had evaporated, to be replaced by cool calm. If he was nervous at all, it showed only in the way he smoked a filtered cigarette. When he wasn't pulling smoke out of it between his lips, he was constantly rolling it back and forth between thumb and forefinger.

Down the hall the pattern room and design studio, the crime scenes, were still cordoned off with yellow plastic tape. It was Saturday in the rag trade, and this entire floor was engulfed in an eerie hush.

Dante introduced himself to the design assistant, and his partner to both of them. The young woman, probably somewhere in her mid-twenties, tried to appear businesslike and didn't quite pull it off. She was obviously upset by her boss's brutal murder. Joe moved to put her at ease.

"We know this has to be hard for you, ma'am. We appreciate your cutting your weekend short to come down here like this.''

She looked, for a moment, as if she were going to burst into tears. "If it wasn't for those damn Japanese, he never would have *been* here. That's what I can't get over. Those bastards are all so arrogant. Peter was furious with them for standing us up.''

Joe turned to Jumbo. "I'd like to get Miss Fox's first impression of the design studio while you wait here with Mr. Rabinowitz. Give us about ten minutes and then come on down.''

The crime-scene tape was pulled away, and they entered

the room. All Hillary Fox could manage was a despondent "Aw, Christ," as she stood there staring at the mess.

"I want you to look around carefully," Joe told her. "Give the whole place a good going-over. And talk to me. Tell me what you're seeing."

She stepped forward now, approaching the pile of debris from the Janet Lake file cabinet, where it lay scattered on the floor.

"Jerry told me that next fall's design books are all missing," she said, kneeling. "He knows them as well as I do."

During their previous day's session, Rabinowitz had stacked some of the ring binders in piles in order to assess the damage. The Fox woman worked rapidly, determining what each pile contained and adding more items to them. Her familiarity with them was obvious. Sorting the entire mess took her less than five minutes.

"He was right," she announced. "More or less."

"You found something else," Dante prodded.

Hillary rocked back on her heels and shrugged. "I don't know if it means anything, really. The summer stuff is missing, too. Lab dips, Cost sheets, Spec sheets—everything. I don't know why summer's missing. Maybe they were in too much of a hurry to look closely. Fall's what they had to be after. If the slopers are missing, like Jerry says they are, somebody got everything they'd need." She looked around the room as she got to her feet; her eyes suddenly narrowed. "Wait a second. . . ."

"What?" Dante prodded.

"The salesmen's samples. *They're* missing."

Joe glanced quickly around. "Salesmen's samples?"

She approached an empty pipe rack standing along one wall.

"They came in Thursday morning. Four cartons of them." And that made her stop again. She turned in apparent confusion and contemplated a large worktable. "They're gone, *too*."

"Slow down. What's gone, too? And *what* came Thursday morning?"

Hillary Fox folded her arms to hug herself. "Two things," she said. "We got the new salesmen's samples for our Janet Lake summer casuals line on Thursday. They came in big boxes. I hung them all out on the rack to be pressed and left the four cartons on that table." She pointed. "Next week is summer sales week. We change all the spring stuff out of the showroom and hang the summer sportswear. The spring garments go into the boxes and are shipped to the warehouse in Brooklyn. We don't throw those boxes out because others are so hard to find. The summer samples *and* the boxes are gone."

Joe thought he'd done a reasonable job of keeping abreast.

"What you're saying is that stealing them, along with the summer design stuff, doesn't seem to make any sense."

Her nod was definite. "None. If they got the fall specs and the slopers, that's all they'd need. You could have carried the ring binders out of here in a shopping bag. Janitorial could have taken the cartons by mistake, I guess. But not the samples."

"Janitorial hasn't been in this room."

She shook her head emphatically. "Then it doesn't make any sense at all."

Dante glanced at his watch and quickly changed the subject. They'd been in there seven minutes. Her boss would be arriving soon.

"Just between you and me, tell me about the politics around here. Any personality conflicts?"

"Sure. Fashion people are temperamental as hell. Especially the creatives."

Joe decided to give a little in the hope of getting something. "We're looking at a possible inside-job angle. There's no evidence of forced entry. The thief knew exactly where to look and what to look for."

She seemed to get his drift and framed her reply carefully. "There are personality conflicts, Sergeant, but no *real* hostilities. People come and go, but mostly to make career moves. There are a lot of people like me. Design school graduates. We've all got an eye out for the next leg up.''

"But you've been here as an assistant, what, four years?''

She smiled at his naïveté. "We all have to pay our dues before someone is going to be willing to cut us loose with our own lines. This is the big time. Here I learn from some of the best. It's not just marking time.''

The door opened, and Jumbo led Jerry Rabinowitz into the room. Dante wasted no time in using his new information. In the presence of Hillary Fox, he started turning the screws on her boss.

"Mr. Rabinowitz. Why is it that you missed the fact that an entire rack of samples is missing from in here, along with the cartons they were shipped in?''

Jerry got a panicked, confused look on his face as he looked around the room. "Jesus. I was so worried about the goddamm fall line. . . . You're right. They're gone.'' He turned his questioning eyes on his subordinate. "They're not in the showroom?''

She shook her head. "I left them right there on the rack for pressing. We weren't going to change the showroom till Monday, so I left the cartons there on the worktable.''

Jerry turned his blank look on the detectives. "I've got no idea why I missed it, Officers. It doesn't make sense.''

"What doesn't make sense?'' Jumbo asked.

"Stealing samples. They got the goddamn *slopers*. If you didn't have them, you'd probably want to get your hands on some of the garments in the line . . . in order to get the fit right. But they didn't need to do that. They got everything they needed.''

Dante asked Hillary to wait for them in the hall and closed the door once she'd left.

"Something interesting came to light yesterday,'' he told Rabinowitz. "Late morning, I came back and had a little talk with your wife. She'd been going through the company's Janet Lake file and ran across the original contract between the model and your company. Only it wasn't between Close Apparel and her, but between you personally and her. In fact, Janet Lake's brother, Peter, signed as an officer in *her* holding company. It looked fishy as hell to her. Looks fishy to us, too.''

Jerry was beside himself with his eagerness to explain.

''My wife's big ideas were bleeding this company dry!'' he exclaimed impatiently. ''We were in the middle of a cash crisis. I gave her an ultimatum: I would take what was mine and leave her high and dry if she didn't give me total operating control. I *saved* this fucking company! As a safety valve I negotiated the Janet Lake deal with Peter as intermediary, creating it as a legally separate entity.'' He paused, shook his head, then continued. ''Landing her was a real coup for us. That line's been a godsend. A cash cow. We've used it to bail out some of Felicity's losers by making absurdly low interest loans. You can look at the fucking *books*.''

''Your wife says the contract in the file isn't the one she approved.''

Rabinowitz clenched his fists. ''Of *course* it isn't. My wife is a jealous, pigheaded woman, Sergeant. To whom I am unfortunately tied by marriage. And I mean *tied*. Half of this corporation belongs to her. She's a paranoid. This was my rescue operation and I'd be damned if I'd risk tying it to an entity she'd just led to the brink of bankruptcy. If I'd shown her the contract the way I wanted it structured, she never would have stood for it.''

Joe wandered to the window, clasped his hands behind his back, and stared out. ''She says that Close Apparel paid for Janet Lake Casuals manufacturing, marketing, and distribution.''

''Bullshit. Same structure and facilities, but everything Close did for Janet Lake, they billed and were paid for. Again, you can check the books.''

Jumbo picked up the ball. ''Wouldn't your wife have checked them already?''

Jerry laughed bitterly. "She wouldn't know an accurate balance sheet if it bit her on the bottom line. Felicity is the public-image side of this company."

"How did she manage to get it into such deep shit then?"

"Her pet losers. Felicity Formals. Close Encounters. The cosmetics line. Party clothes for rich people. High-ticket items. Her promotional budgets were astronomical where the target market was minuscule. You can't run a company spending big money on shit like that. You make money in mass merchandising, selling to the middle class. I didn't realize what a mess she'd made of things until the third-quarter figures came in three years ago. Her Christmas and holiday advertising numbers were crazy. She introduced a new line of knitwear and placed monster orders with a manufacturer in Hong Kong. We wound up barely able to cover the cost. The stuff sat in the warehouse for months. Christ, the *perfume* she spent five million dollars introducing was designed to go for three hundred fifty bucks an *ounce*. Jesus! How many husbands and boyfriends in America can afford to spend like that?"

Neither cop had any way of knowing whether this guy was telling them the truth. Dante had turned away from the scenic view and now walked close to Rabinowitz. He'd had enough of the games fashion people play. They would run all this new information past Dewey Klein and see if he could interpret it. Meanwhile there was still one card left to play.

"You told us yesterday that you left here at one o'clock, Thursday night. Why did you lie?"

Jerry was at a loss for words. It was Joe's turn to smile.

"Forensic pathology is a wonderful science, Mr. Rabinowitz. They keep coming up with new breakthroughs all the time. The latest is pretty slick. A DNA print. It can prove, through a match with your tissue, that the semen we found in Peter Buckley's throat and stomach is yours."

"Funny thing about that semen, Jerry," Jumbo took it

up. "It was bearly touched by digestive juices at the time of death. It'd been in there, oh, no more than an hour or so. Time of death was 'tween two-thirty and three o'clock. What happened? Your watch go on the blink?"

Rabinowitz gathered his wits in a hurry under pressure. He tried his best, disarming smile, like a kid caught with his hand in the cookie jar.

"Just because we had a little fun to kill some time doesn't mean I killed *him*. Hell, we did *that* all the time."

"Lover's quarrel?" Dante said quickly. "Business dispute? Maybe he tried to stab you in the back?"

Rabinowitz had a pleading look on his face. "I left him in his office at one-thirty and went to mine to pick up some things I wanted to take home. Then I left, and that's the truth. I flagged a cab and went home."

"But you didn't get the receipt or the hack number, right?"

The agitated CEO turned on the fat man. "When was the last time *you* did?"

Jumbo's face was impassive.

Jerry wilted. His shoulders sank. "Are you arresting me?" he asked hollowly.

"For what?" Jumbo snarled. "Suspicion of getting your wad wrung? Or are you confessing?"

"I lied about the time I left here. That's all I've lied about."

Dante stepped distractedly away again. After a moment he took up the role of inquisitor in more subdued tones.

"You've got to look at it our way, Jerry. We're cops, and that makes us naturally suspicious. We catch a homicide where the victim has just performed fellatio on his boss. We know the boss was on the scene within an hour or so of the death. These two . . . friends . . . are running their own secret little game with a multimillion-dollar subsidiary of their company, unbeknownst to the other major stockholder. It just happens that the homicide also involves the theft of materials that jeopardize that subsidiary's profit margin for a good chunk of annual sales. The victim and his boss are the two people closest to that material. The thief knew exactly what to look for, and there is no sign of forced entry. To a couple of suspicious cops, that looks a lot like an inside job. You gave us a lot of fancy bullshit to justify why you two were playing those games, and we've yet to check your story out. Meanwhile, the big finger points right at you. We aren't going to arrest you because we don't have enough yet to make anything stick. But I'd suggest you don't take any long trips.''

An ashen-faced Rabinowitz swallowed hard as Dante finished. He could barely get his words out.

"I didn't kill Peter. I'm going to see my lawyer."

Jumbo patted his shoulder.

"I suggest you do, chum. Might come in handy."

Rabinowitz had to see Janet Lake. As soon as the detectives left, he grabbed a cab and rode uptown to her building on Park Avenue. The cops, with his bitch wife's help, had stumbled across the business connection between Janet, her brother, and him. Felicity meant to use the sharp edges of that doctored contract to cut his balls off. But more tormenting than the prospect of that calamity was the grief that tore at his heart. His good friend and lover was dead. Now, with that visit from those two cops, his world had come just a little farther apart.

It was still brutally cold out, and he tightened the belt on his cashmere coat as he hurried past Janet's doorman and into the lobby. His stomach was churning, and all the Tums he'd swallowed weren't helping any. He rode the elevator to the penthouse floor, all the while feeling that his life was being flushed down a sewer.

The Janet who answered the door looked like hell. Her face was puffy, her eyes red-rimmed from crying. She was dressed in a terry robe, and her wet hair framed her face in loose, glistening strands. When she saw the look on *his* face, she motioned him inside.

"The kid's doing homework on the dining room table," she murmured. "Let's go into the den."

73

Jerry nodded and followed her across the living room. A seventeen-year-old blonde with her hair in a French braid poked her head out from the dining room to see who had arrived. She had her mother's angular build and exquisite facial structure. Her reddened eyes suggested that she shared her mother's grief.

"Hi, Jerry," she said softly.

"Skye," he returned with a nod, "I'm sorry about your uncle."

The young woman wiped the end of her nose and turned away without another word. As Jerry started forward and reached to touch her, Janet caught his hand and shook her head. She led the way on to the den, and after she closed the door behind them, her entire demeanor changed. There was a new toughness in her eyes.

"What the *hell* is going on, Jerry? The police were here yesterday with some very interesting questions, a lot of them about a little game you and Peter were playing. With *my* line. They asked those questions like maybe I'm part of whatever it is you're trying to pull. I got the impression they think it's what got my brother killed."

Rabinowitz collapsed into a chintz-upholstered Queen Anne chair. After his recent session with Detectives Dante and Richardson, most of the fight was already gone out of him.

"There isn't any game we were playing. Felicity found the Casuals contract and went to them with it. The whole goddamn scheme is tricky, but legit. It was designed to infuse new capital. You knew that. I've slaved for that company, and now I'm stealing my own designs to tear it down? It's insane!"

She stood her ground, hands on hips. This was her turf, and she felt in control here. The room was decorated differently from the glitzy living room. It was more somber and formal in tone. A massive old mahogany desk had a computer terminal perched on one corner. The blotter was cluttered with the business of running her own little empire. Framed cover shots from *Vogue*, *Glamour*, and *Cos-*

mopolitan were hung on the walls to remind her of a time when having a pretty young face had been enough . . . and to remind her that it wasn't the case anymore.

"I saw him at the morgue, Jerry. Someone caved the whole side of his head in. When he canceled out of Skye's recital, he said you and he had some overdue confirmations you were waiting on. So where were you while some bastard was killing him?"

Jerry covered his face with his hands and started to cry. His words came out choked and muffled, but clear enough.

"I was still in my office. I told the police I'd left, but I hadn't yet. I *saw* the guy, Janet."

Her hand went to her mouth.

"Why haven't you *told* them? Jesus, Jerry!"

His hands came away from his face and dropped to grip the arms of the chair. "He doesn't *know* I saw him. If he did, he would have killed me, too. I was just leaving my office with some papers I'd picked up. The guy was dragging a hand truck through reception, moving in a real hurry. I saw blood spattered on the front of his coveralls. I don't know why, but I knew there was something terribly wrong, and I just froze."

Janet was pacing the floor now, beside herself.

"And you didn't tell the police this? Goddamn it, Jerry. The man had just murdered my brother!"

"I *found* him, on the floor of the pattern room with his *brains* hanging out of his head. And the guy who did it . . . Janet, he was huge. Maybe six and a half feet tall. He must have weighed two fifty. If he finds out I can tie him to Peter's murder, what do you think my chances are? *You* saw what he did to your brother. Am I supposed to trust the cops to protect me? Read the papers. Witnesses to professional crimes are killed all the time."

"So you packed it in and hurried home to bed." She pointed her finger at him. "You saw my little brother there in a pool of his own blood, with half his head caved in. Did you sleep *well*?"

Jerry's face went red with fury. "You know fucking well how I slept! I was in *love* with your brother."

She shook her head in wonderment. "This isn't some tricky little business problem, Jerry. It isn't one of your captain-of-industry games. Somebody was *murdered*." She pointed at her chest. "That somebody was my brother. And your lover. But you're too fucking scared to go to the cops with an *eyewitness* description. I can't believe it!"

He looked up at her, helplessness and fear in his eyes. "Don't do this to me, Janet. Getting me killed won't bring Peter back. I loved him. You know I did."

She laughed loudly. "Don't bullshit me, you phony little coward. It makes me sick. Right now, your *lover* is in a refrigerator at the fucking morgue. You loved him so much, all you can think about is yourself."

The hurt in his eyes overwhelmed the fear for a moment. "You've got a really mean mouth on you, Janet."

"Didn't Peter ever tell you about our wonderful upbringing, Jerry? My father was a long-distance trucker who fucked whores on the road and came home once a month to beat my mom. I learned from the best. He even tried me once. I put a knee in his balls that had him wincing for a month when he walked. When I left home, the world fell in love with my face and my ass, not my upbringing."

"So why don't you call the cops and tell them what I just told you?"

"Because I want to believe that the man my brother loved has a spine. I'm going to give you tonight and tomorrow to work it out. If you haven't gone to them by Monday morning, I'll go to them myself."

EIGHT

Joe Dante piloted his Corvette out the BQE, east on Northern Boulevard and eventually into the handsome College Point section of Queens. The house, near the shorefront park on Flushing Bay, had been in Lydia Lieberman's family since it was built at the turn of the century. Her husband, Gus, was a poor boy from the Grand Concourse in the West-central Bronx, but in his thirties, as a hard-charging New York lieutenant of detectives, he had, as they say, married well. A poor Jewish kid who'd played football at Catholic Fordham, he now lived in the lap of WASP luxury. The couple could gaze on the Manhattan skyline from the security of their tranquil retreat.

The deputy chief's hunger for an update had turned into an invitation to dinner. Such invitations generally came at least once a month. It seemed to amuse Gus that his wife was so taken with his ruggedly handsome right-hand man. The truth was that Gus enjoyed these dinners as well. He was a man with few close friends. Both men knew that these briefings could be handled just as easily over the phone, but Joey was a guy he could sit with in front of a crackling fire, while they smoked cigars and sipped a little prewar vintage port from the Lieberman cellar.

Dante parked his car in the driveway. While he was climbing out, he saw a sparkling white Mercedes 550 slide into the driveway of the adjacent house. A tall, elegant redhead emerged from behind the wheel. She noticed him, too, and they made eye contact. He nodded and smiled. She smiled back before opening her car's back door and retrieving a bag of groceries.

"Careful," the boss man's voice cautioned.

Joe wheeled to find him on the veranda, cocktail in hand.

"That's Carmine DiFranzio's daughter."

Dante threw a quick final glance at the shapely backside in a clinging knit dress.

"Next door? Since when?"

"Not her. The grandmother. The girl shows up every afternoon."

"And you know everything about her, right down to her shoe and cup sizes."

Gus flashed him a smug little smile. "Trust me, Joey. Intelligence knows more about Carmine than Carmine knows about himself. They say this one is supposed to be a nice kid. Raised in a convent school way out on the Island. Her daddy's already had one undesirable's kneecaps customized for looking crosswise at her."

"All I did was smile. How do they feel about Grandma living next door to a deputy chief of police?"

"They like the feeling of security it gives her."

The detective climbed the front steps to Lieberman's level, and the two men entered the grand old house. Tantalizing odors emanated from the kitchen. Lydia Lieberman, wearing an apron, emerged through a swinging door to greet the newcomer.

"Hi, Joe. Give Gus your coat and make him mix you a drink. I'm sorry to be such a lousy hostess, but I promise I'll join you as soon as this is under control."

"Smells like you've got it under control already."

She patted him on the cheek and disappeared.

Gus had some twenty-year-old Scottish single malt that

he wanted Joe to try. One of Dante's rules was never to argue with the boss, particularly when his mouth was watering. They carried their drinks from the bar to chairs in the parlor.

"What happened when you leaned on Rabinowitz this morning?" Gus wanted to know.

Dante sipped his whiskey. Its smoky, cherry-wood flavor went down like nectar.

"When we convinced him that we could tie him to the scene with a DNA print, he admitted being there until one-thirty, but that's no confession that he killed the guy. He made that clear enough."

"And what's your read? Given the stunt he pulled with the contract and all?"

Dante stared at the fire as it danced in the hearth grate. He shook his head. "In my mind, when I got out of bed this morning, he was our guy. But we hit him broadside with the contract thing, with no time to prepare a defense. Fucker argued his case without missing a beat. Claims his wife's big ideas and lousy business sense nearly rode their company into bankruptcy. Says he formed the Janet Lake outfit as a separate entity so they could legally keep profits apart and use them to loan money to Close Apparel below market. Milk it as a cash cow."

"You buying that?"

The reflected flames flickered in the detective's snifter as he raised it to his lips. "I don't know enough about this shit to make the call. It sounded good. The man practically begged us to examine his books. I tried to call Dewey Klein and run it by him this afternoon, but he's on some stakeout up in Inwood."

"He made any progress on the Avenue?"

A shrug. "I'm supposing he would have called if they had. Right now, I'm hoping to God that something breaks loose on that end. We aren't getting too far with our full-frontal attack."

"You got to meet a beautiful movie star."

"Whoop-de-fuckin'-doo, Gus. You put that one in a

tank with a barracuda, I'd give the fish about three seconds.''

"Nasty?"

Dante thought a moment and shook his head slowly. "Not really. Tough, though. Tough as fucking nails. I guess you gotta be . . . to survive in a world like that."

"A huge ego helps."

Joe chuckled. "And we humble servants of the public wouldn't know anything about that, right Gus?"

They sat awhile, drinking in silence and watching the fire. Joe thought it was a lot like watching waves at the beach. No matter how much the same it always was, each flame or wave was fascinating in it's power and subtle differences.

"Where to next?" Gus asked him at length.

"Brian Brennan's place up on the Sound. I'm headed there from here."

Gus nodded his approval. "A little R&R. That guy still shacked up with the little rock star with the incredible body?"

The chief was referring to Diana Webster, Brennan's ladylove.

"When she's not in a recording studio, on tour, or pumping iron at some gym."

Gus chuckled. "Some guys just got it tougher than others. Say hello for me. And Monday, find me something I can feed the PC. It seems that you've done something to rile Bob Talbot, and he's been whispering in Tony Mintoff's ear. The chief of detectives got a call from Big Tony, wondering if you were the right guy to be handling such a high-profile investigation."

Joe broke into a grin from ear to ear. "I made a comment about his dead-fish handshake."

"Something real polite, no doubt."

"Oh, yeah."

It was a rough weekend for Jerry Rabinowitz. All Saturday evening and Sunday morning, he and Felicity kept running into each other. Not a word passed between them. Jerry knew that she had to be gloating over her discovery of that contractual discrepancy. He resolved not to give her the satisfaction of a challenge and forced a cheery smile instead. He spent all Sunday drifting from room to room. He was petrified of talking to the police and just as frightened of walking outside. The killer hadn't seen him. He kept reminding himself of that fact. It didn't do any good. He knew the guy would get him as soon as he opened his mouth to the cops.

The town house on Beekman Place had been another of Felicity's extravagant ideas. In 1982 it had set them back four million bucks, *before* renovation. That project went another million three, the result of it being a residence that was admittedly exquisite. There was nothing too good for Felicity Close, even if she had to spend herself to the edge of bankruptcy in order to get it. She'd been strutting-proud when the *Times* Sunday Magazine did a color spread on her creation and the hard-charging, upstart couple behind it. To her it was the ultimate proof that she had arrived. Jerry could sweat the balance sheets and bottom lines. She was the ringmaster of their circus, and he was the bookkeeper. Even if he survived this crisis, managed to wrest control of the company from her, and got a divorce, he was sure she'd see him in hell before she'd give this place up.

He was in his private study that evening at six o'clock when Janet's call came. With his door locked, he'd been trying to distract himself with a selection from his extensive library of male films. He sat with a stiff Scotch in one hand as *Leather Lads Load Up* whirred silently past the heads of his VCR. He reclined on a brown leather-upholstered chaise, eyes probing every inch of an eighteen-year-old backside he now knew by heart. The twenty-seven inch Sony Trinitron rendered a sharp image of the kid, every finely tuned muscle caught in definition as it flexed. God, he looked like Peter's twin brother. There was envy in his heart as he watched the massively endowed fun-buddy the kid was going down on. With his crotchless leather pants and open motorcycle jacket, he appeared to be enjoying his bird's-eye view.

When the phone rang, he put the VCR on hold. The frame froze with the big biker teetering on the brink of sweet release. Jerry picked up his private line.

"Yeah," he said impatiently.

"Jerry?" He recognized Janet's voice, and his heart fell. His distraction vanished like fog in a stiff wind.

"I can't," he said flatly.

"What do you mean, you *can't?*"

"I've thought over all the angles. First the cops'll try to pin it on *me*. Then the word'll get out that they've got an eyewitness, and the fucker'll get me."

"They'll put you in protective custody."

"Great," he sneered. "And by the time the smoke clears, I walk out to discover that my bitch wife has destroyed everything I've worked the past fifteen years for. I'd *rather* be dead."

"I told you what I'd do, Jerry. I may owe you for what you've done for me, but I don't owe you silence on *this*. It's my brother's killer we're talking about."

"I told you because you *do* owe me," he argued. "That line of yours is selling like bullion in a bear market. I'm plowing every cent of my profit back into keeping Close Apparel afloat. Your piece is making you *rich*."

"Felicity can fuck that up, too, same as everything else you claim is so precious."

"I'm not going to the cops."

"Then I am, Jerry. Tomorrow morning."

"Have you heard anything I've said? The man will *kill* me!"

"I'm giving you until noon, Jerry. I have that bathing suit shoot, first thing, but if you haven't called them, I will. I'll invite them to the studio."

Jerry glanced back to the screen. The massive, leather-clad hips, thighs, and pelvis of the biker were tensed like a snake poised to strike.

"You might as well put a gun to my head." It was a whine, full of despair.

She broke the connection.

The full forensic workup that the partners received Monday morning wasn't much help. They pored over it, looking for some tiny opening into which they could wedge an inquiry. There was simply nothing there that they didn't already know about.

Even in the face of this discouraging fact, both of them were feeling relaxed and revitalized after an entire day off. Jumbo and Agnes had spent it in their new home, trying to get the upstairs rental unit whipped into shape. The big man still had little flecks of paint in his hair. He announced as he entered Dante's cubicle office that he'd lost another five pounds since last week's weigh-in. Joe had nothing so industrious or positive to report, but he had gotten a lot of sleep and managed to lay off excessive quantities of alcohol.

They were drinking coffee, and were just about ready to give up looking for a needle in the forensics haystack, when a uniform from the desk poked his head in the door.

"We finally ran down Dewey Klein for you, Sarge. Way up north on the corner of Dyckman and Payson in Inwood. They been staking out that location since Saturday morning. If you want to go up and talk to him, you're s'posed to look for an alley alongside number 39 Henshaw. You go down it and straight across into the building behind. It's a derelict, and they're set up in the second floor, front. The guy I talked to at Safe, Loft, and Truck was pretty adamant about you not approaching from the Payson Street side."

The partners looked at each other. You couldn't go any farther north on the island of Manhattan without getting your feet wet in the Hudson River. After two days of working his stakeout, Dewey was likely to be in a foul mood. Sitting on your ass for days on end, unable to move from one place, tended to make a man irritable.

"I'll drive," Jumbo said with a sigh. "You wanna leave now or wait till rush hour eases up a little?"

Dante glanced at his watch. It was quarter to nine.

"Now. There isn't all that much traffic heading north at this hour."

Dewey Klein was taking a break from binocular surveillance when Dante and Richardson picked their way through a debris-strewn hallway to enter his temporary abode. The structure was one of several garage buildings in a row. Above were tenement apartments with sheet metal nailed over most of the windows. For their purposes, the Safe, Loft, and Truck boys had bent back the corner of one such sheet, just as a junkie might have done to gain entrance. They'd been careful to make sure that nothing they wore or used as equipment would reflect stray light. Some enterprising individual had tapped into the Con Edison street-side power source in the basement and run a fat, rubberized cable up. A space heater was plugged into it. The place was still cold, but it was warmer than outside.

In lieu of greeting, the partners handed over a cardboard flat filled with Styrofoam cups of coffee and a bag of fresh doughnuts.

"Hear you caught a slow boat," Dante observed.

Dewey nodded, plucked one of the coffees from the flat, and peeled back the lid. "No one's even fuckin' sneezed." He gestured at a low, squat garage building diagonally across the way toward midblock. Another detective was seated on a camp stool, idly staring at the structure through field glasses. "Truckload of cigarettes was stolen off a distributor in Yonkers. The Forty-ninth caught some nasty little scrud behind the wheel of a new Testarossa, and he winged a uniform, tryin' to make his break. Somewhere during the elevator ride between booking and the holding cell, he rolled over on these jokers." He jerked his head at the dead quiet garage.

"How much is a load like that worth?" Jumbo asked him.

"With tax stamps paid for and affixed, probably about three-quarters of a mil. Owner'll probably try for twice that in his insurance claim. So what's on you lucky guys' minds?"

Dante went on to recount the stories Janet Lake and Jerry Rabinowitz had told them. Klein's air of boredom vanished as he listened, locking on every detail. When Joe finished, he took a minute to mull the information over.

"That's the second time now I've heard rumors that Close might have been havin' money troubles. They tend to keep that sort of shit close to the vest, but word sometimes leaks. I can't even remember where I heard it, but it was a couple years back, so the timing's right."

"How 'bout the way he claims to be playin' it?" Jumbo pressed. "This robbin'-Peter-to-pay-Paul crap?"

"Stroke of genius, as long as he's also plugged the leak that got him into trouble in the first place."

"The wife. Felicity Close."

"If that part is true, too. Yeah."

"How about his begging us to look at the books?" Joe asked. "Think it's a bluff?"

"Might be. If I were you, I wouldn't waste my time taking him up on it right now. If he's still your prime suspect in a week, you can subpoena the books and turn them over to the D.A."

Dante reached into the bag of doughnuts and selected one for himself. "They aren't going to mean anything if we can't find a smoking gun somewhere. My guts are telling me there's still a big piece missing somewhere."

"And the Lake broad?"

Joe shrugged. "Another good question. If she's got motive, I haven't gotten even a sniff of it. She lives like the Shah's sister. How about your end? We were hoping for rumors on the street."

Klein gestured around the squalid little room they were gathered in. "I been sorta tied up, myself. There's a couple guys in the unit that have been nosin' around. They ain't heard peep one yet.''

''You think that's odd?''

''Not if they had the whole scam set before they took the place off. Then all they gotta do is deliver the goods and wait for the line to appear in the stores. Once that happens, we've got another angle we can work from. Trace the shit back to the source. But that's months away. The body'll be worm shit in the box by then.''

''Got something, Sarge.'' It came from the guy working the window.

Klein hurried over. Joe and Jumbo followed at a distance. The guy on the camp stool was pointing.

''That Ryder box van just pulled up. There's at least two more, just like it, parked around the corner on Dyckman.''

Dante peered down into the street over the man's shoulder. He watched a short, wiry man with greased back hair hop down from the passenger side of the van and glance nervously up and down the block.

''What are you expecting next?'' Joe asked Dewey.

Klein pointed at the garage. ''There's no one inside, so I'm waiting for the dude in the limo.''

''Come again?''

''Mister Big. There's always one guy who never gets his hands dirty until it's time for the big money to change hands. One of them jokers down there has a suitcase full of green. They hand it over, the dude in the limo has one of his big boys open that garage up, and then off they go. Big load of smokes like that ain't goin' anywhere very fast, so we wait to net the honcho. The *real* prize.''

NINE

Roger Brill moved with practiced efficiency as he directed movement on the studio floor. He'd been up prepping the Janet Lake shoot since six-thirty and was all but set to get under way. He pointed to a pair of Nikon F3 cameras on the studio cart.

"Are those guns loaded?"

Greg Woleski, his young assistant, nodded. "All set, Chief."

"Okay. Let's get ready to check sync."

These two, and the host of others necessary to the smooth running of a major fashion layout shoot, stood around the perimeter of Brill's sprawling studio loft on 21st Street between Fifth and Sixth avenues. The photographer, a recognized heavyweight in the high-pressure glamour business, was lord and master here as he called all the shots. Of the people now crowding the floor, half were his direct employees, either permanent staff or free-lance. Jerry Rabinowitz insisted on having his firm's own wardrobe girl, stylist, hair and makeup people present. The advertising agency had an account manager assigned to the shoot as well, but none of these people could lift a finger without Brill's first giving them the green light. He could get away with being temperamental because of his reputation. He always delivered the goods. The money at stake often ran into the tens of thousands. In this room, it was his responsibility, and his alone, to see that a client got his money's worth.

The photographer and the famous actress–model had a good relationship that had lasted nearly two decades. Her brother had been murdered on Friday, and the funeral would be at ten tomorrow morning. Roger realized that a high-pressure assignment like the one they were preparing for had to be difficult for Janet at a time like this. He was going to handle her with kid gloves. The advertising schedule was tight, or they could simply have postponed for a few days. Janet wouldn't let him down, because Janet was a trooper.

Roger inspected the strobe leads to the last power pack prior to triggering the array of high-intensity lamps rigged around the room. Today's shoot was for a magazine spread featuring the summer line's bathing suit collection. The namesake herself had selected half a dozen garments she wanted to wear. There were four additional models on hand to sport another twenty suits in various groupings. These younger women had been selected specifically because they looked dazzling in skimpy swimsuits. Janet, a full twenty years older than the youngest of them, had decided she would stand right in there among them. If Roger and others thought that took guts, Janet was confident that the three hours she spent every day at her health club had paid off. She'd always had the necessary physical tools, and right now, she was in better shape than she'd ever been in her life. As Brill readied the studio, she was in her dressing room. After an hour of muscle-pumping, low-impact aerobics, and a shower, she was sitting while the makeup person applied her Close Cosmetics face.

Out on the floor Roger waved his studio producer over to take the star's place for the sync tests. The four other models, already in their suits, joined her on the phony poolside set for the first mock shot. The floor in front of a painted backdrop was cluttered with tables, umbrellas, and lounge chairs.

"Just stand there looking ravishing, ladies," the photographer directed. "Okay, Greg. Give me the F3 with the Polaroid back."

Woleski handed him a specially built Nikon with a Polaroid film magazine affixed. Instead of using a direct-line sync cord, Brill employed a remote firing mechanism clipped to his shirt pocket. It allowed him greater freedom of movement. He triggered the array of strobe heads once, manually, just to make sure that every one of them was working. The basic setup had been structured to create the bright, full wash of daylight. They'd done a series of film tests the previous day, but now it was show time, and they had to check the entire system once more to make sure everything functioned perfectly.

"Give me some movement, ladies," Roger cooed. "Toss those heads for me. And let's have some wind, Greg. Gentle."

Woleski kicked on a big mast-mounted fan. The breeze from it tickled the subjects' hair as they began moving from one pose to the next. The models' flesh had been slightly oiled to better define all those curves in the harsh light. The studio producer, in her blue jeans and flannel shirt, looked silly and knew it.

Brill made sure the remote sync was connected to the camera, moved in for the look he wanted, and pulled the trigger.

"Okay," he told them. "Give it a rest." As he spoke, he pulled the Polaroid exposure from the magazine and set it on the studio cart to develop. The stylist appeared from the dressing rooms. "How's it looking back there?" he wanted to know.

"Two minutes, Roger," the tall, severe brunette told him. "You know Andre. He won't let her pass until it's perfect."

Brill rolled his eyes. "This is a swimsuit shoot, not a *Vogue* cover."

She just smiled indulgently and headed for the coffee urn. Brill picked up the Polaroid print and studied it. Everything looked good; all the strobes were firing in sync, and the color was as true as a Polaroid could get it. His test strips, sent to the lab on a Sunday rush, had also looked good when they showed up first thing that morning. He was ready to go.

Janet Lake hadn't gotten much of a night's sleep. That fact and the toll her grief had taken combined to make Andre the makeup artist's task a formidable one. He was having one hell of a time getting her to sit still in the chair. She apologized repeatedly and struggled to get a handle on her agitated state. Jerry had left the responsibility for his future in her hands. She supposed that he was right, that what he'd seen could end up getting him killed. Right now, she was feeling terribly torn. Before she went to the police, she thought she needed to seek a friend's advice about it. And a friend was nearby, prowling the studio floor outside her dressing room.

Roger Brill had just been making his breakthrough and a name for himself, aggressively charging onto the scene, when the young Janet Buckley first arrived in New York. The two of them had worked together back then, with Janet building up her portfolio by giving Roger free time in the studio and on various locations. Until a time, a year later, when the aspiring model met and married financier Carl Lake, her money troubles suddenly and forever over, she and Brill had comingled ambitions for mutual benefit. When a big agency spotted her on Carl Lake's arm, she landed a lucrative contract. Those thousands of pictures Brill had taken of her were an entree all their own. They'd drifted in and out of touch but remained friends. She still liked working with him better than with any other photographer in the business.

The door to the dressing room opened, and Janet stepped forth in all her glory. The swimsuit she'd chosen to wear didn't make any exceptions for a forty-year-old body. It swept high over her hip bones, exposing a long expanse of tightly muscled thigh and posterior cheek. The back was all but nonexistent. Her tightly packed breasts swelled above the cut of a plunging neckline. Her hair was pulled back in a French braid to accentuate those world-famous facial bones.

"You look fabulous, sweetheart," Brill exulted. There was nothing insincere about it.

She rolled her eyes. "This is the first time I've been in front of a camera in a bathing suit in seven years, Roger. I feel absolutely *naked*."

He beamed benevolent reassurance. "We're all friends here, darling. And you've got absolutely nothing to be embarrassed about. Places, everyone!"

The entire studio sprang into action. Roger directed Janet out onto the set, flanked her with two models on either side, and then posed all five in attitudes of leisure. As he set up with the first of his cameras, Woleski kicked the wind on. As the light breeze touched the edges of Janet's coiffure, Andre the makeup man looked like he might faint.

In the middle of shooting that first camera's full roll, Janet saw Jerry Rabinowitz ease through the lounge door onto the set. Try as he might, it was impossible for him to remain invisible. His eyes were darting furtively. One by one, as his own employees spotted him, they began to fidget. The big boss's putting in an appearance on a shoot, unannounced, was an unsettling event for them. Theirs was tenuous employment, subject to many whims and fancies beyond their control. Andre, of them all, was the only one assured of long-term security. He'd been with Jerry and Felicity since the beginning.

"I don't like it," Roger announced as he set the camera, load now spent, on the studio cart. He beckoned to Woleski and pointed to the bank of strobes on a bar suspended directly over the set. "Those guys are firing just a tad out of sync, buddy. Yank that power pack, huh? Take five, everybody. Don't wander off."

As Janet stepped to the edge of the floor, Andre hurried over with his bag of tricks, brandishing a brush. At the same time Jerry stepped between them and held up a hand.

"I've got to have Janet for a minute, Andre." He looked at her beseechingly. "Can we talk somewhere?"

The weight of her exhaustion descended on her shoulders again as Janet looked quickly around and found Brill.

"Roger? Jerry and I have to talk a minute. Mind if we use your office?"

Brill, busy helping Greg with the power pack, shook his head quickly and waved her on. "One sync shot just to make sure we're on track, and then we're back at it, babe. Try not to be all day, huh?" He glanced around, caught Jerry's eye, and nodded.

"Did you call them?" Jerry demanded. They were shut into the confines of Roger's cluttered office, Janet in her swimsuit, perched on the edge of the desk while Jerry faced her, leaning against the door.

"When would I have had time, Jerry? I've been up since five o'clock for this goddamn shoot. I humped an exercise routine for an hour, and I've been in a chair most of the morning since."

"But you haven't changed your mind."

She shook her head emphatically. "If you hadn't shown up just now, I might have used the break to call them."

Rabinowitz thought that her face betrayed some slight indecision that her voice did not. He leapt at it like a drowning man grabbing a life preserver.

"You haven't called them because you're having second thoughts! You know the son of a bitch will hunt me down and kill me!"

"Jerry. Please."

A heavy knock came at the door, causing Jerry to jump.

"All set, Janet," Greg Woleski's youthful voice announced. "Everyone's waiting."

"Have lunch with me," Jerry begged in hushed tones.

"We've talked this all out, Jerry." She moved past him

to reach the doorknob. As she preceded him down the short hall to the studio, Jerry hurried along at her heels.

"I'm going to sit here until the lunch break," he hissed stubbornly. "You can't sign my death warrant without hearing me out again."

They broke into the busy, brightly lit studio. All eyes of the loitering crew turned.

"Go, Jerry," she whispered hoarsely.

He shook his head, a maniacal smile stretching his lips. "I'm staying right here unless you say yes."

In exasperation she relented. "For Christ's sake! All right!"

His smile broadened as he turned away and headed for the lounge door. "That bagel place around the corner on Sixth. I'll be there."

Flustered, Janet moved to rejoin the models on the set. Roger moved to put her at ease as Andre scurried in for a quick dusting of the famous face.

"Everything all right?" Brill asked.

She waved it off. "You know Jerry," she told him.

"Okay," Brill announced to the room, "one more time and then a quick suit change." He peered at his watch. "It's ten now. Let's see how much of this we can get on film before we break for lunch."

At the third suit change of the morning, Janet asked Roger if he could join her for a moment in her dressing room. As soon as the door was closed and they were alone, she started to talk. The straps of a breathtaking mono-suit came away from her shoulders, as she peeled quickly out of it and let it drop to the floor.

"We've been friends for a long time, right, Roger?"

Unselfconsciously she was already taking the next suit off the rack, the consumate pro just doing her job in the company of another consumate pro.

"A long time," he agreed. "What's it been now? Almost twenty years?"

She smiled and stretched out a hand to pat him on the cheek.

"No almost about it, chum. Twenty long ones. Some of it still seems like yesterday though, doesn't it?"

His smile was pensive. "Long ones, maybe. But they've been kind to both of us. You've never looked better, babe."

"Jerry saw the guy who killed my brother, Roger."

It struck him like a lightning bolt.

"He didn't tell the cops because he's frightened to death that the man will get to him and kill him before he could ever make a positive identification."

Brill stared at her. Jerry didn't know the half of it. He didn't know Murray Chopnik.

"But he told *you*. Jesus Christ. Why?"

She shrugged. "Guilt, I guess. He thought Peter's sister should know what a chickenshit he is."

"So what are you *doing* about it?"

"I gave him an ultimatum. Either he goes to the police today, or I do. I haven't had a spare minute, and now he's begging me to hear him out, just one more time."

Brill had the picture now and nodded. "At lunch . . ."

"Right. To appeal to my sense of compassion as a friend. And you know something? In a way he's right. He risks his life, and no matter how it turns out, it can't bring Peter back. So what the hell am I supposed to do? Let my brother's murderer go scot-free? Not to mention that he also stole the designs to our fucking fall line?"

As she was stating her case in these linear terms, Brill was frantically thinking rings around her. He couldn't act too interested in the specifics of Jerry's revelation, but visual identification of Murray was a deadlock if he was ever caught. And if Murray was ever caught, there was little doubt in Roger's mind that he, too, would take a fall. That meant being charged with murder.

"What's another hour, Janet?" he asked sincerely, his voice dripping with understanding and sympathy. "You sound like your mind is already made up. So hear him out another time, just to ease your own conscience and convince yourself that you've given him all the breaks."

She was into the next suit now and wiggling to adjust it. After surveying the fit in the full-length wall mirror, she took a deep breath, pushed it out quickly and nodded.

"You're right, I guess. Thanks for listening, Rog. Let's get on with it, huh?"

TEN

The windowless, one story target of Klein's three day stakeout was isolated midblock in this fringe section of Inwood, with empty lots on either side of it. Red brick, it stretched back from Payson Street to touch Riverside Drive where it terminated at Dyckman Boulevard. On the island of Manhattan, this was the boonies. Just down the block from where the cops now sat Dyckman Boulevard threaded through the sprawling Inwood Hill Park, ducked beneath the Henry Hudson Parkway and met the Hudson River. At the other end of Payson Street, where it intersected with Riverside Drive, Fort Tryon Park climbed steeply through granite outcroppings toward the tranquil seclusion of The Cloisters, the medieval art museum. And down in this little saddle between the Henry Hudson Parkway and Broadway lay a neighborhood of drab Depression-era apartment blocks and rows of squat, dingy garages. The predominant makeup of the local population was European. The streets themselves were quiet, and the commerce of these scattered garages appeared to move at a lazy pace.

Now that the rental vans were in place and the trap was set to be sprung, Dewey called in the unmarked backup he would use to seal off both ends of the street. Once the real quarry entered the trap, those units would roll into position as Klein got on the hailer and apprised the guilty parties of their options.

Halfway between her talk with Roger and the break for lunch, Janet made up her mind. This wasn't some sort of friendship and betrayal game they were playing. This was murder. When Brill called a ten-minute break between shots, she changed quickly into her next suit and used one of the phones in the lounge to call the number on the card Sergeant Dante had left her. Informed that the detective was not in, she asked the woman taking the message to convey that it was urgent, and gave both the studio's phone number and its address.

With each passing minute, Dewey Klein became increasingly impatient. Dante knew the feeling and watched sympathetically as the sergeant clapped the cop on the stool, Rudd, on the shoulder for the third or fourth time.

"As soon as you see it, buddy."

"You want to hear about it. Gotcha." The younger detective was still peering intently back and forth to both ends of the block. Then, without any apparent excitement, he grunted. "How about now, boss?"

Klein did a double take and stooped to take the proffered binoculars. And sure enough, a big white Lincoln limousine with Jersey plates glided around the corner off Dyckman and rolled cautiously on toward the sidewalk rendezvous directly below.

Dante and Jumbo both hurried into the next room, where another window's tin had been partially folded back. They crowded in to watch developments on the street below. Dewey could be heard transmitting the order sealing off both ends of the street. As soon as the stretch-limo came to a halt, the man riding shotgun in the front passenger seat hopped out and sauntered toward the first box van. He was big for a South American, at least six feet, and pushing two and a quarter on a broad-shouldered but still narrow-waisted frame.

"That guy looks like some heavy muscle," Jumbo observed. "Lookit the cannon bulge under his left arm. Dude must have a Howitzer under there."

The muscle and the smaller, wiry man from the truck stood conversing on the sidewalk for a brief time before the little guy signaled to his driver. The door of the truck came open, and a cheap zippered suitcase was pushed out onto the street.

As he watched the big man stoop to retrieve the case and then set it on the hood of the limousine, Dante saw the first of the unmarked sedans creep into view at the south end of the block.

"Here we go," he muttered.

The hijackers and their buyers still hadn't noticed the sedan's arrival. Their attentions were fixed on each other. There was obviously no honor among thieves here. The bigger guy unzipped the case, flipped back the top, and inspected the contents. Even from where Joe and Jumbo sat, they could see the thing was crammed full of cash. The big henchman displayed dexterity in pawing through it. When he seemed satisfied, he pulled the lid back over, tugged the zipper, and lugged the thing back along the car to the right rear door. The smoked glass, which to that point had obscured the interior, came slowly down.

Dewey decided it was time to spring the trap and ordered the seal-off units to advance and establish barricades.

"Park the cars in the street and get the hell to cover," he directed. "Anyone who exposes himself could get cut to ribbons in cross fire. Trust these crazy fuckers to decide they want to play it John Wayne-style. Now go!"

And go they did, descending to within twenty yards on either side of the action as Klein's amplified voice boomed out over the scene.

At the first word, the big guy with the money pushed it through the open window and had his Ingrahm MAC-10 machine pistol out in an instant. The little guy from the other team never knew what hit him as a short burst from that wicked weapon tore into his chest.

Dante saw the next move coming, and was wondering if anyone else had as he started toward the door. "The garage!" he yelled. "They're gonna *crash* it!" He was off at a dead run.

Jumbo, dumbfounded and still not getting it, bounded up out of his crouch to back his partner up. Dante was headed out of the building the way they'd come, not toward the scene of the shooting on Payson, but through the back alley. He reached Henshaw Street way ahead of Beasley, got the car started, and swung it around on smoking rubber.

"Shit!" Jumbo gasped, gulping air as he collapsed into the passenger seat. Dante didn't even wait for him to get his legs all the way in or close the door before he tromped the accelerator to the fire wall.

"That garage is double ended!" Joe barked above the growl of the Plymouth's power plant. "Even if they're stacked right in front of the entrance, cigarettes can't offer much resistance!"

"You think they're gonna try to go through?"

Dante cranked the wheel hard, squealed around the corner onto Dyckman, and headed toward the intersection where it met Riverside Drive and Broadway.

"Wouldn't you?" he demanded. "The big guy just killed that poor fucker. Even if Dewey's people managed to get *him*, everybody in that car's an accessory."

"Not that you ain't, but you'd better hurry, dude. We ain't got a clue what any of the others look like, and there's a subway station right up here. They get down onto that platform, it's just two or three stops before that train intersects with the IRT at 168th Street. That complex is a motherfucker."

"One of 'em will be carrying a suitcase," Joe assured him. "There's no way they'll leave all that money behind."

* * *

Lucho Falco gripped the handle of the suitcase and crouched on the spacious backseat of his Lincoln stretch limousine as Jaime, his driver, accelerated up across the sidewalk and crashed headlong into the roll-up metal door. Fortunately for them the thing wasn't built to withstand that sort of impact. Unfortunately for the cases of cigarettes stacked directly behind it, neither were they. The big engine snarled beneath the hood as they thundered through half a million dollars worth of Phillip Morris offerings. Lucho knew the warehouse was less than half-full; the Riverside Drive end empty. Hoche, the poor bastard, was cut to ribbons in the street back there, and half the glass in the car was on the upholstery all around him, but they had a shot at it. Those dumbshit cops hadn't counted on one street-bad Ecuadorian who thought nothing of walking or driving through walls. They were still back there scratching their cojones and wondering what had happened. He and Jaime were fifty feet from reaching the daylight at the other end of the tunnel.

The limo hit the roll-up at the opposite end of the garage with a deafening crash. Just as Falco suspected, there was no one around to stop them.

"We've got to get rid of the car! Pronto!" he ordered his driver. "I don't care where. We are better off on foot now."

Because he had demanded the payoff be in small, easily negotiable bills, the five hundred thousand was heavy and difficult to move with. He needed to get to ground as quickly as possible and then sort out their next move. When a subway stop suddenly materialized directly ahead, it seemed as much a miracle as the apparitions of the virgin at Fatima and Guadalupe.

Dante and Jumbo spotted the battered Lincoln within seconds of entering the intersection of Riverside, Dyckman, and Broadway. The damn thing was double-parked in front of a newsstand, with both the driver's and left rear doors hanging open.

"Seconds," Jumbo guessed. "The door handles must still be hot."

Dante brought their Fury up to a screeching stop and leapt out, while Jumbo did his best to keep up. As Joe hurried forward, he was pointing to the subway entrance, dead ahead.

"Get on the horn and call in some backup," he yelled. "And keep an eye peeled up here. They could just be using the subway to throw us off."

The familiar weight of his Walther automatic gave him something less than complete confidence as he descended the subway stairs without backup. He flashed his tin at the woman in the token booth as he edged along the turnstiles and slid under the one offering the best protection. There wasn't much of a crowd here on the uptown platform, with only one stop to the north before the IND line ended. But as he gazed across the tracks to the downtown side, he found it to be considerably more congested. There were maybe as many as thirty people over there.

His eyes slowly scrutinized every one of them. As yet, he could hear no train rumbling toward the station from either direction and decided he could afford to take this time. Mothers with toddlers. Mothers with babies in strollers. A knot of loud kids. A young woman in a business suit, gripping a briefcase. Two men standing casually, smoking and talking with animated gestures. A mother with a stroller, and a baby in her arms.

From the downtown direction, he could hear a train now approaching the station. In another moment, his vantage would be cut off as the train rolled in to stop, discharge passengers, and then get going again. He headed for the stairs leading down to the crossover tunnel.

The train approached the station, its brakes emitted a crescendoing banshee howl, and it came, finally, to a halt. By then Dante had traversed the tunnel, and was emerging on the downtown side. Cautiously he approached the two gesticulating men, pitched one forward onto his face with a vicious sweep kick to his feet, and wedged his pistol up under the other's chin. With his free hand, he caught a fist full of the man's shirt and propelled him face-first into the nearest wall. Judging from the sound of it, the man's nose shattered on impact. Dante left him holding his face, leapt onto the fallen man's back, and quickly cuffed him.

"I still don't get how you *knew*." Jumbo marveled. They were back in the Plymouth now, parked at the scene on Payson Street, waiting to give the local duty captain their statements. "You were down there less than three minutes."

"It was the mother with the stroller and the baby in her arms. The kid wasn't crying, and he looked pretty big to be held for long. It made me curious about what was in the stroller. Those two were standing a good twenty feet away, cool as ice. Then I saw the way the mother looked at them."

The big Ecuadorian bodyguard, the skinny little guy from the truck, and one other man had been killed in the exchange of gunfire surrounding Lucho Falco's break for freedom. Two other men from the rented trucks had been wounded, one critically in the abdomen and the other superficially in the right leg. With that much blood spilled, there was going to be a lot of bureaucratic red tape to wade through before the partners could cut loose, even though they hadn't been directly involved in the gunplay.

That detective, Sergeant Dante, still hadn't returned Janet's call by the time Roger had them break for lunch.

"Just half an hour, right, people? I want us all out of here at a reasonable time tonight."

Janet changed quickly into street clothes, not bothering to worry about the glistening oil and heavy makeup. Jerry had to be crawling out of his skin, and she felt she owed him the courtesy of telling him that she'd already placed that call.

The weather had warmed considerably since the last time she'd been outside, before sunup. She hurried along 21st Street toward Sixth Avenue with her coat hanging open. It was still a few minutes before noon, and the early lunch rush hadn't begun. Pedestrian traffic on the sidewalk was light, and this was a neighborhood where she felt comfortable on foot. Most big photographers had studios within just a few blocks, and models were a common sight. Laborers on the street might hoot appreciatively, but no one ever bothered her.

Jerry, impeccably turned out in tailored business attire, sat impatiently stubbing out a half-smoked cigarette as she entered the restaurant and crossed to peck him on the cheek. He'd been busy, by the look of it. His ashtray was brimming with crushed butts.

Before Jerry could utter a word, she leaned across the table toward him, her elegant hands splayed palms outward.

"I left a message with Sergeant Dante, Jerry. He wasn't in, but when he calls back, I *am* going to tell him what you saw. You can't talk me out of it. My mind is made up on this, so please don't try."

The wind went out of his sails. He slumped back in his chair and abandoned his groping for a fresh cigarette. As he contemplated her with accusing eyes, his fingers closed around the near-empty pack and slowly crushed it.

Against that baleful stare, she could only lift her chin in regretful defiance. This wasn't easy for her.

"Demand protective custody."

He snorted derisively. "A lot of fucking good *that* will do. Do you have any idea how long it takes to bring a man like that to justice? If I demand protective custody, I might as well apply for Social Security while I'm at it. I'll be eligible by the time they finally turn the key on him, if ever."

A waitress approached the table and asked Janet if she would like to order. The model shook her head and said no thanks, she wasn't staying. As the waitress moved on, Janet stood up.

"I'm sorry, Jerry. If this affects our business relationship, then that's the way it has to be."

"I loved him, too, you know," he murmured.

By the time he said it, she was already too far away to hear him.

Murray Chopnik was sitting in his car, parked by a hydrant across 19th Street. He'd gotten there fifteen minutes after Roger's call. That was an hour and a half ago, and now he watched as the model got up abruptly from the table inside the restaurant. As she hurried out, the big Texan smiled to himself, watching her move. Goddamn, that was one finely tuned filly. He wondered just how much she knew of what Jerry-boy actually saw that fateful night. From what Roger had told him, it sounded like she only knew that the squirrelly little faggot had seen him. The tête-à-tête they'd just had in the bagel joint couldn't have done much to broaden her knowledge. She'd been in and out as quick as a tornado through a one-horse prairie town. He hoped he was right about what she knew. The world couldn't afford to lose that kind of female beauty.

Inside the restaurant Rabinowitz could still be seen sitting at his table, looking agitated as hell, when one of the brown-uniformed personnel from the city's traffic bureau approached Murray's midnight-blue Buick from the sidewalk side and rapped on the window. She pointed at the hydrant and gestured that Murray should move it along. In response he reached into his breast pocket, extracted a small leather wallet, and flipped his Federal tin and identification at her. Until Jerry was finished, he wasn't going anywhere.

ELEVEN

It seemed that one thing had just led to another. After on-the-scene questioning and then hours of statements, the day was shot. En route back toward midtown, with Jumbo behind the wheel this time, Dante struggled mentally to get some momentum back into their investigation. Even while distracted with his cigarette heist, Dewey Klein had sent a couple of men sniffing around the Garment District for leads on the Janet Lake design theft. The weekend was admittedly a bad time to conduct such inquiries. On the Jewish and Christian Sabbaths, Fashion Avenue was a virtual ghost town. Now, with these trigger-happy Ecuadorian factions in the bag or in rubber bags, Klein would be able to devote direct attention to their problem. Still, Joe couldn't shake the feeling that they were all becalmed while their perp was sailing merrily along.

Nothing they'd heard led them to believe that Jerry Rabinowitz was lying about the contract or the way he was conducting business. When Felicity Close had first shown Joe the document, his immediate conclusion was that Rabinowitz and Buckley had something shady working. That it had gotten nasty. That the semen in Buckley's dead guts proved that his boyfriend had been lying about his whereabouts for good reason. The finger was pointing straight at the Close Apparel CEO. Dante had seen Jerry's motivation as being money, plain and simple. He wasn't blaming himself for taking the bait. In ninety-nine percent of all homicides, the most obvious trail leads to the killer. Jerry still had to be their prime target, but the focus on him was getting fuzzier by the minute. After him came Janet Lake and her possible conflict of interest. Her tie-in with Close Apparel through her brother and his action as signatory on her contract struck him as a potential time bomb. But to what purpose? The killing of her own brother? And why had the perp stolen those salesmen's samples if the design theft in no way required them? The design assistant, Hillary Fox, had seemed more perplexed by this question than any other.

Jumbo got them out onto the Henry Hudson Parkway in hopes of avoiding the early-rush-hour midtown snarl. Spring had sprung out of nowhere, and the sun danced dazzlingly out on a river caressed by balmy breezes from the south. Joe had the window down and his elbow hanging out for the first time since Halloween. Idly he reached for the radio mike and thumbed the transmit switch on. When the dispatcher answered, Joe requested that he be patched through to Borough Command for messages. The desk at Manhattan South relayed Janet Lake's urgent request that they get in touch, along with a phone number and address.

The address was a four story loft building on the north side of West 21st Street just east of Sixth Avenue. The afternoon delivery snarl Jumbo encountered was typical of the entire midtown area between 42nd and 14th streets. Trucks of every configuration were parked every which way in relation to the curb: perpendicular to or diagonally, half up on the sidewalk or half blocking traffic. It was a tight squeeze, but the big man eventually found a hydrant slot he could shoehorn it into.

The photographer's studio was easy enough to locate. It

occupied the entire top floor of the address. After riding up to it in a painfully slow converted freight elevator, they stepped off to be confronted by a flannel-shirted watchdog behind a massive Formica desk.

"Help you gentlemen?" the young woman asked.

Both detectives extracted their wallets and showed her their tin.

"We understand that Janet Lake is here today," Joe said. "She left a message asking us to get in touch."

The receptionist's demeanor changed swiftly. Having the cops show up in unlikely places generally forced such transitions.

"She is, uh . . ."

"Detective Sergeant Dante. This is Detective Richardson."

"They just finished a swimsuit shoot in there, and my orders are to keep everyone out, no exceptions . . . but then I guess you are an exception to the exception, huh?"

Dante smiled indulgently. "That's right. Could you let the lady know that we're out here?"

"Mr. Brill's producer is going to chew my head off."

Jumbo spoke softly. "If you think maybe you're gonna have a problem, we'd be glad to back you up. We're the cops, remember?"

She seemed to like that idea and nodded eagerly. "Sure," she agreed. "I'd rather risk *her* yelling at you."

They followed the young woman through a big office-type area cluttered with worktables and desks before entering the studio lounge. It looked a lot like someone's living room, only larger, with several different groupings of furniture. The walls were done in oak wainscoting to waist level and wallpaper in a bright floral print to heavy crown moldings. The appointments, from the leather couches and chairs to ornate brass-and-glass wall sconces, looked expensive. A zinc-wrapped wet bar sported a coffee machine and refrigerator beneath. All the comforts of home.

At yet another door the watchdog suggested they "hang

on a minute,'' while she opened it to poke her head through into the studio itself. From where they stood behind her, the detectives could see stacks of poolside gear, people coiling cables, and others just milling around.

"At least there's no one naked in there," the girl told them and then led them inside.

"Holy shit!" Jumbo murmured into Dante's ear. "Did I just die and go to heaven?"

Joe jabbed an elbow into his partner's ribs. By all appearances this was a fashion shoot that was just wrapping up. People were busy packing cases and moving equipment around as, over to one side, half a dozen voluptuous women clad in the skimpiest of bathing suits conversed with two women in business suits. Janet Lake was among them, and it was another moment before it occurred to Joe that the rest of these women had to be fifteen to twenty years younger than she. Yet, from where he stood, and with only a few square inches of fabric between her and the altogether, that age disparity was minimal. The famous face was a bit more chiseled, perhaps. The musculature tighter and more readily defined. Indeed, Janet Lake was in superb physical condition.

"Close your mouth, or we're gonna need a crowbar to pry your tongue up off the floor," he muttered to Jumbo.

The big guy turned to scowl at him. "I suppose you *ain't* enjoyin' the scenery?"

From a room off the side of the studio, a boyishly handsome man of perhaps forty-five emerged carrying one of those aluminum cases photographers always seemed to sport.

"I'm off," he announced to the room, aiming it toward the cluster of bathing beauties and their suit-clad cohorts. "Got to get this film to the lab if you people want to see something by tomorrow afternoon."

"Mr. Brill always hand carries the film from his shoots," the watchdog informed them. "He won't trust anyone with it."

So this was the famous photographer. Dante had heard

108

his name bandied about, as much in social columns as in reference to his work. The man was a bona fide fixture with the glitz-and-glitter crowd. And he certainly looked the part. He carried himself with a jocular bounce in his step and was Hollywood-handsome in that Bob Wagner sort of way.

It was time to find out what the model's urgent message was all about. Joe was heading toward the cluster of women when another, significantly less attractive number moved to stop them.

"What's the meaning of this? Who the hell are you?"

This had to be the studio producer of whom the watchdog was so fearful. Joe could see why she wouldn't want to be chewed on by this one.

"Police officers," he told her. "We have a message from Ms. Lake saying there's something urgent she needs to speak with us about."

The producer's head swung back and forth, eyes blazing bright fury as she scanned the crowd of hired help.

"Brigette! How the hell did they get in here!"

Jumbo set a heavy hand on her arm and squeezed just enough to get her attention. "Hold on, lady. Maybe you didn't hear the man. He said police officers. We *walked* in here. On our own flat feet."

The producer's demeanor changed. She swallowed hard, scowling but no longer the aggressor.

"We're awfully busy at the moment. Couldn't this happen a little later? I'm on a tight schedule and trying to get things wrapped up."

"She called *us*. And believe it or not, we're busy, too."

The scowl dissolved in surprise as Janet Lake spotted them and came hurrying over. "Sergeant. I left my message at your office this morning. It's been *hours*."

"We got caught up in a shooting incident, ma'am."

She suggested they follow her as she led them through the lounge and into the privacy of a workroom beyond.

"What's this about?" Dante asked. He'd turned to face her as she closed the connecting door.

Janet had grabbed a robe off a chair. She pulled it on. "Jerry Rabinowitz saw the man who killed Peter."

"What?" Both cops blurted it at once.

"He lied to you about when he left that night. He'd gone to his office to pick up some papers. He got side-tracked. He was on his way out when he saw a man with a hand truck in the reception area. A big guy in building-maintenance coveralls."

"When?" Dante pressed. "Did he say when this was?"

"Quarter to three. The guy was just pushing the hand truck out the door, and Jerry's sure he didn't see him."

"He didn't say anything?"

"He told me that the guy had blood on his coveralls. He was confused, but even more frightened. Then he went looking for Peter, and found him on the pattern room floor."

"How long have you known this?" Jumbo demanded.

She turned to meet him head-on. "Since Saturday night."

"And you're just tellin' us now?"

"Jerry's scared to death that if you know he can identify the man, the man will hunt him down and kill him. I told him he had to go to you with what he knew, that I'd give him until this morning. I talked to him last night, and he still wasn't willing to contact you, so I did."

Dante shoved his hands deep in his pockets and began to pace. "Do you believe him?"

She seemed startled by the question. "What's *that* supposed to mean?"

"Only that another scenario also occurs to me. Jerry has now admitted that he was on the scene at the time of your brother's death. He doesn't admit that to us himself, but feeds it to you, along with this story about a mysterious janitor. *You* feed that story to us."

"Are you saying that you don't believe he saw someone?"

Head down, eyes on the carpet ahead as he moved,

Dante said, "I'm saying that right now, I don't know what to believe, Ms. Lake. Your confidant has been playing a lot of curious games lately. What you just told us makes me wonder if maybe he's playing another one."

"I think I *know* him," she argued. "Believe me when I tell you that the man is scared silly right now."

"Did he describe this man to you?"

"Just that he was big. Six and a half feet tall and maybe two hundred fifty pounds."

Jumbo snorted. "That's not big, lady. That's *huge*. How good's your friend at estimating size?"

"He's in the fashion business, *Detective*. His business is people's sizes."

"How about hair color?" Dante asked. "What his face looked like?"

She shook her head. "We never got that far. But I know Jerry well enough to believe that he isn't pulling some sort of trick here. He's scared to death, and I'm telling you this, even though he begged me not to, because I want my brother's killer caught. If you think Jerry did it, you're barking up the wrong tree."

"Let us worry about where we bark, ma'am," Jumbo suggested. "If your brother's boyfriend convinces us he's tellin' the truth, we'll get him into protective custody. We don't like the idea of losin' a primary witness any more than he does."

Jerry Rabinowitz was struggling hard against coming completely unglued. Doom was right around the corner. He was just as sure of it as he was sure he was not a brave man. Clever, yes. And a bright, able tactician. But not brave. From the restaurant on Sixth Avenue he'd called the office to inform his secretary that he wouldn't be coming in at all that afternoon. Then he went to the Excelsior health club on East 57th for a long work-out and an hour of steam. Exercise and steam always seemed to melt the tension away, but not this time. He already knew exactly how it would happen, and he couldn't stop thinking through every step of the journey. That tall, rangy cop and his fat black partner would come. Then the newspapers and TV stations would carry the story of an eyewitness to the spectacular Close Apparel murder. Then the killer himself would begin stalking him. Death would come, as the Bible put it, like a thief in the night.

So he sat at home in his study, waiting for those cops, a stiff Scotch in one hand and another of his favorite tapes in the VCR. In *Lube Rack*, a host of muscled-up pump-jockeys cavorted in the grease-smudged confines of a filling-station garage. The same kid who was in *Leather Lads*, the one who reminded him so much of Peter, was featured in this film, too.

Downstairs, the front doorbell rang. Jerry peered at the face of his watch and thumped the arm of his chair with a clenched fist. Since Janet got up and left him sitting alone at his table, a mere four hours had passed.

Reluctantly he pushed himself to his feet, hit the stop and off buttons on the remote, and shuffled forward to meet his fate. Before he could get to the intercom panel in the hall outside his study door, it blared a second time.

"What?" he snarled into it.

"Mr. Rabinowitz? Police officers. We'd like to talk with you."

Jerry nearly sneered something obscene into the mouthpiece. Talk with him. That was a joke. Hand him his death warrant was more like it.

His scowl of irritation was still fixed on his face as he threw the security deadbolts and yanked the front door open. Monday was the maid's day off, completing his indignity.

The scowl changed to confusion as he recognized the lone man on the stoop. It was just a glimpse of him, moving through the front doors of Close Apparel. A janitor pushing a hand truck. But the curly gray hair and extraordinary size were unmistakable. The man raised a

112

noise-suppressed 9mm automatic and aimed the muzzle between Jerry's eyes. Without a word, he pulled the trigger.

The top of Jerry Rabinowitz's skull exploded into a pulp of bone fragments and brain matter. It made a real mess of an impeccably maintained entry hall. Murray Chopnik casually returned the gun to his coat and reached to pull the door behind him before turning away. He had just cleared the stoop of the brownstone and was beginning a stroll up the sidewalk toward First Avenue when a late-model maroon Plymouth Gran Fury rolled through the intersection ahead. He was well clear of the mess he'd just made, but it would be nice to be clear of the vicinity as well. A quick glance around revealed no opportunity for an inconspicuous fade. The last thing he wanted to do in a neighborhood like this was quicken his step. The key was not to draw attention.

He was a hundred feet clear of the brownstone's front stoop when the Fury passed at normal speed. His peripheral vision caught the driver flick a look at him in passing. Bareheaded and without time even to tug his collar up, he opted to carry on with head held high. There was no way any occupant of that car could have seen him descend those front steps. He was just a casual pedestrian out for a stroll.

The car slowed with a flash of brake lights. Even without his turning to get a fix on it, Murray's sense of timing told him that it had come to a stop near the address he'd just left. He thought about the pistol in his coat pocket. There were six rounds left in the seven-shot clip, and one in the chamber. He eased his right hand in to wrap fingers around the butt of the gun. When he reached the corner of First Avenue, still walking without breaking his pace, he turned into the cover of a phone booth, and allowed himself a cautious look back.

The Fury was parked directly in front of the town house where he'd just left Jerry Rabinowitz convulsing on the foyer floor. Two men were getting out. The confident way they moved screamed cop. The driver was a lanky, fair-haired white man. His partner was black and huge, going at least two fifty and probably more. They made for the stoop and started up it. Murray marveled at just how close he'd cut it. He didn't worry about looking conspicuous now. He got the hell out of there.

TWELVE

The front door of the Close-Rabinowitz town house was slightly ajar; the throw rug from the vestibule was bunched beneath it. In an ultraexclusive residential enclave like Beekman Place, Dante thought this made about as much sense as the conflicting stories they'd been fed recently. Then he saw the spattered blotches of blood.

"Whoa." He touched Jumbo lightly on the sleeve. "Any second now, I think you're gonna be glad you had a light lunch."

"Aw, Christ!" Beasley spotted the tiny streaks and droplets.

Both of them drew their weapons, assumed crouches, and moved to either side of the doorway. When Joe gave him the signal, Jumbo flicked one of his size fourteens out and shoved the door open. It moved quickly inward, came up hard against an obstruction, and stopped with a dull thud. A human hand was now visible in the soft interior light. A pool of bright crimson crept toward it across the white marble floor. Blood also streaked the adjacent wall, along with bits of blackened tissue. Dante abandoned caution and hurried forward with Jumbo backing him.

It was Rabinowitz all right, with the top half of his head

blown off. Blood had barely stopped pumping from that gaping wound. His body was still warm to the touch. He'd been dead for a scant few minutes.

Dante's mind raced back over the landscape of their approach to this place. It picked up a lone pedestrian. A tall, heavyset man in an expensive-looking topcoat. Curly gray hair. Janet Lake reported that Jerry had described the janitor as huge. Six and a half feet tall and two hundred fifty pounds. This guy wasn't quite that, but he'd been big. Maybe six four and two twenty-five.

"Call this in." He was already pushing himself to his feet and making for the sidewalk. The guy had been headed toward First Avenue. This block, jammed up against the East River, was a short one. His conscience brimming with self-reproach for not taking *this* wild story more seriously than the others, Joe sprinted for the corner.

At the intersection with First, he stopped to spin and scan in all directions. There were very few pedestrians about. He spotted a couple strolling toward him from the north and decided to take a flyer. He dragged out his shield and approached them.

"Did you happen to see a big man go past?" he asked, tin extended for their examination. "Curly gray hair?"

These people were in their late sixties or early seventies, affluent in dress and demeanor.

"Bloody rude, he was," the old fellow said crossly. The accent was clipped British. "Nearly knocked the missus down. Didn't even have the decency to apologize."

"He was in a hurry then?"

"He was *running*."

"Did you get a good look at him?"

They glanced at each other and shook their heads.

" 'Fraid not, old boy," the Brit confessed. "Elspeth's got a bad hip. I was most concerned with protecting her. As soon as I realized he was on a collision course, I pulled her out of harm's way. He was a big bruiser."

Dante thanked them and retraced his steps to the scene of the homicide. Just driving past, he'd gotten a pretty good look at the guy. He hoped it would be enough to get them a workable sketch.

It had to be thirty degrees warmer than when he'd left the house that morning. After having sprinted a quick hundred yards, he could feel himself sweating through the shirt and sweater he wore under his tweed jacket. His weapon was in the clip holster at the small of his back, so he stripped off the jacket and carried it over his shoulder. He could hear the distant wail of approaching sirens.

Jumbo was sitting on the front stoop.

"You wanna tell me what all that was about?"

"A guy I saw on the street as we drove up. Not huge, but big. When I felt Rabinowitz was that warm, something just kicked in."

"And?"

"Long gone. Almost knocked down a couple of geezers on First Avenue. They said he came on them at a dead run."

Jumbo considered this information. "The somethin' that kicked in. The description our dead guy gave the Lake broad? I don't remember seein' no guy on the street. He was big enough to maybe be our perp?"

Joe shrugged. "He was in an awful hurry to get the hell away from here. I'd say he had two inches and twenty-five pounds on me."

"That ain't six and a half feet."

"But maybe close enough, huh?"

The big black man sighed and shook his head. "This fucker's only four days old and already it's got more dips and turns than the Coney Island Cyclone."

A pair of blue-and-whites screeched to a halt at the curb. Four uniforms piled out. In this neck of the woods, the department didn't like radio calls reporting gunshot victims. The local precinct reacted with real speed. Even as the uniforms were hurrying toward them across the sidewalk, an unmarked Plymouth Reliant full of detectives arrived. The partners knew that before long, half the brass in the job would be there. When a designer went down in an office tower, that was one thing. When a CEO got it in the head at home on Beekman Place, that was altogether another. A whack job like this one was certain to have political repercussions.

Forty-five minutes later, the sidewalk outside the town house was a three-ring circus. Dante had managed to sneak away from all the madness and was poking around upstairs, while the lab technicians combed and dusted the foyer. By the time Jumbo managed to break away and join him, he'd already caught a few frames of *Lube Rack* in Jerry's study. He'd run across nothing else even mildly intriguing, but detectives learn to grab any opportunities to poke around in dirty linen before it's too late. Lawyers and bereaved loved ones prefer to tie up embarrassments with red tape.

A hubbub of raised voices on the sidewalk outside prompted Beasley to spread the heavy curtains and peer out the window.

"The widow. Just pulled up to the curb. Mercedes stretch. Half a fuckin' block long. White. Must be nice."

Dante slapped a file folder closed against his knee and returned it to the drawer he'd been pawing through.

"I don't know. Think of all the energy you'd have to expend, just keeping up appearances."

"*And* the lousy gas mileage. You find anything?"

Joe shook his head and stood. "You as pissed off as I am that Janet Lake waited all that time before she called?"

"You mean that earlier mighta saved the dude's life? Forget it, Joey. Us skippin' lunch mighta saved his life. But he's dead. Bottom line's gotta be that he chose to keep his own mouth shut."

"To everyone but her."

"So maybe that was dumb of him. You think *she* called the shooter?"

Dante led the way from the room. "Would that surprise you?" he asked.

"Yeah," Jumbo muttered. "That's somethin' that

would. Unless she was hopin' the guy'd get caught. Two fewer red lights on the way over here, and we *mighta* got here."

The two men descended a magnificent mahogany staircase to the ground floor. The entry area at the foot of the stairs was a maelstrom of dusting-lab men and strobe-popping photographers. The front door was tightly shut against the more public chaos outside, with a uniform leaning against it to make sure it stayed that way. Through the Tiffany stained glass on either side of that ornate oak panel, the partners could observe a riot of flashing squad car lights and the bright kliegs of the television news crews.

"Okay!" It was almost like a bark from Bernie Horvath, the lab crew chief, who indicated with a beckoning finger that a couple of the medical examiner's men could now bag the corpse. At the movement on the stairs behind him, he glanced around.

"Dante. Heard you guys were around here somewhere."

"How's it look, Bernie?"

"The guy's real dead, cowboy. And the scene's very clean. You got any special requests?"

"Just the usual. Ballistics on the slug. A miracle or two."

They waited until the zipper on the body bag was tugged all the way closed before opening the front door and proceeding out onto the stoop. The uniforms behind the yellow tape were keeping half a dozen different news teams at bay. Beyond them, isolated between a couple of unmarked cars, Gus Lieberman, Chief of Detectives Murphy, and Commissioner Mintoff were locked in animated conversation with Felicity Close. Dante slipped under the tape and sidled over as unobtrusively as he could manage.

"You don't think the public is going to hear about this outrage?" the Close woman seethed. She seemed to be aiming the bulk of her invective at the PC. "My husband is dead in there, and you refuse to let me into my own house to be at his side!''

A sawed-off little runt of a man with a reputation for taking no shit from anyone, Anton "Tony" Mintoff was trying his damnedest to keep cool. "Chief Lieberman just explained that you don't want to see your husband in his present condition, ma'am."

This was a different Felicity Close. The mild-mannered facade Dante had seen early Friday morning had vanished. This persona was accustomed to giving commands. She was having none of Mintoff's mollifying.

"Instead of worrying whether a widow can handle being at the side of her murdered husband, you people ought to be out trying to find the monster who did this to him!"

"We've got every resource available to the department working on it," Mintoff replied. "We're operating on the assumption that this is directly tied to the homicide on the premises of your corporation's offices last Friday morning. Chief Lieberman has already assembled a special task force. They're pressing full ahead."

The front door of the house opened and a gurney bearing the corpse was rolled out into the fading light of early evening. The uniforms on the street worked to push the news hounds back. Others, on the stoop, attempted to mask the gore still visible on the entry hall walls. The door closed on that grisly scene just as quickly as the body could be dragged through.

While following the gurney's progress onto the sidewalk, Dante spotted Rosa holding court with reporters. At her side stood Captain Bob Talbot, looking slick in his neatly tailored dress uniform.

Gus broke away from the confrontation between Mintoff and Felicity Close to join his team leader.

"What the hell's going on here, Joey?" he asked under his breath.

"If it gets out, it's gonna get messy for us," Dante replied. "Rabinowitz was on the scene Friday morning and saw Buckley's killer."

"Jesus *Christ*!"

"I know. The son of a bitch was so afraid this would happen that he lied to us. We just found out about it." Joe went on to describe Janet Lake's involvement and the guy he'd seen on the sidewalk. "We were inclined to believe Rabinowitz fed the model a line of shit, Gus. Hell, that's all he'd been feeding *us*."

"So how did the perp know he'd been seen? The timing of this whack job and your getting this news from the Lake broad are too close to be coincidence."

Dante took a step back to lean against the fender of the squad car behind him. With his arms folded across his chest, he contemplated the toe of one shoe.

"That's one of the questions I'm wrestling with right now, boss. It's hard to believe that Janet Lake is involved in something that could get her brother killed, but anything's possible. It's also possible that either she or Rabinowitz told someone else about what he'd seen." He looked up into his old friend's eyes. "And then there's something else we've gotta consider. If she *ain't* one of the guilty parties, she could be in real danger now."

"He told her what the man looked like?"

Joe shook his head. "He didn't tell her enough. But the perp doesn't know that. What he most likely *does* know is that Rabinowitz did talk to her. This guy strikes me as someone who leaves nothing to chance."

Gus digested this. "You wanna protect her."

"It's also a good way of keeping an eye on her. And just think how hot Felicity Close is gonna make it for us if this maniac whacks the namesake of her most profitable clothing line. According to what we've been able to dig up so far, it's the one thing that brought them back from the brink of bankruptcy."

Gus promised that he'd look into getting some men assigned to the actress and left to rejoin Felicity Close and his fellow brass hats.

"What can you give me to feed the jackals, Joe?"

He looked up to find Rosa confronting him.

121

"I'm fresh out of dog food, babe."

"Table scraps, then. Something. This thing's gone sensational on us. They're at my throat."

"Man name of Gerald Rabinowitz was killed in the foyer of his home here on Beekman Place. President and chief executive officer of Close Apparel, Incorporated. Top of his head blown away by a well-placed shot, right between the eyes."

He let it hang there as Bob Talbot approached.

"Afternoon, Bob. Nice change in the weather, huh?"

"Nice work on this thing so far," Talbot countered. "Dead people everywhere you go. I hear you were up in Inwood this morning."

"Who taught you your manners, Bob? They suck."

"So does your investigation, Dante."

"That your *expert* opinion? I'm dying to hear everything you've got to say about investigative procedure, Bob. You wrote the book sitting on your ass, didn't you?"

Rosa decided it was time to get between them. "Bobby, please. This isn't productive. I've got a job I'm trying to do here." She turned back to Joe. "I could get what you just gave me out of the *Daily News* tomorrow morning."

Dante contemplated her beautiful face. "You're a cop, Rosa. No one can stop you from going inside and looking at the brains on the wall for yourself. Beyond that?" He shrugged. "Unlike your friend with the manicure there, you used to be a street cop. You know as well as I do that a street cop, in the middle of an investigation, doesn't give away *shit* to the press." He turned to go, stopped, and addressed Talbot again. "If you decide to go in and take a look, careful of that fancy uniform, Bobby. Blood's hard as hell to wash out once it's dried."

Jumbo was standing behind him when he turned away.

"For a sec there, I thought the dude was gonna swing on you."

Joe grinned. "I guess I could wish, huh?"

THIRTEEN

It was late, but Dewey Klein answered when they called and said he'd still be there. He was sitting with his feet up on his desk when Joe and Jumbo entered the Safe, Loft, and Truck offices. Beasley was pretty quick on his feet for a shrinking fat man, as long as the ground covered was either level or downhill. Now, after a five-flight climb in steam heat, his breathing was labored and he was sweating profusely.

"It's sixty-five fuckin' degrees outside," he grumbled, collapsing into one of the unit's chic dinette chairs.

Klein dropped his feet with a heavy thud and handed his empty coffee cup across to Dante. "Fill that while you're at it, eh, buddy? Hey, you two are the only detectives in the city with a body count almost as high as mine."

"You can't include yours in our total."

"Naw. I fucked that up, not you."

Dante filled Klein's mug and a couple of Styrofoam cups for himself and his perspiring partner.

"Tough break," Klein told them once they were settled. "What the hell happened?"

Joe let Jumbo relate the depressing details this time. As

Dewey listened, he ran his fingers through his unruly mop of salt-and-pepper hair.

"I wouldn't want to be in your shoes right now, gents. This one's gonna be big news, and that means heavy pressure."

"Tell us about it," Jumbo said. "Bob Talbot's already let Joey know what a hot job he thinks we're doin'."

"Talbot's a prick."

"We know that. But Tony Mintoff's more politician than cop. Talbot's his boy. He *listens* to the butt-sucker."

Dante waved off the problems of job politics. "There's nothing we can do about the daisy chain downtown. We've got other problems, too. The way I see it, we're still as far behind the eight ball as we were on Friday. Have you had a chance to talk to your guys? See if there are any whispers on the street?"

"Nada. It's quiet as a tomb out there."

"How far have they dug?"

Dewey grinned at that one. "Rag trade's a lot smaller than you'd imagine, Joe. Especially the underbelly. They didn't find shit because there ain't shit to be found. Not even the vaguest rumor of anyone lookin' to knock off Janet Lake designs. Not fuck-all."

Dante absorbed this thoughtfully. "What's bugging you?" he asked.

Klein threw a leg back up over the corner of his desk and sighed. "A lot of people on Fashion Avenue owe this unit a lot of favors. It's a society within a society. Close-knit. People hear things. Maybe not all the people hear the same things, but we've got a lot of 'em listening out there. What's buggin' me is that I find the silence odd. That there ain't even a whisper out there. It's like the theft didn't happen and no plot exists."

Interest piqued, Dante leaned forward in his chair. "What's that mean to you? You sound like you've got some real faith in this network."

"You bet I do. I helped build it. And when the street's this quiet about a specific takedown, I start thinking diversion. I ask myself if what it looks like they were after is what they were *really* after."

"They've done a pretty thorough check," Jumbo said doubtfully. "Ain't nobody there that's found another thing missing, except for them salesmen's samples from that rack. What else could it be?"

Dewey pushed out a lower lip, pulled it back, and smacked his lips. "Beats the fuck outta me, pal. Somethin' worth killin' for. Twice."

"The leak is *plugged*, baby. And funny contract or no funny contract, you own that subsidiary outright now. Damn. You had it all planned, didn't you?"

Roger Brill was pacing the living room floor of his Murray Hill triplex apartment. Felicity Close was lounging on the sofa. She had a glass of white wine in one hand and looked completely relaxed.

"He had us strung up by the thumbs, Roger. What was I supposed to do? Continue to lie down and let him walk all over me? *You're* the only reason he didn't throw us to the wolves three years ago. Not me."

"You think he can't add two and two?" Brill was obviously beside himself. "That man's a *maniac*. I know him better than you do. He already knows you crossed him up the other night. And he's too smart not to guess why."

She graced him with a smug little smile. "Then he will have also guessed that we are all on an equal footing now. I'm not just the third wheel on his bicycle anymore. The three of us are equal partners in this. I want an equal share."

"You don't care that he killed *Jerry*, do you?"

Her smile stayed right where it was. "Jerry was conspiring with that little faggot to screw me out of something that is rightfully mine, Roger. I may be stuck with that bitch, but I'm in the driver's seat now."

"She did some wonderful work for you today. You'd be a fool to alienate her."

Felicity took a quick swig of wine and laughed. "I'm not stupid, Roger. We're going to enjoy a wonderful business relationship."

"I'd check out that holding company Jerry set up before I started counting my chickens," he advised.

A look of alarm crossed her face. "What are you saying?" she demanded.

It was his turn for smugness. "Just that you and I got into this mess in the first place because all your extravagance was running that company into the ground. You needed cash, and you didn't want to give Jerry control. We fucked it up and Jerry *got* control. Whether you respected him as a person, you should at least respect his business acumen. I'll bet that contract is the only Janet Lake document you looked at."

"It was the only one in the goddamn file!"

"Just my point. I suggest you pay your attorney a visit. He should have copies of the structuring agreements. Or you could go see Janet. It's my bet that she's got copies, too. I'd also suggest that you start shopping for an operating officer who knows his ass from his elbow. You never did."

If he hadn't seen it coming in her eyes, the glass she flung at him would have hit him in the face. As it was, he ducked just in time to see it sail past his ear and smash into the wall behind.

Janet Lake hated exercise more than anything in the world. On the other hand, she believed in it with the unquestioning passion of a religious zealot. In the world she had made her fortune in, you either got past the pain and did the work, or you lost your edge. Tonight the exercise was easier to take than usual. She'd been looking for an escape when she arrived at the club. Something to numb her and shut out the gnawing reality of what she'd done.

Jerry was dead. She'd heard the news over the radio in the cab on her way home. A policeman had met her there and said he'd been assigned to protect her. At the time it seemed like a ludicrous, cruel joke. Jerry had been killed just as he'd predicted. It was as if *she* had killed him. Jerry hadn't had a chance.

After two complete circuits of the Nautilus equipment and a half dozen less than wonderful games of racquetball with one of the instructors, she took half an hour's steam, showered, and collected her watchdog downstairs. Officer Vincent Santacroce was a patrolman assigned to a plainclothes protection detail out of the Seventeenth Precinct. Janet supposed that at another time she might have found him handsome in that outer-boroughs sort of a way. He had swept-back hair, a clipped mustache, and a bodybuilder's physique. He'd told her during the ride to the club that he was generally assigned to United Nations Mission protection, roving from one embassy to another as the demand dictated. He was polite and seemed competent, but not competent enough to alleviate the fear that gnawed at her gut. Now *she* was terrified of what might threaten her. Her protection, at least fifteen years her junior, was in awe of her public image.

Santacroce drove her back uptown on Park Avenue and pulled up in front of her awning. The two of them were getting out when the doors of a maroon Plymouth swung open, just ahead. Janet's heart leapt in her breast and continued to pound furiously even after she recognized Sergeant Dante.

It was late for a couple of guys who'd been on the street since eight A.M. In the balmy darkness they had waited a full hour for the actress to return from her gym, the windows of the car rolled down and WFAN all-sports radio playing low. As they wandered up the sidewalk toward the new arrivals, their jackets hung open.

Joe flipped his buzzer out where the heavyset young patrolman could scrutinize it.

"Santacroce, Sarge," the young guy introduced himself.

"How's it going?"

"No problems. I'm just driving the lady back from her health club."

Dante turned to Janet and nodded. "We wanted to do a little follow-up. It shouldn't take long."

"I killed him," she said hollowly. "He begged me not to go to you, and now he's dead."

"If he hadn't lied to us at the outset, we might have been able to protect him," he replied. "You didn't kill him. The same maniac who killed your brother killed him."

She turned without another word and preceded them through the lobby door. No matter how good an actress she was, the emotion that gripped her was genuine. It led Joe to suspect that perhaps she *wasn't* the one who fed Jerry Rabinowitz to the wolves. In a way, that was a relief. From the outset he'd appreciated her no-bullshit approach. In this investigation, it was like a breath of fresh air.

So if she wasn't the one who'd flipped on poor old Jerry, who had? Who else had known what she knew about what he'd seen? If it was someone she could say for certain that she'd spoken to, they had a shot. If it was someone else, someone Rabinowitz had talked to, chances were that the identity of that person had died with Jerry.

The lights of Central Park West and midtown kissed the huge expanse of shadow that was the park itself. This spectacle filled the windowed wall of the living room as they entered it. The place looked just as opulent as it did the last time Dante had visited. The only difference now was a beautiful young blond woman whose bare feet were dangling over the back of one of the sofas. She was reading the most recent issue of *Vanity Fair*.

The young woman sat up quickly, startled by the intrusion. Joe realized then that she was just a girl.

"Hi, honey. Sorry. These men are police."

"I heard about Jerry, Mom. God, what's going on?" She tossed her magazine aside and stood with a graceful energy that was astonishing to all three men. She was not nearly as tall as her mother but she somehow seemed to command the space she stood in. Her body, in faded blue jeans and a sweater, was lanky, like a race horse. The eyes were frozen blue.

Janet shook her head in exasperation. "None of us knows, honey. It's like the world's gone mad out there. They believe I might be in some danger."

When the kid moved to throw her arms around her mother, Dante got what he thought he'd been seeing. She was a dancer. She stood and walked in that funny way they did, with feet splayed just slightly and back ramrod straight.

From over her daughter's shoulder, Janet Lake introduced her. "Officers Dante, Richardson, and Santacroce, this is Skye."

The girl pulled back and tried to smile, not quite managing it.

"Officer Santacroce and other men from his detail will be around here until this thing blows over," her mother explained. "Right now, these other officers want to talk to me. We'll be in the study."

They left Santacroce and the girl in the living room, retiring to the model's more austere inner sanctum. She closed the door as Jumbo passed, and indicated chairs. Dante picked a spot on a green leather settee. Jumbo and the woman each took wing chairs. The cops glanced around the room, taking in the framed magazine covers and movie posters as they tried to formulate their thoughts into questions.

"We know you're tired and you've got to bury your brother tomorrow, ma'am," Joe started in. "But right now, there are too many holes in our investigation. We're hoping you might be able to help us plug some of them."

"Just point me in a direction," she replied. Her tone was almost begging. "My whole world is coming apart."

Dante shifted position on the settee, trying to get comfortable. The thing had been built more for show than for sitting.

"The shooter knew the same things you did, apparently.

129

We have to wonder if Rabinowitz had any other confidants. His wife was feeling less than cooperative when we last saw her, so we thought we'd start by asking you. Who were his friends?''

"Certainly not Felicity," she shot back. "I think it's okay to say that now. While he was alive, he tried hard to keep up the facade. Now that he's dead, I don't think it matters anymore. Frankly, they loathed each other."

Jumbo came forward in his chair. "Because he was gay?"

She shook her head slowly as she thought about it. "That was secondary, I think. It was more because of their contrasting visions. She's an elitist, and he's strictly mass-market oriented. Their first falling out was over how to create a focus for the business. She won out at first because she was better at cultivating heavyweight connections. Money people. Jerry started to get more and more control when a lot of her great experiments turned into fiascos. All along, his sportswear division was carrying them."

"So he wouldn't have confided in her?" Dante asked.

Idly she'd pulled the tie off the end of her braid and begun to work it loose. "Not much chance." She bit her lower lip now, and, when the braid was unraveled, shook her head slowly. Thick blond hair cascaded over her shoulders. "Peter was Jerry's only real, close friend. . . ." She stopped, her eyes suddenly narrowing.

"What?" Joe prodded. "What is it?"

Her eyes widened again, and her hands stopped fiddling with her hair to fall into her lap.

"Roger. This morning it was tearing me apart. What I was going to do. And I talked to Roger about it."

"The photographer?" Jumbo asked. "Why him?"

A real confusion of emotions could be seen raging within her. That drawn, work-weary face was touched by the bewildering contradictions of something she was trying to think her way through.

"God," she murmured, shaking her head slowly. "I've

known Roger Brill for ages. Twenty years ago, we were both just starting out at the same time. We've drifted off into different worlds over the years, but he's always been someone I could talk to.''

Dante was on it like a bloodhound catching a scent. ''You told Brill what Jerry told you.''

''This morning.''

''When?''

''Jerry showed up at the studio. He wanted to talk me out of contacting you. I agreed to meet him during our break for lunch. I was really torn, and Roger was being a friend, wondering what Jerry was so worked up about. When I told him, it was his feeling that I should at least hear Jerry out one more time . . . that I owed him it as a friend. During our next suit change I made up my mind and tried to call you. I left that message and then met Jerry about an hour and a half later. I told him I hadn't changed my mind and that as soon as you two contacted me, I was going to tell you everything.''

The two detectives glanced at each other.

''What's this photographer's connection to the company?'' Jumbo asked. ''Neither of us know much about this game, but we gather he's big-time.''

''Top level,'' she affirmed. ''For years now. Jerry and Felicity have always used him whenever they could. A shoot like the one we did today is actually sort of beneath him now, but Close Apparel is an old account . . . and he's always liked working with me.''

''Could anybody else've overheard you . . . when you were laying this on Brill?''

''We were in his office. With the door closed.''

Jumbo turned to Joe. ''Interestin', huh? Same morning Jerry's gonna get pushed into singing, he gets whacked. I was thinking maybe our perp *did* know he'd been seen. That he'd been layin' for Rabinowitz ever since Friday. Now, I'm not so sure.''

''It bears checking,'' Dante agreed. ''How are you feeling about being here?'' he asked Janet. ''We can't honestly tell you what sort of danger you might be in.''

She hugged herself and took a deep breath. ''I think I'm okay. After the funeral tomorrow morning, I'm going to send Skye to stay with her father. That will get at least one worry off my mind.''

They agreed that it was a good idea. Unable to come up with anything terribly encouraging to say, they eventually said their good-nights and headed for the barn.

132

FOURTEEN

Murray Chopnik was getting impatient. He'd been waiting for Brill to connect with him here at the South Street Seaport for over an hour past the time agreed upon. Come the weekend, this place turned into the world's biggest meat market, and then he wouldn't much mind being forced to sit here and watch some of the generally spectacular scenery. But Monday wasn't a big night for players in the mating game, and the whole of Fulton Street was dead. No parading little fillies with tricked-up hair, wiggling fannies, and come-fuck-me pumps out trolling for the investment banker of their dreams.

The bar was Fluties, the joint opened by that jockey-sized pro quarterback with the draft-horse heart. Murray had himself a corner table and was sitting with his back to the wall. That way he had a view of the whole place, sorry as the scene was. There were a few yuppie assholes in off-the-rack suits and phony Rolexes, getting sloppy at a couple of tables near the bar. All the women he'd seen enter the place that night had been dogs. The yuppies made fools of themselves, sniffing around them anyway. As much as he liked almost any woman with a little fire in her, Chopnik couldn't be bothered with this scene. He had things on his mind and wished like hell that Roger would show up.

A few minutes later Brill pushed in through the door and scanned the room before spotting him. Murray ignored a wave and leaned forward to flag the bored looking cocktail waitress. She wasn't bad, compared to the rest of the talent in here tonight, with plenty of the right equipment packed into a tight little ultrashort outfit.

Brill arrived just as the waitress did and pulled out a chair. Murray touched the girl lightly on the forearm and beamed one of his winning smiles.

"Get me another Corona, will you, sugar? And whatever my buddy here wants."

Brill asked for a Dewar's and soda.

"Where the fuck've *you* been?" Chopnik asked irritably as the waitress moved off. "I've been waitin' for a fuckin' hour."

"The queen bee wanted to be held and stroked, buddy. I couldn't very well jump up and say I was running off to meet *you*."

Chopnik shook his head in disgust. "I can't see how you can still stomach it. Dude like you, knee deep in world-class horseflesh all day and then havin' to face that. It's a cryin' shame."

Brill grunted. "Just holding up my end of a deal, amigo."

Compared to Murray's big, pro-athlete build, Brill was almost diminutive in stature. They made an unlikely looking pair of conspirators.

Chopnik sighed and smiled at him. "I guess we're all animals when you get right down to it, capable of any animal act. How's she takin' the mess I made of her entry hall?"

"You know how she feels about you in general, Murray. I'm not sure whose guts she hated more, yours or Jerry's. I'm guessing that the way she's looking at it, at least Jerry isn't living in the same house with her anymore."

"She set us both up."

Brill shrugged, a smug smile playing across his lips. "Maybe. You can't think you're the only clever bastard on the block. Not in Bigburg. You've got to have eyes in the back of your head and tungsten balls to survive playing your game."

Chopnik scowled. "With what she has on me now, we're gonna have to pay her off equal. Chunk of that'll come out of your end, too."

"There's plenty to go around, Murray."

Over Brill's left shoulder, Chopnik saw the door swing open. Three good-looking young girls, dressed to the nines, pushed their way inside. These were hot little broads from the boroughs, by the look of it, each of them glancing coyly from side to side as they paraded to a middle table. The yuppie guys near the bar didn't miss a jiggle.

He leaned forward, forearms flat on the table. "There's real heat building under this thing now, buddy boy. I did what I had to do, but all this cleverness on your girlfriend's part ain't gonna make life any easier. The cops are gonna be diggin' *every* fuckin' where. They're gonna grill your good-lookin' blond friend, and she's gonna remember she talked to you."

Brill waved it off. "Jerry was a hysterical faggot. He could have told a dozen people what he saw. I was just a shoulder Janet needed to cry on. End of story."

"You better tell it with a straight face, friend. Ain't much question in my mind that you'll get your chance."

Brill scowled now as the waitress brought their drinks. Murray tipped her a five and met her appreciative smile with a lecherous leer. When she'd left, the Texan leaned back into the conversation and fixed Brill with hard, intense eyes.

"I want your read on what the blond bitch really knows."

Brill blinked. "Janet? Jesus, Murray. I know what you're thinking, and you're out of your mind."

"She's a loose end, bright boy."

Roger shook his head with emphasis. "A big guy pushing a hand truck. That's *all* Jerry described to her. I *asked*. He didn't even tell her your hair color.''

For all Brill knew, it had fallen on deaf ears. Murray was suddenly lurching forward and squinting hard into the middle of the room.

''Damn! Get a load of the *nipples* on that filly!''

Astonished at the abruptness of this explosion, Roger twisted around in his seat. About fifteen feet away a pert little dark-complected woman stood facing a drooling young guy in a badly tailored suit. Her jutting breasts strained the fabric of a belted, T-shirt tunic, and Murray appeared to be in danger of going into a feeding frenzy.

''They're stickin' out like *thumbs*!'' the Texan gasped. ''Holy Christ, I'm gonna wet my pants!''

Dinner was Chinese food in cartons, dragged up the block from one of the neighborhood places on Hudson Street. Sunday, *yesterday*, that day of sweet idleness up on the Sound, was no more than a vague memory now. By the time he'd dumped dirty tableware in the dishwasher, filled his tub, and stripped to climb in for a long, hot soak, Joe Dante wasn't sure he'd have the energy to climb back out. Between the Ecuadorian hijack episode in Inwood and finding Jerry Rabinowitz all over the walls of his entry hall, it had been a very long day. The direction his investigation was moving in had suddenly become a dead end. Along the way there'd been frustration at every turn.

Something Dewey Klein said was really eating at him. Safe, Loft, and Truck had been unable to locate even a whisper regarding a Janet Lake Casuals design theft. Dewey seemed to think that was significant. He'd suggested the possibility of a diversion, something Dante had dismissed earlier. Now, in the light of recent developments, he was being forced to reexamine it.

The lights of the bathroom were switched off, and a food warmer candle flickered on the edge of his washbasin. Joe leaned out of the tub to pour himself two fingers of his favorite Irish whiskey. Then he settled into the depths of the intense heat surrounding him to drink and think. If that theft was no more than a red herring, it was a whopper. Intricate and elaborate, yet confusingly ineffective. Two people had lost their lives because of something it was designed to cover up. Something, obviously, of immense value. But what? Another sip of the amber liquid in his glass contributed nicely to his warmth. He began to make a mental list of everything taken from Close Apparel that night:

The design specifications themselves. Buckley's assistant, Hillary Fox, contended these could have been just as simply carted off in a shopping bag. Slopers, from the pattern room, scene of the actual homicide. Dante had examined any number of other slopers that remained hanging on the rack. They were posterboard and bore no apparent intrigue. Four cartons full of new salesmen's samples the owners hadn't even noticed were missing.

Something struck him about this last item. The samples appeared to be of no significance to either Jerry Rabinowitz or Felicity Close, and yet they were far and away the *bulk* of what had been taken in the theft. He thought back over what Hillary Fox had told him about those items.

They'd just arrived Thursday from the warehouse in Brooklyn. The previous season's line was to be taken down and packed into those same cartons for shipment *back* to Brooklyn. Did that mean that the contents of those cartons had originated from Brooklyn? Or was he overlooking the obvious here? Maybe they'd been forwarded to midtown *through* some shipping facility. Maybe they'd originated from somewhere else.

His imagination kicked into high gear. The stuff in the boxes arrived Thursday and was stolen that same night. Timing. Again, there were those nagging suspicions of an inside job. If the samples were what the thief had really been after, he'd known precisely when they'd arrived and where they'd be. Garments shipped in boxes. From where?

Potentially containing what else, other than the obvious? Something worth killing over.

Hell, half the manufacturing done for U.S. companies was done offshore nowadays. Clothing, specifically, was being manufactured all over the Orient, from Hong Kong to Thailand. The night Peter Buckley was killed, he'd been staying late in anticipation of a transmission from Tokyo. If those samples had been manufactured and shipped from some point in Asia, they could have also contained all manner of contraband. Drugs. Gemstones. Pirated technology. Microfilm. His imagination started *stripping* gears. Two people, both witnesses to this theft, were dead. They'd been usable to catch even the scent of a lead in pursuit of the obvious. Here was something less obvious, and it looked for all the world like a sore thumb.

Joe drained his glass and put off refilling it to run a little more hot water into the tub. Then he eased down deeper to luxuriate in that womblike warmth. Tomorrow morning he was going to string a hook on the end of his new line of thinking and start fishing untried waters. He'd had all the red herring he could stomach.

Their father had tried to contact her about ten years ago. By that time she was so well known that even he, in his drink-sodden state, had become aware of his little girl's success. He'd come to New York in an attempt to contact her, and she'd had her attorney tell him to go to hell. About a year later their mother died of lung cancer. Peter was already attending Parsons by then. He'd escaped Ft. Wayne, like her, in search of a better life. Janet Lake saw no reason to send Peter back there now.

It was a gorgeous spring dawn, and Janet, in her robe on the terrace, watched the sun make its way over the buildings to the southeast. She hadn't slept well, but she didn't feel particularly tired. This was the day she would say good-bye to her little brother and it seemed fitting that it would also be one of the first truly springlike days of the year. Peter had always hated winter so much.

She contemplated the rising sun and hugged her robe tightly to her. There were no more tears right now. She'd cried all Friday and most of Saturday. She would cry again when they wheeled that long box past her in the church. Right now, there was only emptiness.

The newspapers Officer Santacroce had brought lay strewn across the coffee table, full of stories of Jerry's murder. Peter's murder was suddenly taking on much weightier significance now that it could be directly tied to a gangland-style slaying on Beekman Place. New York City was riveted to this gruesome drama. Front and center, Felicity Close had gone on record demanding that the mayor do something to stop the campaign of terror being waged against her company. She stated that Close Apparel would actively consider relocation outside New York, to some place where her employees wouldn't have to live in fear for their lives.

Janet pushed the latest edition of the *News* aside and slumped back into her glove-soft leather chair. It was still early, barely past eight. She'd shaken Skye out of bed just minutes ago, and was going to have to start getting dressed soon herself. Peter's funeral was at ten.

Vinnie Santacroce was in the dining room eating the light breakfast Ellie had prepared for him. He had arrived as Janet was coming in off the terrace half an hour ago, replacing a big, redhead named Boyle who worked the night shift. Santacroce seemed genuinely concerned about staying out from underfoot through this difficult time for the family. His presence could be felt, but he wasn't in the way, something Janet appreciated.

Ellie, the Jamaican-born housekeeper, poked her head through the doorway to the dining room.

"Where's that Skye? Her food's gettin' cold in here."

Janet rolled her eyes and pushed herself from her chair.

"She spends more time in the bathroom than *I* do. I'll get her."

The model was halfway down the hall toward Skye's

room when the doorbell rang. The pivot hinge of the dining room door could be heard to squeak as Santacroce double-timed it out and across the living room.

"I'll get it!" he hollered.

FIFTEEN

Vinnie Santacroce wondered who would be paying a visit at such an early hour. There had been a steady stream of flowers and messages of sympathy the previous evening. He'd had to be careful to intercept all that stuff in the elevator lobby and inspect it before allowing it into the apartment. When the job bigwigs suspected there was enough danger to warrant putting a citizen under round-the-clock protection, the protection had to stay on its toes. The way Vinnie looked at it, he could get dead just as easily as the target. He was always watching two asses, hers and his own.

The door opened to an imposing, gray-haired guy in a charcoal pin-striped suit. Nice tailoring. Commanding glint in the guy's eyes.

"Special Agent Chopnik, Treasury," the man announced, producing his documentation and little gold Fed buzzer in a leather case.

"Santacroce, NYPD," Vinnie responded. "What's up?"

Janet Lake, followed by her sleepy-eyed daughter, entered the foyer just as Santacroce was ushering this other man in and closing the door behind him.

"I'm sorry, Ms. Lake," he said. "This man is a Federal Treasury agent. He wants to ask you some questions. I'll be in the dining room if you need me."

The model, confused, looked the new guy over as Vinnie led Skye off toward her breakfast.

"I don't understand, Agent—?"

"Chopnik, ma'am." There was a slight drawl in it. Oklahoma or Texas, she thought. "We're conducting our own investigation into the robbery at Close Apparel and the two subsequent murders. I can't say why, specifically. It could have something to do with an investigation we've been pursuing for some time now. Something delicate, I'm afraid."

Janet pursed her lips, nodded, and led him toward the living room. "My brother's funeral is this morning, and I haven't even started getting dressed yet. I hope this won't take long."

The agent was carrying a folded copy of the *Times* in his right hand. He waved it in a gesture of dismissal.

"Just a few minutes, ma'am. A couple of clarifications is all I'm after."

As he said this, the paper flew loose from his grasp, hit the carpet, and flopped open beneath a marble-and-chrome side table. The agent dropped to one knee to retrieve and refold it. Then he and Janet sat on sofas facing each other across the table strewn with that morning's tabloids.

"I want to emphasize that this is confidential, ma'am," the agent started in. "Our investigation may or may not parallel the homicide investigation being conducted by the New York police. We aren't working with them on this thing, and it's critical to avoid leaks. If we uncover anything they should have, you can rest assured that they'll get it. The commissioner is being updated on a need-to-know basis."

Janet contemplated the man speaking to her. He was huge, perhaps six feet three, and well over two hundred pounds. Even though his full head of curly hair had gone entirely steel-gray, he couldn't have been over fifty. He looked extremely fit.

"I don't understand what Peter and Jerry's murders could have to do with the United States Treasury," she told him. "Am I missing something?"

He smiled indulgently. "We're operating on the theory that the homicides could be incidental to the break-in, ma'am. That's really all I can say to you about it. You're gonna have to take my word for that."

"Okay." She sighed. "What did you want to ask me?"

Chopnik cleared his throat and leaned forward in a pose of confidential intimacy. His outstretched fingers came together in a steeple and then touched his lips.

"I understand that before his death Gerald Rabinowitz revealed to you certain circumstances he observed the night of the break-in."

Janet contemplated him. "That's right. He lied to the police about being there. He was in his office when Peter was killed."

"And as he was leaving, he saw something," the agent prodded.

"That's right. He saw a man leaving. Pushing a hand truck out the front door."

"And what did he tell you about this man?"

She shrugged. "That was it, really. Just that he was dressed in a janitor's jumpsuit and that he was big."

Chopnik's interest appeared to be piqued. "Anything else? Ethnicity?"

Again she shrugged. "You have to understand that I didn't press him for details. This man was most likely my brother's killer, and I wanted Jerry to go to the police with what he saw. To tell them, not me."

"So you're saying that he gave you no description of this man at all?"

"Only that he was big," Janet replied impatiently. "The way Jerry saw him, the guy was huge. Six and a half feet tall. Heavyset."

The Fed digested this. He nodded his head slowly as he

tapped the end of his nose with those peaked fingers. "And that is how you're going on record? That what you've just described to me is as detailed a description of the intruder as Gerald Rabinowitz imparted to you?"

"Going on *record* as saying?" she demanded. "What kind of a question is *that*?"

Chopnik ignored her anger. "And the man was pushing a hand truck. Did he describe the contents of it?"

Still perturbed, Janet contemplated this arrogant son of a bitch and tried to keep a lid on her temper.

"No."

"Nothing?" he asked. There was condescension and disbelief in his tone.

"A hand truck. Big guy in coveralls. That's *all* I know."

He dropped his hands down between his knees and scowled, his shoulders hunched. Janet could see the muscles of his jaw working.

"I and my superiors at Treasury understand your fears and anxiety, Ms. Lake. You believe there might even be reason to fear for your own life. But those fears are no reason to obstruct a Federal investigation."

"I've told you *everything* I know. Jerry was there. He *saw* somebody. That somebody was pushing a hand truck out the front door. Period. And I resent your coming into my home and treating me like I'm a liar. It was my *brother* who was murdered, for Christ's sake!"

"I can hear you without your raising your voice," the agent assured her coolly. "You can also bet money on the fact that if I think you're holding out on my investigation, I'll drag you in as a material witness in a red-hot second, and I don't care *who* you are."

As he said this, Skye and Vinnie Santacroce appeared in the dining room doorway, drawn by the raised voices. Janet was truly upset now.

"I think that red-hot second might be up, Agent Chopnik. I suggest you either arrest me or get the hell out of my home. I refuse to be questioned like a criminal by you or anyone else, without my attorney present."

Chopnik pushed himself to his feet and glared down at her from his considerable height. For a moment Janet thought he might hit her. It scared any confidence right out of her.

"You might just get that chance," he said through clenched teeth. "If what you just told me doesn't check out, we'll throw the book at you and any high-priced attorney you care to bring along."

He turned, strode across the room to the front door, and yanked it open.

Santacroce was scowling, and Skye stood in wide-eyed astonishment as the door slammed behind the T-man.

"What was it that set him off, ma'am?" Vinnie asked. "That is one pissed-off Fed."

Janet's knees were shaking. She had to grope to get her thoughts to fall into any semblance of order.

"I hope it was just about arrogance. That man had the bedside manner of Attila the Hun."

"If he wasn't a policeman, I thought he might've hit you, Mom," Skye said. There was awe in her voice.

"So did I, honey. For a second there. Jesus. Where do they get those guys?"

"That's Secret Service, ma'am," Santacroce offered by way of explanation. "They can be a pretty wild bunch."

In an attempt to pull herself together, Janet glanced at her watch. "We've got to get moving, young lady," she announced.

When Skye moved off to get dressed, Janet took Santacroce to one side.

"That detective, Vinnie. Sergeant Dante?"

"That's right, ma'am."

"Do me a favor while I'm getting dressed and see if you can get hold of him. That monster who just left was feeding me a line about how his investigation is confidential. I resent the way he just tried to walk all over me. Maybe Sergeant Dante can find out what all that was about."

* * *

First thing Tuesday morning Dante and Richardson took a trip downtown to visit a sketch artist at One Police Plaza. Joe fed the woman his best recollections of the face he'd seen the previous afternoon on East 50th Street. The resultant rendering was of a square-jawed, lean-faced man of perhaps fifty. He had gray curly hair cut close to the head and a slightly prominent, fight-broken nose. While they waited, the artist ran off a dozen copies for them.

On their way down to the big building, Joe had outlined the conclusions reached in the tub the previous night. Jumbo liked this new tack, confessing his frustration at the lack of progress made on other fronts. It was Joe's turn behind the wheel, and he now piloted them north on the FDR toward midtown.

"So what you want to do is talk to the design assistant. Find out where that shit originated from and how it was shipped."

"You got it. I called Close Apparel when I got in this morning. Hillary Fox and the rest of the design staff are taking the morning off to attend Buckley's funeral."

The service was being held at St. Thomas Episcopal Church on Fifth Avenue. As they approached the site on foot after parking nearby, both cops could tell that Janet Lake had spared no expense in paying her last respects to her dead brother. The casket coming out of a hearse at that moment must have cost some real money. Bronze with brass fittings. There were three open-backed Caddies filled with flowers.

The crowd thronging into the church was surprisingly large. Dante estimated it at close to two hundred. Most of the mourners were Buckley's age. An even mix of men and women. Once inside, the detectives took up positions toward the rear and off to one side, scanning the crowd.

Janet and her daughter could be picked out easily in the front row on the aisle. Directly across from them, Felicity Close sat flanked by some of her minions. After a few minutes Jumbo spotted Hillary Fox. She was seated about five rows back, huddled close with a tall, angular man of about her age.

The ceremony was mercifully short. The priest gave the eulogy, and a soprano soloist sang the Lord's Prayer. The body was being cremated that afternoon. As the mourners filed out of the church, Vinnie Santacroce spotted the investigating detectives, whispered something to his charge, and stepped over. The model was surrounded by well-wishers and not in any danger he could hope to prevent.

"How's it going, Vinnie?" Dante asked.

Santacroce wiggled an open hand. "So-so, Sarge. Lady had a strange visit from the Feds this morning."

That caught Joe's attention. "From the who?"

"Treasury agent named Chopnik. He was kinda rough with her. I thought he was way outta line. Typical Fed with a hard-on."

"Rough in what regard?"

"In regards to your investigation. Laid some shit on her about them conducting a parallel inquiry. All hush-hush."

Dante and Jumbo frowned at each other.

"You got a good look at his ID?" Jumbo asked.

"Legit. Sucker was huge, too. I consider myself to be pretty good size, but I'm not sure I coulda taken this one."

Dante considered this. Santacroce was probably just under six feet, but he had good muscle bulk and must have weighed a little better than two hundred pounds. He'd seen the way the kid moved and was pretty sure his build didn't just look good at the beach.

"What exactly about our investigation?"

"Mostly about her conversation with Rabinowitz. What he told her he saw. It was like he didn't want to believe she was telling him everything, which wasn't much."

"Treasury," Joe mused. "A parallel investigation."

Santacroce nodded. "The way she tells it, he claimed they were worried about leaks, but the PC was being kept abreast."

Dante reached out and patted the kid on the shoulder. "Get her home and keep a sharp eye out until I can get to the bottom of this, huh? And do me a favor. I don't care if it's J. Edgar Hoover's ghost, you don't let anybody else in to talk with her unless I'm there, all right?''

''You want to talk to her now? She's pretty freaked out. She actually thought this character might hit her.''

''Later this afternoon. We're on the trail of something right now, but we'll finish it up and drop by.''

While he was wrapping it up with Santacroce, Dante watched Jumbo spot the Fox woman as she passed and hurry to stop her. By the time he could join them, Beasley had already offered the diminutive design assistant a lift back to work.

''What was that all about?'' Jumbo asked him.

''Beats me,'' Joe admitted. ''I'll get Gus on it and see what he can turn up. I can't figure what the hell Treasury could have to do with this thing.''

With Hillary Fox in the back seat of their sedan, they moved across town in sluggish midday traffic. Dante twisted around in his seat to face the young woman.

''Those salesmen's samples that were taken the night of the break-in,'' he asked, ''where did they come from?''

''Our warehouse facility in the Brooklyn Navy Yard.''

''But they weren't manufactured there.''

She smiled and shook her head. ''No. South America.''

He perked right up. ''Let me get what you're saying straight now. The samples are manufactured in South America, shipped up to the Brooklyn Navy Yard, and then sent to you here.''

''Just the Janet Lake sportswear samples, so far. We just finished building a big new manufacturing facility in Barranquilla, Colombia. Most of our other stuff is still cut and sewn in the Orient.''

The mention of Colombia set all sorts of bells ringing in the detective's head. A few years back he'd worked undercover for Manhattan South Narcotics.

''Who unpacked that shipment?''

''I did.''

"Did you notice anything out of the ordinary about it? Anything at all peculiar?"

She shook her head. "Not really. Customs always inspects the stuff and reseals it. Everything gets pretty wrinkled in transit, so before it goes on the showroom floor, we hang it on the rack for pressing. I'd done all that, and it wasn't any different than usual."

From inside his jacket Joe extracted a folded sketch of their mystery man and handed it across to her. "You ever see this guy?"

She flattened the drawing out on her lap, peered down at it, and slowly shook her head. "I don't think so. No. Who is he?"

"We're not sure. Just another random piece in the puzzle right now. Could be that he turns out to be nobody."

At the Close Apparel building they let the young woman out of the car. When the door closed, leaving them alone again, Jumbo turned his head toward his partner.

"You're thinkin' dope."

Dante nodded. "I'd be too dumb to live if I wasn't."

"What's the next move?"

Joe glanced at his watch. "Let's run this latest stuff by Dewey. I need to get in touch with Gus and now that the Feds are involved, I don't want to use the radio. Both sides can play this bullshit confidential game."

"Barranquilla," Jumbo murmured. "I'm surprised it's Treasury. I would've expected DEA."

SIXTEEN

Klein was furiously thumping the keys of a beat-up old Underwood. He glanced up and scowled, as the partners strolled in and pulled up chairs. With a sweep of his hand Klein indicated the mess on his desk.

"I'm up to my ass in this shit."

"Fallout from yesterday?" Dante asked.

"What do you think? The bullshit they're making me sling would grow mushrooms for months. I ask you, is this any way to run a police department?"

Joe and Jumbo knew all too well that on every case, win, lose, or draw, the huge amount of paper generated remained the same. Not many cops were also crackerjack typists.

"Take a break and talk to us," Dante suggested. "That crap's got nothing on what we want to tell you."

Klein jerked the triplicate form out of the carriage, tossed it on the blotter with a host of others, and kicked away from it in his rolling desk chair. Fingers intertwined, he cradled the back of his head and regarded his visitors.

"Good news?"

"Barranquilla, Colombia. It's been staring us right in the face."

150

"I'd like to buy a vowel, Pat."

Dante grinned. "You remember what you were saying yesterday? How the quiet on the street had you thinking diversion?"

Dewey nodded.

"It wasn't the Janet Lake designs that our perp was after. He also stole four big cartons and a load of salesmen's samples that had just been shipped up from Barranquilla. They arrived Thursday, and the guy broke in that night."

"We just left Buckley's assistant," Jumbo added. "She can't see any reason why anybody'd want that shit. The designs they stole were for a different line."

Klein's hands had dropped to his lap and he was sitting forward.

"Bingo. You just might be onto something."

"Drugs are what comes to mind," Joe told him. "That your reaction?"

Klein spent a moment contemplating the possibilities and eventually shook his head. "When Customs opened the boxes and emptied them, weight would've been a factor if they had false bottoms. Those boys see 'Columbia' on a shipment, they give it a little extra attention. Uncut smack is a maybe. Half a pound per box might've gone undetected. Risky for the smuggler, though. They check close for that sorta shit."

"You have a better guess?" Jumbo prompted.

"How about gemstones? With the right connections, you could have them sewn right into the garments themselves. A good quality, single-carat emerald is worth a couple thousand bucks. Dogs can't sniff 'em, and they ain't bulky like dope."

Joe and Jumbo digested this information.

"I like it," Dante murmured. "The way you tell it, as few as a hundred stones could be worth a quarter million."

"And there's a huge underground market for them," Dewey added. "Undocumented means untaxed. Once a stone is inside this country, it's hard as hell to keep track of how it's traded. The black market in them is immense."

"That means a lotta new rocks to hunt under," Jumbo murmured. "Dope and gemstones. Joey used to work Narco and probably knows someone we can lean on there, but what *about* this gemstone angle?"

Klein wiggled his eyebrows and smirked. "You happen to have come to the right place. There ain't much gem traffic off of 47th Street. The Chinese play a little game downtown, but the Diamond District's pretty much got the city sewn up. That's part of the Safe, Loft, and Truck beat. Midtown North handles purse snatchings and tourist muggings, but we investigate crimes on the inside. The ones we find out about, that is. They've got a self-policing system of their own that'd put most countries' intelligence networks to shame."

"You willing to run the gem angle while we chase dope?" Dante asked.

Dewey shrugged. "My Ecuadorians oughta be lickin' their wounds for awhile yet. I can probably even put a few more of our guys on it."

Joe wanted to contact Gus to discuss these developments. Dewey turned the phone on his desk around and pushed it at him. As Joe dialed and waited for the connection, he mentioned one other thing that was on his mind.

"The idea that this is something organized from the inside of Close Apparel looks more and more appealing to me. It's too well orchestrated. I'm going to have their personnel department put together a list of everyone on their payroll, both here and South America. We can run the list against the FBI, Interpol, and NCIC data banks. They might kick a connection out."

As the other two cops were agreeing that this was a priority idea, Lieberman came on the line.

"Joey. I was just trying to get you in the car."

"What's up, boss?"

"Tony Mintoff's dander. I heard from Pat Murphy this

morning, and he's getting heat from the PC's office. It seems that your buddy Bob Talbot's been whispering in his boss's ear. There's flack coming my way for leaving you as head of this investigation team.''

''And?''

''Just the usual big-building back-stabbing. Thought you'd want to know that the going could get a little rough before this is over. Talbot's doing his best to send you on a white-water canoe trip up shit creek.''

Dante pushed down his rising anger and told Lieberman about the latest emerging theory. ''Dewey's gonna go with the 47th Street end while Jumbo and I chase Narcotics. As soon as that list is ready, we'll want Jim Hanrahan to run it.'' Captain Jim Hanrahan headed Borough Command Narcotics and had been Dante's commander when he was attached to the Special Narcotics Task Force. Toward the end of Joe's tenure there, the wings had come off an investigation into East Village motorcycle-gang trafficking interests. The thing had crashed and burned nasty, with Hanrahan left to fight the heat. There was no love lost between these two.

Lieberman sounded relieved to learn of the new direction. ''This is just the sort of chum I needed to toss those barracuda,'' he said. ''Should do to keep 'em off our backs for a coupla days, anyway.''

''Another thing,'' Dante mentioned. ''Some storm trooper from Treasury paid Janet Lake a visit this morning. He laid a story on her about a parallel investigation they're conducting. Confidential and the other usual hogwash. She's upset with the way he handled her, and we're gonna have to take time out to go over there and stroke her a little. We want to know what the hell they're up to.''

''Treasury?'' Gus asked.

''That's what the kid, Santacroce, tells me. He checked the guy's ID pretty carefully. Guy named Chopnik.''

The deputy chief was as baffled by this development as Joe and Jumbo were. He promised to check it out and get

153

back to them. As soon as Dante cradled it, Klein spoke up.

"Treasury. What do you make of it? You think we're overlooking something here?"

"You tell me," Joe said. "There's just as much chance that we've got some badge-happy Fed using the excuse to get a close-up look at his favorite movie star. The way Vinnie Santacroce describes him, this guy is the type who's used to going anywhere he wants to."

"Big?" Klein asked.

"Huge."

The Safe, Loft, and Truck cop nodded. "Probably outta the protection detail. Secret Service. Overseas, those fuckers give new meaning to the words *Ugly American*. Party hearty is the lead item in their code of conduct."

The two partners eventually left Safe, Loft, and Truck, with Klein promising to start accessing various data banks as soon as they got him some names. A call to Linda Cooper at Close Apparel personnel got the wheels rolling.

From the day Felicity had first talked him into her hare-brained scheme, Roger Brill's life had changed. But the only external evidence of this would be the lines now etched in that once-boyish face. Otherwise all the trappings of his existence remained exactly the same. Same reputation as a topflight fashion photographer. Same fashionable brownstone duplex on 38th Street in the Murray Hill section of Manhattan. Same elaborate studio facility on West 21st Street.

They'd been caught with their fingers in the criminal pie. Felicity was struggling to hide the toll of her extravagances from Jerry by attempting to replace some of the funds she'd recklessly squandered. Murray Chopnik had been waiting for them. Murray, part T-man and part high-wayman. The ultimate opportunistic machine. He'd seen them coming, caught them red-handed, and pinned them. His proposition had been easy enough to understand. There were two options. Twenty years in Federal stir or a chance to play the game his way. With a Treasury badge behind them. The choice was clear to Roger Brill. Felicity would be allowed to tag along for the ride, simply because she represented liability if allowed off the hook. But Roger was the guy Murray was really after, because Roger had a special skill.

In the wake of the previous day's bathing suit shoot, Roger had scheduled a couple of down days. The flow of work had been less than steady for many photographers in recent months as ad agencies devoured one another. Many established photographers found themselves forced to scrape for new accounts as old ones vanished. Roger counted himself among the fortunates. The old demand might not be there right now, but the old demand had always been for more time than he could spare. His schedule was manageable. Now he could squeeze in a few days off here and there. After the cleanup of yesterday's shoot, he'd sent his staff home this morning, just before lunch, and paused to contemplate his situation.

His ruminations were interrupted when the intercom panel blared out in reception. He'd propped the door to the lounge open so that he could hear the thing, and disturbed now by the distraction, he considered ignoring it. Then, thinking better of it, he pushed himself from his seat.

A minute later the two cops, that tough looking one and his enormous black partner, stepped off the freight elevator. The tall white guy nodded to him and reached for his wallet. Roger waved him off, knowing exactly who he was.

"Terrible, what happened to Jerry," he told them after inviting them into the lounge. "I guess that's what you're here about, huh?"

The cops chose seats and waited for him to get settled.

"As a matter of fact," the tall guy said. He'd introduced himself as Sergeant Dante of the Special Task Force, whatever that was. "We understand Mr. Rabinowitz paid a visit here yesterday morning. Janet Lake tells us he was quite upset. Did he seem that way to you?"

Roger feigned thinking about it for a moment and then lifted his hands in a gesture of uncertainty.

"That's a tough one, Officer. I was busy as hell all yesterday. But in light of what Janet told me later in the morning, I imagine he must have been. It's just that I couldn't swear to it, one way or the other."

The big black guy, Richardson, jumped in here. "And just what was it that Ms. Lake told you?"

Roger feigned surprise now. "She didn't say? The way she told it to me, Jerry had come to her on Friday and told her he was there that night. He'd caught a glimpse of the man who killed her brother."

Richardson continued to bear down. "And what did you tell her when she told you this?"

Roger shrugged. "That I thought she should at least try to reason with him . . . for his sake. I didn't think it would look all that good to you people if he insisted on holding out and she was forced to go to you."

Dante picked up the ball. "After you had that exchange with her, did you happen to mention what she told you to anyone else?"

Roger paused, frowned, and shook his head. "Not that I can recall. Like I said, my mind was on a host of other things. I think she went and saw Jerry at lunch. She wasn't gone long, if I recall."

"If you *recall*? Wasn't it a bit more of a bombshell to you than you're making out?"

Brill nodded emphatically. "I'm sorry. Yes, definitely it was. I was distracted just now, thinking about how it turned out exactly as Janet said that Jerry feared it would."

The black cop reached into the breast pocket of his jacket, extracted a folded piece of paper, flattened it, and handed it to him.

"You ever see this man?"

The shock of seeing Murray's face was something Roger had to scramble to mask. He was not at all convinced that he was successful. He'd already swallowed inadvertently. His eyes must have widened at least a bit.

"No," he said, maybe a little too nonchalantly. He shook his head. For effect, he pretended to regard the face a second time and then shook his head again. Overacting? God, he was swimming blind through these waters. Boldly he passed the paper back. "At least, I don't recognize him. Who is he?"

The fat black cop refolded the sketch carefully and returned it to his pocket. "We're not sure. He's just a hunch we're runnin' with right now."

Five minutes later, the cops were gone, and Brill sat staring at a wall, his heart rate up and his mind reeling.

"What did you think of that squirrelly little fucker's reaction to the sketch?" Jumbo asked.

They were headed uptown on Park Avenue toward Janet Lake's building, Dante still behind the wheel.

"Same as you did. He knows who that son of a bitch is."

SEVENTEEN

Janet Lake's daughter, Skye, had been shipped off to stay at her father's place in the northern suburb of Bedford Hills. That meant limo rides into the city every day and a real crimp in an active teenager's social schedule. To her credit Janet had stood firm against the kid's understandable protestations. Skye disliked her dad nearly as much as her mother did. Nonetheless, people were getting dead on their home turf. The inconvenience could be endured.

When Dante and Richardson arrived at the Park Avenue penthouse, they found the model in pretty good shape for someone who'd just buried her brother. Her red-rimmed eyes were dry now. She'd just returned from taking her pent-up frustrations out on some Nautilus equipment, and her skin glowed with the residual effects of exertion.

Vinnie Santacroce sat alongside her on a sofa as they settled in the living room. The dazzling light of midday poured in through that monster window that was the west wall.

Dante addressed the young cop first. "The way I understand it, you left the T-man in the room with Ms. Lake. Right?"

Santacroce nodded. "Just after I'd examined his ID and

let him in, Sarge. I went into the dining room with Skye and finished my breakfast. Ellie was sitting in there with us, drinking coffee.''

Joe's eyes moved to Janet. She was dressed in loose-fitting gray cotton sweat clothes, not the current-vogue workout gear that makes women look like Olympic skiers or circus clowns.

"We're trying to make sense out of this, ma'am. We have a request in with Chief Lieberman, asking him to chase this Chopnik guy down and find out what he's up to. Still, we'd like to hear it from you in your own words. Just what he was after."

Anger flashed in her crystal blue eyes. "He treated me like a criminal. Like I was holding something out on him."

"Specifically," Joe prodded.

"He wanted to know whether Jerry had given me a description of the man he saw that night. When I told him just what I'd already told you, he practically insisted that I wasn't giving him everything." She paused, glancing over at Santacroce. "We had strong words when he started talking about obstruction of justice. That's when Vinnie came in."

There wasn't that hard edge to her speech that Dante had noticed in prior conversations. Events of the past few days seemed to have taken a little of the starch out of her.

"The guy was pretty charged up, Sarge," Vinnie offered.

"I swear I thought he might hit me," Janet added.

Something was eating at Dante about this entire episode, but he couldn't put his finger on it. He turned to Jumbo and gave him a questioning look.

"Sounds fishy to me, too, Joey. Dude comes in here messin' with our homicide investigation, talking confidentiality. We ain't heard a thing about this parallel investigation of theirs. It rubs me all wrong."

Joe focused on the model again. "I'm sorry this had to happen. We realize what sort of strain you've been put under. You can rest assured that we'll find out who this character is and what he's up to. Meanwhile, we had an interesting chat with Roger Brill just before coming here.''

She perked up. "He confirmed what I told you?"

"Top to bottom. He was very up-front about all of that. And then"—as he spoke, he dug into his jacket for his own copy of the artist's sketch and started unfolding it— "we showed him this.''

Janet leaned across the coffee table to take the sheet of paper extended toward her. It was a drawing of a man's face, upside down. As she reversed it, her nostrils flared.

"It's *him*!"

All three cops came forward in unison.

"Who?" Jumbo asked.

"Chopnik. The Treasury man."

"Whoa!" Dante was reeling. "Run that by us again."

Janet handed the thing to Vinnie Santacroce. The young cop glanced over it, nodded, and handed it back.

"Dead ringer, Sarge. Where'd it come from?"

Dante was evasive now. "Just something we're following.''

"Something to do with Roger," Janet jumped in. "What?"

Joe shook his head. "We're not sure. He seemed to recognize this guy, too. Only he denied it. Chances are that this character paid him a visit, too, and laid the same confidentiality crap on him. Sometimes a visit from the Feds'll put the fear of God in people.''

"But you've got other suspicions," she pressed.

The shake of his head was emphatic this time. "You're jumping to conclusions. The water's gotten a little muddy. That's the whole of it, for the moment.'' He paused to think, trying to process all this recent input. "Run the whole thing by us again. I want to see if maybe we're missing something.''

The model sat back, took a deep breath, and pointed toward the foyer. "I was down the hall there, trying to get Skye to hurry it up. We were due at the church in a little more than an hour and she hadn't eaten her breakfast yet. When the doorbell rang, Vinnie said he'd get it. I came up the hall to discover"—she pointed to the sketch on the table—"that man in the entry. He explained who he was and why he wanted to ask me some questions."

"And you walked over here?" Joe asked.

She nodded. "I invited him to have a seat. He dropped his newspaper under the side table over there and had to get on his hands and knees to pick it up. Then he sat right where—"

"Hang on," Jumbo interrupted. "He dropped his paper, and had to get on his *hands and knees* to pick it up?"

"It went almost to the wall under there. He was waving his hand about something and the paper flew out of it."

As she picked up the narration of events, Jumbo pushed himself casually to his feet and wandered over to the table against the wall. There was a folded *New York Times* lying on top of it next to a vase of fresh flowers. There were a lot of flowers all over the place, sympathy gifts from well-wishers. The table itself was one of those half-round jobs, the top cut from marble and the legs polished chrome like everything else in the room.

"It started out being friendly enough," Janet was saying. "Like he was trying to take me into his confidence. He asked questions, and I answered them as frankly as I could."

The big detective lowered himself to his knees, planted his left hand, and bent to peer up under the table.

The listening device was one of those tiny multi-directional units, mounted on a suction-cup and affixed behind the top of one leg. Back while Joey was working undercover Narcotics, Jumbo had done a stint in Intelligence Division. They had to yank him after the city came down hard on a militant radical group, because his face had become too well known. But in the course of his infiltration assignment, he'd planted a dozen of these sneaky little devices himself.

While listening to the model's account of the morning's

events, Dante watched his partner's progress out of the corner of his eye. When Beasley's head came up, Joe turned his full attention toward him. The big guy smiled and held an index finger to his lips. Joe rose from where he sat, motioning that Janet should continue to talk as he walked to where his partner knelt.

Janet Lake finished her story and stopped. All attention in the silent room was focused on that spot where both detectives now crouched alongside the wall table. Dante acknowledged Jumbo's discovery. With his own fingers he indicated that Jumbo should plug his ears. Then he placed those fingers on either side of his mouth and blew a shrill, deafening whistle directly into the highly sensitive microphone.

For an instant Murray Chopnik thought he might pass out. He clawed frantically at the earpiece and managed to get it loose as a knifelike pain shot through his head.

"Fucking hell!" he screamed. In the confines of his car, parked alongside a hydrant on East 66th Street, no one heard his shrill curse.

Gus Lieberman frowned. He had a Carlton out and had paused with his thumb on the wheel of his battered Zippo. He hated smoking this antiseptic brand but did so as a concession to Lydia. Quitting had made him too ornery to live with.

"There ain't no way he coulda gotten his information from inside this department, Joey. I've been feedin' Tony Mintoff *shit* because that's all I've *got* to feed him."

"Okay," Dante allowed. He and Jumbo had divided forces. The big guy was gone to pick up the Close Apparel personnel roster from Linda Cooper while Joe ran this latest development past the boss. "She and Santacroce may have talked some about Brill's connection to this. I doubt it, but I'll allow it as a maybe. But if I'm allowing that, I've also got to consider the other side of the coin."

"Which is. . . ?"

"That Brill recognized this guy for some other reason. Hell, Gus. The thing that's eating me is *where* this sketch came from in the first place."

Gus sighed and leaned back, his coffin nail afire now.

"You could be wrong about the exact time of death, Joey. The ME can't fix it to the minute. You say the guy was still bleeding out. Maybe, but with that much blood, he coulda been dead for ten minutes, and the pool was still growing. Our T-man coulda been just a little closer on the killer's heels. Because he's operating on the QT, he got the hell out of there in a hurry so you two couldn't put the screws to him."

"And maybe the Love Boat will tie up in my back garden tonight."

Gus snorted. "What's the alternative? That some Treasury agent is also a crazed killer?"

"There are eight million ways to die in the naked city, Gus."

"But that ain't one I'm ready to consider."

"So what *about* this Treasury investigation? The sons of bitches are planting *bugs* on my work. It stinks, and I want to know why."

"That hook's in the water, but no nibbles yet. Instead of going after them directly, I thought I'd let the PC handle this one himself."

Joe puffed his cheeks in frustration, pushing a breath out quickly. "And Hanrahan? I'll bet he's just dying to see me, huh?"

Gus grinned. "I'm not sure I'd put it quite that way. On the other hand, you need Narcotics, and he's got little choice."

"Jumbo's picking up a list of foreign and domestic personnel from the Close people right now. He'll drop it by Dewey's office so those guys can run it by their sources. We'll leave another copy with Jim and call it a day. I'm hoping to God that Big Tony will have turned up something with the Feds by morning."

Lieberman leaned forward to stub out his half-smoked

cigarette in disgust. "I like this angle you're running with, Joey. You got that look in your eye like you're onto something, and that makes me sleep better, nights. What's your opinion of how Janet Lake is holding up?"

After a moment's thought Dante said, "She's rattled. I'm all but totally convinced now that she's got nothing to do with this thing, but her luck's sure running bad. If you're referring to the protection on her, I'd say we leave it. Bad luck like that, you don't press."

Gus started to shake another Carlton out of the pack. Knee-jerk habit. When he realized what he was doing, he tossed it onto the blotter. "Commander of the Seventeenth's house-protection detail called to tell me some Palestinian is coming in to address the UN. They're pulling out all the stops, laying on some heavy security. Figures to leave him shorthanded."

"When and for how long?"

"Tomorrow till Friday morning."

Dante pinched the bridge of his nose, squeezing hard. "If it comes down to it, Jumbo and I will split the detail ourselves."

"I'll put her into protective custody before I ask you to do that."

Joe sighed. "That'd look good, wouldn't it? NYPD has the manpower to protect some controversial camel jockey but nobody to protect a high-profile movie star. I'd like to see the way a rag like the *Post* handles *that* one."

A few minutes later, Joe was back in his Task Force cubicle, mulling over the more subtle nuances of life, death, and perpetual confusion, when Jumbo huffed his way in. It was nearly quitting time, and the big man had been gone about forty minutes longer than Joe had expected.

"Traffic?" he asked.

"Little detour," Jumbo said, pulling up a chair. "On my way upstairs I stopped by to drop the list off with Jim Hanrahan myself."

Dante's eyebrow went up, and he started to open his mouth. Jumbo held up a hand.

"It's no secret, the way you two lovebirds get along. I thought I'd save myself the aggravation of having to pry you apart. He says they'll run it and have the results by the start of business tomorrow."

Dante abandoned his protests. "And Dewey?"

"He could take a little longer. NCIC and the FBI are no sweat. He's leaving straight from work to meet some Bureau pal for a drink. Interpol requires that he go through a coupla more channels."

Joe kicked back, rose from his desk, and reached for his jacket. "Then let's call it a day and meet here first thing in the morning." He related the news about protection and the possibility that one or both of them might be pressed into emergency service.

"I'd hate it." Jumbo was grinning. "Havin' to sit around looking at Janet Lake for hours on end. There'd be some compensation for hazardous duty, right?"

Joe rolled his eyes. "Maybe to her, my married friend."

"I fell in *love* with Agnes," Jumbo protested. "I didn't go blind."

Roger Brill heard the elevator door open, and then Felicity emerged into the lounge from reception. Dusk had a grip on the city outside, but the photographer hadn't bothered to turn any lights on yet and was sitting alone in the dark.

"Roger?"

"Over here."

"Why are you sitting in the dark? And what the hell was that panicky call all about?" She found the light switch on the wall to her left, and the room was flooded with soft incandescence.

From his chair Brill contemplated the ever-confident figure she cut. "We've got to do something, babe. They've got a picture of him."

"What? What picture? Of whom?"

165

"That tall, dirty-blond cop and his fat-man partner. They came here this afternoon asking questions. The black guy showed me a sketch that's a dead ringer for Murray. Wouldn't tell me who it was or where it came from, but they're on to him."

"And how did you react when they showed it to you?" she asked, suspicion in her voice.

He snorted derisively. "How would you have reacted? It hit me like a left hand from Mike Tyson."

"You blew it, didn't you?"

He shook his head.

"I can't honest-to-God say, babe. They were grilling me pretty good over what Janet told me yesterday morning. I was riding it out just the way I'd rehearsed it in my mind. Then came the KO blow. They blindsided me. I didn't *tell* them anything, but my heart was pounding up between my ears."

"You fucked it up, or you wouldn't be telling me this now." Her voice was cold as stainless steel.

A heavy silence confirmed the truth of her accusation. Finally Brill sighed and shook his head.

"Whether I fucked up or not is immaterial. You brought all this down on us with your power play. While you're blaming everyone else for your problems, try not to forget that."

Felicity crossed her arms and gazed up toward the ceiling. "You amaze me," she said flatly. "Do you have any idea how pathetic you sound? My 'power play,' as you put it, got us both off that monster's hook."

"Temporarily. It also got us implicated in two murders."

"We're just this far away, Roger." She held up two fingers, a quarter of an inch apart. "When it's over, Murray goes off to Rio or wherever, and we go back to our lives. Free of him and richer by eight million dollars. *Each.*"

"Dreams, babe. As long as he's in Rio and out of reach of the law, he's got us by the short hairs. When that eight million runs out, he can make us jump through hoops to get him more. You and I will both still be guilty of those murders in the eyes of the law.''

He was amazed by the look on her face. It was as if it had never occurred to her. And hell, he supposed maybe it hadn't. Felicity spent her life with her head in the clouds. It was still up there now as she spoke.

''I did what I thought was best for *us*, Roger. I actually thought that we had something, the two of us.''

''I stopped thinking that when you came to me with your jackass plan three years ago. It didn't take two shakes for me to see you were using me. You still are, on some pathetic level. I don't know what it was that I thought we had, but I'm sure now that it wasn't love. Some people are just incapable.''

''You're a fucking prima donna *prick*, Roger.''

''Fine,'' he replied. ''A prima donna prick who regrets not having the guts to face the music back when it wasn't so loud, when it was only *you* who had me by the balls. Now get the hell out of my studio.''

EIGHTEEN

Murray Chopnik, his right ear still hurting, lounged in the opulent den of a sprawling Staten Island home. The room was crammed with memorabilia from the owner's trips to his family's Sicilian homeland. Bits of stone from Mount Etna. Big, expensive enlargements of richly evocative scenes. A street in Palermo. The plain of Catania. Various seafront villages. The man fancied himself a photographer, and it was difficult to argue with this evidence. The rest of his decor was distinctly Mediterranean in accent. The furniture was alabaster-and-gilt Italian Provincial, as rococco as the stuff got and a bit much to take. Hunting trophies were hung above the wet bar.

Murray's respiration rate belied the relaxed attitude he strove to project. Everything he'd been working toward was sitting in some unseen back room. The man was examining the goods he'd delivered for quality and easy marketability. If Brill had delivered, and no more fag designers stumbled on the main shipment, everything was fat city from here on in.

A pair of huge double doors swung inward, and a smug, silver-haired man in an elegantly tailored European-cut suit entered the room. He walked to where Murray sat and paused to contemplate him sternly. Then, slowly, his teeth began to show as his eyes crinkled at the edges.

"Excellent, my friend. Perhaps the very best I have ever seen."

"You can move it? I mean, that and more?"

The man laughed lightly. "Oh, I assure you. As much as I can get my hands on. There is always a market for such quality."

Chopnik took a deep breath, let it out, and started to relax. "That's real good news, friend. When it comes to this sort of thing, I hate to think of having to go somewhere other than the top. It makes everything so much easier."

The slightly built older man nodded. "I am glad you came to see me first. I am confident enough to know that when I see what I want to see, I can pay top dollar. How soon can you make a larger delivery?"

"Inside the week, I hope. I can't say precisely. It depends on some delicate shipping schedules. Soon, though. Can we settle up on this one?"

With his look of benevolent good nature still in place, the man stepped to a low cabinet, swung the doors on it, and stooped to spin the combination dial on a safe. From it, he extracted a tightly packed nine-by-thirteen-inch envelope.

"One hundred and fifty thousand." He handed it to Murray. "Please check it."

Chopnik undid the string clasp, riffled through four thick stacks of hundreds and pulled notes randomly from each. With apparent expertise, he crumpled, straightened, rubbed, and scrutinized the bills.

"Fine," he announced. "I'll trust the count."

The man closed the safe and then the cabinet doors before approaching the bar. "It is nice to encounter a professional of your caliber in this business. There are so many amateurs. Riffraff. Would you join me in a cognac?"

Murray told him that he thought he would.

* * *

In his bedroom Joe Dante lay with his knees bent and his feet wedged under the cushioned restraints of a slant board. His body streamed with the sweat of exertion as he reached the hundreth of these murderous abdominal tighteners and collapsed backward. His breath came in labored pants. The blood throbbed at his temples. Two hundred push-ups and one hundred slant-board sit-ups. It was a short workout, but after it, the tension of a frustrating day in the trenches drained slowly out of him.

As he swung his legs around and stood, he reached for the beer on his highboy dresser and took a long swallow. Then he set it back down and began to stretch out. Dead ahead he could see beyond the open patio draperies, through security gates and French doors to the garden beyond. If the weather hadn't insisted on remaining so lousy lately, he'd have already done some prep work on the flower beds out there. Right now they were a mess of mulch and dead leaves. The patio chairs were stacked against the round metal table and covered with a tarp. The herringbone brick surface beneath was littered with more dead leaves. Winter always refused just to leave. He had to get out there and sweep it away.

A half an hour later, after his cool-down and shower, he set the alarm for an early start and crawled between the sheets. He knew he wouldn't be able to get to sleep immediately, no matter how early he intended to get up. Instead of even trying, he propped the pillows and lay wedged up against them. Copter the cat hopped up on the bed and crawled in next to him. Joe reached down to scratch him idly between the ears.

A host of new pieces had been added to the puzzle now. Everything pointed toward a contraband smuggling operation, but contraband covered a lot of ground and any of a dozen enforcement agencies might hold the key. It was possible that they still hadn't thought to ask the right one.

Eventually sleep seemed as if it might be ready to come. He sat up, rearranged his pillows, and nestled his weary head into one. As he closed his eyes, the image of Bob Talbot, naked and in Rosa's arms, flashed before his mind's eye. Try as he might, he couldn't shake the revulsion that image caused him. In the past few days, since their talk that evening in his living room, he'd begun to accept that it was over between himself and Rosa. Still, he loved her in that strange way ex-lovers so often continue to do. Talbot wasn't right for Rosa. He represented all the worst tendencies in her, all the things she needed to overcome.

Dante was no longer angry with himself for their failure as a couple. He'd had his shortcomings, surely, but he wasn't the one who'd taken it behind the shed and shot it in the head. That had been her decision. She'd made her bed, and somewhere tonight, with Talbot stretched naked beside her, she was sleeping in it.

Copter was purring contentedly as Joe rolled over. It was easy to envy the cat his simple contentment. Scratch him, feed him, and change his litter once in awhile. That's all a cat asked.

Murray was feeling pretty good about life. About the hundred and fifty big he'd stashed in the closet wall safe. About the fact that it represented the mere tip of a very lucrative iceberg. His ear still throbbed where that prick cop had whistled into the bug, but the wop capo's cognac and a couple of shots of his own Maker's Mark were easing that pain. Not to mention the satisfaction of a job nearly done. Hell, in another week he'd be basking in the sun of Ipanema. Hot-and-cold-running-sixteen-year-old girls. A beachfront apartment with a view running all the way to Africa.

He was stripped to a sleeveless tank shirt and gym shorts, and the pieces of his Beretta model 92F were spread before him on the coffee table. With painstaking care, he caressed each component of the weapon with an oiled cloth. Johnny was just finishing his monologue on the big Zenith.

When the intercom in the kitchen buzzed, he scowled.

He looked at his watch and saw it was ten to midnight. Still, in his line of work, it could be just about anybody. He rose to check it out.

It was Felicity, insisting that they talk. He depressed the button that would release the downstairs door, left his own front door ajar, and returned to his chair in front of the tube.

After a minute, the door came open, and Felicity edged tentatively into the room.

"Any chance you were followed?" he growled without looking up.

"I took two cabs and a crosstown bus, just like you told me that time." She stood with her back to the door, clutching her purse in both hands.

He looked up at her. "You've been awful clever lately, ain't you? I mean, two cabs, a bus, and the double cross the other night at your office. You proud of how you got me to kill that squirming worm of a husband for you?"

She met his gaze defiantly.

"You've always done what you had to do," she replied. "Why did you think I would be any different?"

"Because I underestimated you, sweet tits. Plain and simple. You proud of how you foxed old Murray's box? You come here to gloat?"

She shook her head as she stepped into the room. "Not really. I came here to tell you I think Roger is coming unraveled."

He guffawed, as he methodically began to reassemble the automatic. "Your loverboy? No shit, sweet tits? And you just thought you should drop on by here and let me know that? That's wonderful. Heartwarming. Who *are* your friends?"

Her jaw tightened, and anger flashed in her eyes. "*I'm* my friend, you fucking hillbilly. You aren't, and he isn't."

"I hail from Midland, Texas, missy. There ain't a hill within a hundred miles."

"They showed him your picture today," she said. "He

172

admitted to me that he doesn't think he handled it very well.''

Murray smirked. "A sketch? Well, well. Who from? The Lake bitch?''

"They wouldn't say.''

He shrugged it off. "So I paid him a visit in the course of my investigation, just like I did to the model. I leaned hard on him to keep his mouth shut. That's why he looked so shifty when they showed him the drawing.''

He'd completed assembling the Beretta and checked the action with a quick tug.

"You've got an answer for everything, don't you?'' Felicity stepped to the cabinet that served as a bar. With a deft twist of the cap, she upended the bottle of bourbon and poured herself a stiff belt.

"Make yourself right at home.''

She downed most of the whiskey in one gulp and closed her eyes tight as it burned south toward the pit of her empty stomach.

Murray eased back in his chair, the pistol held loosely in his lap. "Roger's a bit of a nervous Nellie. A fabulous photographer, though. Does some of the nicest work I've seen. Just beautiful. You? You're a whole other piece of work, princess. Hell, instead of hating me, you ought to be thankin' me for leaving that faggot fool's brains all over your front hall. Probably made you a hundred million bucks in the process.''

"It's a house of cards, Murray. Funny money. Not the kind you could take to the bank tomorrow and spend. The cops are crawling all around that house, trying their damnedest to figure a way to blow it down. They know you stole the boxes now, not just the Janet Lake designs.''

Chopnik snickered. "So what the fuck does *that* tell them? Fuck-all. It's in the bag, baby. The show is on the road. A week, tops, and I'm outta here. They can't stop me now.''

He brought the pistol up, thumbed back the hammer and aimed it right toward the center of her chest.

"You know, I've always wondered what sorta head a tight-wound little cunt like you gives. Why don't you come on over here and show me?"

Felicity tried to swallow her horror and got it caught in her throat. Tears welled up in her eyes. All the while, she couldn't tear her gaze from the menacing muzzle of the pistol's four-inch silencer.

"C'mon, baby," he crooned. "Tit for tat. It's only fair, huh? You jerk my chain, I jerk yours."

She approached him and three feet out, her eyes still locked on the gun, she went slowly to her knees. Murray reached out with his free hand, caught hold of her blouse and tore the front of it away. She stiffened in horror.

"Unhook the clasp on that there sling, sugar. Murray wants to see the job that South American surgeon did on your duds."

Face hot with shame, she fumbled open the clasp on her brassiere. As it began to fall free, her tormentor reached out with the barrel of the pistol to push it aside.

"My, my," he murmured. "Your boyfriend told me you had a great set. Who woulda guessed, with a nasty disposition like you got."

The tears ran hot down her cheeks as she reached slowly into his lap and caught hold of his shorts. The cold steel of the muzzle touched her temple as she leaned into him.

Murray brought his hand around a little so she could see him exert pressure on the trigger out of the corner of her eye. Her hot breath was on him as she squeezed her eyes shut and held her breath. When the hammer came down with a sudden snap, he knew that her heart exploded in her chest. That knowledge released his maniacal laughter.

"Whooee! Lucky I didn't have my thing in your mouth, sweet tits. You would'a bit the sucker clean off!" When he'd recovered himself, he picked the clip out of the chair between the cushion and side, fitted it into the butt and slammed it home.

Felicity had collapsed back onto the floor where she was

hugging herself and shuddering in a sudden cold sweat. The surge of high-voltage terror had filled her veins with adrenaline. She'd gone into shock.

Chuckling, Murray stepped over her to pour himself another drink.

"Teach you to fuck with a *master* mind-fucker, little lady."

NINETEEN

Gus Lieberman visited the partners in Dante's Task Force cubicle first thing Wednesday morning.

"Jim Hanrahan called to say that none of the names on that list raised any red flags with Narcotics. The ballistics tests on the bullet that killed Jerry Rabinowitz didn't tie in to any other weapon. The Protection Detail whip at the Seventeenth called to say that he can leave a uniform at the Lake place until end of shift this afternoon. From then until Friday, he can't spare the manpower. We're on our own. I called the duty captain at the Nineteenth, and he tells me they're stretched thin as hell right now. Same with the Thirteenth and Midtown North and South. I haven't gotten to the rest of my Command yet."

Dante glanced at Jumbo, who shrugged apologetically. "College Night at Kathy's school. The girl's got her mind set on Bryn Mawr or some shit. I say over my dead body, but I'm the one forcin' her to go to this gig."

"All right," Joe muttered. "Save yourself the time, Gus. I'll go on up there this evening and see if there's a friend she could stay with for a couple days. If not, I'm on protection detail."

"What about the list you gave Klein?" Lieberman asked.

"Good question. We left him a message to get in touch. Guy on the unit says he was dropping by the FBI Field Office on the way in this morning."

After the deputy chief left them, Joe and Jumbo sat down to map out their day.

Eventually Dante tossed a pen onto his desk and rocked back in his chair.

"I've been thinking about the actual smuggling process. You know, Barranquilla to Brooklyn to midtown. No matter what the contraband is, the method should stay the same, right?"

Jumbo gave the idea some thought and nodded. "Stands to reason."

"So," Joe continued. "I'd like to spend a little time tracing out the mechanics of that first route. Dates, times, means of transport, the names of people involved in the actual handling. It could help us narrow down any other information we get."

Jumbo thought it sounded like a good idea. While they awaited Dewey Klein's call, they contacted Felicity Close's secretary and made an appointment for just before lunch, figuring that the quickest way to get their shipping information was to go straight to the horse's mouth.

At nine Klein called and told them he didn't want to relate the particulars of an unnamed discovery over the phone, so they drew a Fury from the Borough Command pool and headed uptown to Safe, Loft, and Truck.

It was a lovely spring day. The temperature was around sixty-five, and the partners rolled with the windows cranked down. Pedestrians walked coatless on the sidewalks, and Dante thought he could detect a decided bounce in their collective steps.

"You seem to be in a better mood this fine morning," Jumbo commented from the passenger seat. "Something good happen I ain't heard about?"

Dante snatched a quick glance over his shoulder,

wedged the car into the next lane, and shook his head. "Naw. I think it's just this weather. Nobody hates winter as much as this boy. Look at 'em out there." He gestured at the world with a sweep of his hand. "People are enjoying themselves instead of fighting to survive. Even the bums look happy."

"Happy . . . *er*." The fat man corrected him. "I ain't heard any of them singin' the 'Alleluiah Chorus' on the sidewalk yet."

They pulled to a stop at a red, and Dante looked at Jumbo and frowned. " 'Alleluiah Chorus on the Sidewalk'? I'm not sure I've heard that one. Who does it? Michael Jackson?"

"Stevie Wonder, asshole."

Dewey Klein was sitting with some of the other guys around the big table in the middle of his squad room. He picked up his coffee mug as they entered.

"You two are just gonna love this," he crowed. He pushed his plastic dinette chair back beneath the table and led them toward his office. "How'd you do with Narcotics?"

"Struck out," Jumbo muttered.

Klein waved it off. "Better yet. I was hoping to Christ you wouldn't come up with something there, *too*."

"Spill it, man," Dante begged, pulling up a chair and perching on the front edge of it.

"Treasury." He said smugly.

Joe and Jumbo looked at each other.

"You gonna squeeze it outta him, or can I?" Jumbo growled.

Klein laughed. "Easy, gents. That visit the T-man paid Janet Lake is what set some of my inquiries off in that direction. I didn't want to access them directly, so I took it to my pal Bobby Thornhill at the Bureau. They got ways around usual channels."

"And . . . ?" Dante urged impatiently.

"One of the names raised a big red flag. Roger Brill.

He was under investigation for about six months three years ago. The agent running the investigation is a character named Murray Chopnik. The information gets a little fuzzy here. Bobby called a friend at Treasury in D.C. Chopnik was running a counterfeit investigation out of the main office back then. Two years ago his name was dropped from the Federal payroll.''

Dante's imagination was running amok. The photographer had been under investigation for counterfeiting. And the agent who'd planted a bug on Janet Lake wasn't part of the Treasury picture any longer. A renegade ex-Fed? Either that or deep cover, with his file and records of payment expunged.

''Was Brill ever arrested?'' he asked.

''No record of it.''

''Any specifics on just what he was being investigated for?''

Klein shook his head. ''We'd need to access the actual file for that. I didn't want Thornhill to press it and let Treasury know we're snooping in their sector.''

Dante eased back off the edge of his chair, took a deep breath and let it out slowly. ''Paper,'' he mused. ''Dope, gems, electronics . . . all that other shit, and it never even occurred to me. Any other names raise any flags?''

''Couple of warrants for unpaid tickets. An accountant who's behind on his child support. The list goes on, but nothing like the fireworks Brill set off. You ready for the rest of it?''

Dante was back on the edge of his seat again. ''There's *more*?''

Klein pulled a printout from a manila folder and shoved it across to him. ''That's from Customs and Immigration. I got curious about the Barranquilla connection and had them run Brill's name.''

According to the sheet the partners were putting their heads together to scan, Roger Brill had made four trips to Colombia in the past eighteen months, all of the flights on

Avianca out of JFK. As they read, Dewey shoved across another sheet from the folder.

"Airline flight information. As you can see, all four trips were paid for by Close Apparel, Incorporated. The plot thickens, huh?"

Jumbo stood and started to pace the stained linoleum floor. "Interestin' game. Slick. The way I see it, Brill and somebody on the inside at Close are printing *outside* the country and smugglin' the shit *in*. From what I've heard, the toughest part of a funny-money scam is keepin' the press under wraps. They've solved that problem."

Dante frowned. "So why don't they just *mail* the shit? Dope or gemstones, I can understand something this complicated. But paper?"

"Mail's got a name and address on it, dude. It might be ninety-nine percent safe, but that ain't good enough. One freak postal inspection, and you're takin' a ride up-river to the house with bars on the windows. Same with smuggling through Customs at an airport. The risk is personal. These guys figured a way to short-circuit all that."

"Customs would be looking for bulk when they inspect a shipment of garments," Klein agreed. "Unless he was working with a tip, no inspector would hunt for paper."

"Right." Jumbo stopped his pacing to stand facing them. "And our theory of there bein' someone on the inside is probably accurate. They'd know just when the shit arrived and whether the coast was clear for waltzing in and carting it off. Only the inside man fucked the dog. The coast *wasn't* clear. The best laid plans and all that shit."

Dante was amazed at how it all fit. He tried to think ahead.

"We're gonna have to hope they didn't shoot their wad this one time. That there'll be another shipment."

"If you want to catch them red-handed at it," Klein agreed. "And the evidence is on your side. That was a pretty elaborate red herring they generated. They want us to be thinking design theft, and I can't imagine why, unless they want the way clear for another shot.''

After she reluctantly told her secretary to show the two detectives in, Felicity Close checked her makeup in a compact mirror and straightened several items on her blotter. As they entered and crossed the expanse of carpet, she rose from behind her island of a desk and asked them to take seats. As a recent widow she wore black wool crepe, cut to accentuate height and flatter her well-maintained physique. The two cops pulled up a pair of burgundy leather chairs and sat before her.

''So what can I do for you gentlemen?'' Her voice was cool, corporate, and devoid of any emotion.

The tall, rugged one took the lead. ''We're following up a couple of recent developments. Several things. But first, we'd like you to tell us everything you can about your manufacturing facility in Barranquilla, Colombia.''

It took her by surprise, but she wore such an impassive expression that none of it registered.

''Barranquilla? It's our pride and joy at the moment. All the latest technology. Labor and shipping costs way below anything in the Orient. We feel it's the wave of the future, and we've had the foresight to ride the crest of it.''

The detective sergeant nodded. He had a notebook out but failed to make any notations. ''Those samples that were stolen the night Peter Buckley was killed. They'd been manufactured and shipped from down there, hadn't they?''

The alarm bells were ringing now. Something had turned their attention away from the design theft. She had to be careful.

''All of our Janet Lake sportswear is manufactured in Barranquilla, Officer. And like all of our other offshore manufactured items, it is shipped to our warehouse facility at the Brooklyn Navy Yard.''

It was the black detective who took up the thread. ''Our

investigation has revealed that Roger Brill, the photographer, has taken several extended trips to Colombia in the past year and a half. Trips paid for by this company. Should we find that unusual?''

She was scrambling now and trying to keep a serene, straight face at the same time. "Not at all." She displayed an amused smile. "Those trips came out of discussions with our PR and advertising people. They encouraged us to take advantage of the potentials the venture embodies. Hemispherical goodwill. Hands across the Americas. The financial boost we are giving an economically troubled Third World country. All of that. One of the ad people mentioned our discussions to Roger, and he came to us with the idea of his going down there to document our progress on film. For the money we ended up paying him, he worked awfully hard. He shot some strong stuff for an industrial that's been shown at several trade shows. I think it's had the effect of putting us in a very good light.''

They looked as though they'd bought that one. But why this focus on Roger? What could have pointed them in his direction? She decided it was time to go on the offensive.

"I'm afraid I don't see what any of this has to do with the investigation.''

The sergeant answered her. "We have to consider the possibility that the whole design theft was a diversion.''

"A *what*?" She came forward quickly and planted her hands on the edge of the desk. She heard her voice go cold as steel. "My husband is dead, gentlemen. Peter Buckley is dead. I'm looking at the possibility of some pirates stealing millions of dollars from my organization. So what is the New York City Police Department trying to do? Those murders and that theft happened in New York, gentlemen. Not in South goddamn America!''

The detectives weathered her tirade impassively. When she'd settled back in her chair, face hot and breath coming quickly, the one named Dante smiled a patronizing little smile.

"We appreciate your explaining all that to us. It's always refreshing to have a concerned citizen point out how we might better do our jobs. We won't take up any more of your valuble time this morning, and we're sorry if we upset you." He pushed his chair back and stood. "I can see that you've got a lot on your mind."

The black man rose and followed his partner out the door. When they'd gone, Felicity sat in her huge rosewood-paneled office staring her undoing in the face. Somehow those two bozos had stumbled onto Roger. As much as she loathed the idea, Murray had to be told. He would surely get the message. And it was only right. When a ship started sinking, women and children were supposed to get off first.

Joe and Jumbo had more questions they wanted to ask about shipments from Barranquilla, specifically any due in the near future. Rather than do any more snooping around Close corporate headquarters, they thought it best to try the source this time and head for Brooklyn. Before driving away from 39th and Broadway, Dante dropped a quarter and called upstairs to Peter Buckley's design assistant, Hillary Fox. In short order he had the name of the warehouse facility manager. It was moving on noon already and time to start thinking about lunch as he climbed back behind the wheel and fired up today's Plymouth.

Almost as they pulled away from the curb and into the snarl of midtown traffic, the radio crackled, and the dispatcher announced their call sign. Jumbo snatched up the mike and answered. A few seconds later Gus came over the speaker.

"A little powwow at the big building, Joey. Two-thirty this afternoon, PC's office, and he wants you on the carpet there with me."

Joe gestured for the handset, and Jumbo passed it over.

"What's the scoop, boss?"

"Beats me. Maybe all he wants is an update. See if you can be no more'n fifteen minutes late, huh?"

Dante racked it, rolling his eyes. A summons to an audience with Tony Mintoff at One Police Plaza was the last thing he needed today. This investigation was just starting to move. To make matters worse, he found himself in a wild snarl of cars on Broadway that had traffic frozen nearly solid.

"What do you want for lunch, Mr. Diet?" There was little enthusiasm in the way he asked it.

TWENTY

In deference to the big man's crusade, Dante allowed himself to be led into one of those glorified salad bars which had sprung up just about the same time Jane Fonda started making exercise tapes. He ordered and ate something they were calling the Taco Supremo Salad and washed its phony south-of-the-border taste away with sparkling apple juice. It left him feeling mean. They discussed the afternoon's meeting and agreed that once Tony Mintoff got his hooks in, there was no telling how long it might be before he took them out. The uniform assigned to baby-sit Janet Lake was due to swing out at four. Chances were that Joe wouldn't be on hand for the changing of the guard. Jumbo agreed to cool his heels up there until Joe could relieve him.

After dropping his partner on Park Avenue, Dante fought the snarl of traffic going downtown and parked in the garage beneath the big building with time to spare. He wasn't feeling any less mean, and there was something rubbing him the wrong way about this meeting. When a cop was in the middle of an investigation and on the verge of a breakthrough, it was kind of a jinx to discuss it with outsiders. Technically the big boss wasn't an outsider, but on the other hand, anyone not directly connected to the street seemed like an alien to a street cop. Tony Mintoff had long since divorced himself from the street. Everything was spit-and-polish in his world. In the big building everyone looked as if he was either going to a funeral or playing dress-up.

To add to his uneasiness, Rosa was standing in front of the elevator doors when they opened on the PC's floor. Her hello seemed as sterile as the atmosphere.

"You got any idea what this is all about?" he asked.

"The mayor's been bringing a lot of pressure over your investigation, Joe."

"And good old Bob's gone on record that maybe I'm not the guy to be handling it, right?"

She was noncommittal.

Dante shook his head, a weary smile crinkling the corners of his eyes. "What the fuck would *he* know about it? Tell me that."

She started to move off. "I'm through discussing what Bobby does or doesn't know with you, Joe. All of our personal failings aside, I still think you're the best street cop in the job. He knows I feel that way. How he chooses to view my opinion is his business."

Dante watched her go and then walked toward the PC's outer office. Upon entering, he met Bob Talbot almost head-on. The dapper captain wore his immaculately tailored uniform with every bit of gold braid he was entitled to sport. Dante had to admit that the man wore it well. His WASPish good looks and bearing gave him just the right amount of pretension necessary to support such a get-up. Gus Lieberman and C of D Pat Murphy were standing next to him, neither man shining quite so brilliantly. Joe looked right past Bob to Gus.

"When's show time, boss?"

Talbot sneered. "We were waiting for you."

Dante held up his watch. "Mickey's big hand is still on the five, Bob. I was told two-thirty."

Talbot turned away with a look of pained contempt and

disappeared through the door to Mintoff's inner office. Joe took the opportunity to bring the chiefs up to date.

"I think we're finally getting somewhere," he told them. As quickly as he could, he filled them in on the progress Dewey had made with the personnel list and how it had turned up Roger Brill as the subject of a Treasury counterfeiting investigation.

Pat Murphy, on the verge of retirement and, in the view of many, just marking time, nodded solemnly. "You're convinced that this design theft is a decoy, then."

"Sergeant Klein's convinced me of it, Chief." He jerked his thumb toward the PC's closed door. "Any indication of what all this is about?"

"Talbot's been working the knife into your back with real zeal," Gus muttered. "My bet is that we're in for a lecture on negative press and lack of progress. The captain has the boss man's ear, and he hasn't made any secret of the fact that he thinks you're the wrong man for this job."

Dante had to make a real effort to control his anger. In the big building, the buck never stopped until they could find someone out on the street to pass it to.

"I like that. Two corpses in four days. A sneaking Fed planting bugs on us. A smokescreen burglary. Not a latent print to be lifted. Not a smoking gun or a hair out of place. We're less than six days into all *that*, and I've just finished explaining some actual *progress*. What would that fool do that we haven't?"

Gus was about to say something when the door opened and Talbot invited them into the inner sanctum. In addition to the captain and the commissioner, there were two other men present. Dante was startled to recognize one as the guy he'd seen walking away from the Close town house on Beekman Place. The T-man. Agent Murray Chopnik.

"Gentlemen," Tony Mintoff said, "I know we're all busy, and I thank you for coming down."

The PC was wiry and built low to the ground, like a

jockey just a little too big for flat-track racing. He wasn't much more than five and a half feet tall and moved as though his motor was forever stuck in high gear. His face was framed by a mane of perfectly coiffed silver hair. There were rumors about heavy drinking and extracurricular activities on the city's clock, but try as the press might to nail him, nothing ever stuck. He spoke without a hint of his Spanish Harlem upbringing. Anton Mintoff. Maltese in heritage . . . and you'd better not even *think* he looked Italian.

"It would seem that we've encountered a rather messy problem," he started in. "These two men with me are from the United States Treasury." He turned to indicate the man closest to him, a tall drink of water in a blue Brooks Brothers suit. His face was etched with deep lines like the Marlboro cowboy's; his hair was a dull steel gray, and his eyes were a piercing blue. They reminded Dante of the sort of eyes he'd seen in photographs of birds of prey.

"This is Wes Wainwright, agent-in-charge, Treasury's New York field office. With him is Treasury field agent Chopnik. They've come to me with a disturbing story." With that said, he introduced Gus, Pat Murphy, and Dante before suggesting the boss T-man take it from there.

Wainwright clasped his hands behind his back and started to pace the thick pile carpet. After walking a few yards, he turned to face them.

"Commissioner Mintoff tells me that you are the three men responsible for the current investigation into the break-in at Close Apparel and the two murders associated with it. I'm here to tell you that your investigation directly jeopardizes a tightly choreographed Treasury operation that has been in the hopper for over two years."

This guy was fascinating. Joe watched his every posture and overall attitude as he spoke. Supreme confidence there. Absolute command. He was the perfect embodiment of Fed arrogance.

"Agent Chopnik has been deep cover in an effort to break a major counterfeiting operation."

That explained why his name didn't show up on any current Treasury roster. Deep cover meant ceasing to exist in any traceable capacity.

"He has been on this trail, risking his life, ever since a load of security paper was hijacked en route from the place of manufacture. Four of our people lost their lives in that hijack. Agent Chopnik was the only one escorting it to survive. He managed to foil the complete theft of the load, with the aid of his mortally wounded partner. The hijackers got away with one thousand sheets of Government security, or money, paper." He paused at this juncture to pace a little again. When he stopped, he fixed New York's Finest with a no-nonsense glare. "We have been trying to track that paper ever since. The implications of such a theft are unthinkable."

The drama in the guy's voice was a bit much for this small gathering. The man assumed they were all standing in awe of who he was and what that represented.

"You said directly jeopardizing," Joe piped up. "You mind explaining that?"

A quick flash of irritation crossed the Fed's brow. He glanced first toward Mintoff, and then back to this lowly detective sergeant.

"You're the man actually running the street investigation, correct?"

"That's right."

"Well, *Sergeant*, we don't feel free to reveal specifics at this moment, but you can rest assured that your heavy-footed plodding has already spooked a number of birds to cover. Birds we are hoping to shoot down in flight." He forced a condescending little smile, as if he were addressing a dog with no pedigree. "Agent Chopnik and others like him are highly trained in this sort of operational situation. You and your fellow officers are not. It's a very fine line we're treading here."

189

Before Dante could crawl down this arrogant asshole's throat, Gus jumped in.

"You're outta line there, friend. Fine line or otherwise, you call the best detectives in my command heavy footed, you better back it up with specifics."

Wainwright turned impatiently to the commissioner. "All I've got to do is get a Federal restraining order, Tony. The potential damage runs into the tens of millions here." He held up two fingers, shaking them for emphasis. "We're this close. There is no way I'll let your people blow it for us. Once we've dropped our net on this, *if* we can still drop the net, then your team can come around and make your arrests for the murders." He turned to Chopnik and directed him toward the door with a slight nod. "I mean that about getting a Federal judge to step in. Don't force my hand."

Chopnik was already on his way out. Wainwright followed on his heels. The five cops remaining in the room stood facing each other as the door closed.

The anger was evident as Mintoff withdrew a good-looking cigar from his desk humidor and occupied himself setting it afire. The rest of them waited for the legendary volcano to blow.

"Great!" he snapped, slamming his lighter down with the flat of his hand. "I've got two high-profile citizens dead, the bitch of Fashion Avenue crawling up the mayor's ass, the mayor crawling up *my* ass, and now *this*! And what have you gentlemen got to give me? Other than fucking heartburn?"

Gus warned Dante back with a look and fiddled for a Carlton.

"Something fishy goin' on here, Tony," he said with utter calm. "That big joker who just walked outta here? He's been stumbling all over *my* investigation. I know your friend there"—he glanced at Talbot—"has been whispering sour nothings about who I've got conducting this investigation and how he's goin' at it, but let's put the back-stabbing bullshit aside a minute." He shifted his gaze from the PC and trained the full heat of a whithering glare on Talbot. "I was slogging shit in the sewers of this city when this guy was still in some Connecticut prep school. You let him talk that MBA shit to you, and now you just let that Treasury asshole walk in here and jump on all of us. I'm where I am because I'm the best you've got. Sergeant Dante's where he is because he's the best *I've* got. So far this week, that big T-man's been seen leaving the immediate area of an NYPD homicide, has threatened one of my prime witnesses, and planted an electronic listening device on her. Who's city *is* this?"

The room fell deathly quiet as Lieberman stuffed his cigarette between his lips, lit it, and snapped the lid of his Zippo shut.

"Bob?" Mintoff said at length, nodding toward the door in dismissal.

Talbot, obviously incensed at being stripped naked by the deputy chief, opened his mouth to protest. The PC narrowed his eyes. The captain got the message and vacated without further ceremony. Once the door had closed on him, Mintoff regarded Gus with a wry smile.

"Touché, big fella." He turned to contemplate Dante. "You've stepped on some big toes, mister. I don't suppose I have to remind a street cop of your savvy that we have always maintained the best mutually beneficial relationships with the various Federal enforcement agencies."

Dante shoved his hands deep in his pockets and took a deep breath. "No, sir. You don't need to remind me of that."

Mintoff nodded. "Good. There seems to be some sort of personality conflict between you and Captain Talbot. I realize he can rub some of you guys the wrong way, but my word is law here, not his. So talk to me. Enlighten me a little. Give me some idea why Wes Wainwright came down here so fired up."

Joe lowered his head, turned away, and walked toward a window overlooking the Brooklyn Bridge.

"I've got two murders in four days, both of them apparently committed to cover up a break-in at Close Apparel." He described the misleading nature of the actual theft, and the Barranquilla connection. "Just this morning Sergeant Klein at Safe, Loft, and Truck uncovered the Treasury connection to an actual name in the case. A photographer who does a lot of work for the company. Fashion layouts. He's made four trips to Colombia in the past eighteen months."

Mintoff digested this while working to keep his cigar alight. Dante was perched on the windowsill now, framed by the top cop's magnificent downtown view.

"This Chopnik actually *bugged* the model's place? You're sure it was him?"

Joe pushed himself back off the sill and shrugged. "He also told her that you were fully aware of their investigation."

That got him. "He said *what*?"

"That this office was cooperating on a need-to-know basis."

Pat Murphy, silent up to this point, cleared his throat.

"While you were in here with Wainwright and Chopnik, Dante brought Gus and me up to date, Tony. We were going to ask you about all this and see if you could get some answers out of the local field office."

"There's something wrong here," Gus added. "It's the first time in my thirty years in the job that I've known any Fed to run an investigation parallel to one of ours without at least touching base with the commissioner's office. And I've *never* known them to try and run a municipality off a *homicide* investigation."

Emboldened by this exchange between his superiors, Dante decided it was time to go for broke. The air had been clouded this afternoon, and he wanted it cleared.

"*My* homicide investigation," he interrupted. "There's a maniac out there, butchering citizens in media-grabbing, high-profile situations. My job is to stop that maniac before he can kill again, not to back off because some Fed threatens me with a court order that doesn't even exist yet. If you want me to tuck tail and fake going through the motions, find yourselves another boy. I can't.''

Mintoff scowled in open irritation. ''Nobody's telling you to do anything but the job this city is paying you to do, Sergeant. Just do us all a favor and try to proceed delicately, huh? No more requests to Federal agencies for data checks.'' His expression softened. Joe would have sworn that the little tyrant had even hinted at a smile. ''Tuck tail, you said? I doubt the agent-in-charge has heard as much about your exploits as I have, Sergeant. *Kick* tail is more like it. Keep up the good work.''

Joe drove Gus Lieberman uptown to the Borough Detective Command through early rush-hour traffic.

''What's your read on that charade we just witnessed?'' Gus growled. They were pulled up to a red where the Bowery crossed Delancey.

Dante flashed a smug smile at his passenger. Gus read it without too much difficulty.

''You smell something as fishy as I do.''

Joe nodded and spoke calmly. ''You bet I do. I know firsthand just how unorthodox a deep-cover operation can get, but this one's got stink on it.''

''That one of your hunches?''

Joe lifted his hands from the wheel in a gesture of futility. ''Call it what you want. That big guy *ran* to put some distance between him and the Rabinowitz murder scene. If he's got that kind of weight behind him, why'd he do that? Just to avoid being questioned?''

''Maybe.''

''Then why did he turn up at Janet Lake's first thing the next fucking morning?''

The light went green, and they started to roll again.

''Okay,'' Gus murmured. He shifted in his seat and tugged the brim of his Resistol hat down lower on his brow. ''I ain't askin' you to back off even one iota, Joey. Not because some Fed asshole with a studio tan threatens us with a court order. Just watch your backside from here on in. This thing has more sharp edges than a roll of razor wire.''

TWENTY ONE

Dante dropped Gus at Borough Command and continued uptown to Safe, Loft, and Truck. One aspect of Wainwright's story had piqued his interest, and he wanted to run it by their resident expert. He found Dewey in his characteristic pose, feet up on the big battered table. A freckle-faced younger guy with crew-cut red hair sat opposite. He wore sneakers, jeans, and a faded blue work shirt.

"Day is done, huh?" Dante nodded at the open can of Genesee Cream Ale that Klein was cradling.

"You bet. Want one?"

Joe wrinkled his nose. "Genny? No thanks."

Dewey introduced the redhead as Fred Peterson, and Dante pulled up one of the plastic chairs.

"How'd it go down there?" Klein asked.

Dante related all the gory details, tossing in plenty of flowery expletives to season the stew.

"A big boy," he concluded. "Built like a pro tight end. He's been running with this thing, deep cover, since the hijack. And that's why I thought I'd drop by. The hijack itself. That's up your alley, and I'm wondering what you might be able to tell me about it."

Klein gazed over at Peterson, puckered his lips, and wedged his knuckles up under his chin. "The item is fact, right, Freddy boy?"

Peterson took a swallow on his beer and nodded. "Oh, yeah. Huge stink at the time. Four guys from the Treasury side and two from the other were killed, if I remember right."

"Four Feds dead, compounded by the fact that the government just doesn't lose blank security paper," Klein confirmed. "If I'm not mistaken, there's only been one other loss in the history of Treasury. The other one, they located. This load's been missing for two years. Shit, I figured they'd seen the last of it a long time ago."

"And what about the actual job?" Joe pressed. "Did it go down the way they're saying it did?"

Klein removed his chin-supporting fist as he shrugged. "Beats the fuck outta me . . . and them, too, I'll bet. Nobody survived but the one agent and some guy in a van from the other side. I don't think the escape vehicle was ever found."

Dante leaned back, contemplated Klein's can of Genesee, and was momentarily tempted. "So what does Roger Brill have to do with all of this?" he wondered aloud.

"Maybe tomorrow will shed some light," Klein replied. "I've got a buddy of mine in San Francisco checking into it. The FBI records had him born in the Bay Area and going to school out there. He moved to New York twenty years ago, but he was already working some as a photographer."

"Who's this buddy?" Dante asked.

"Inspector with their hijack unit. Sort of my opposite number. He promised to do some digging."

Roger loved the challenge of printing perfect money. Getting that crackling-clean image on film. Burning the super-sharp negative onto the litho plate. Mixing smudge-free gray and green inks with a critical eye for exact color. And then there was the paper.

The paper was the hardest obstacle to surmount. While at art school, Roger took a course in papermaking. He became obsessed and actually built a makeshift laboratory in his China Basin loft. Over on the streets of Haight-Ashbury the flower children were milling in stoned hordes. The Jefferson Airplane was taking off, Moby Grape wasn't a soft drink, and the Summer of Love was still a year away. But Brill gave all these developments only the most fleeting attention. His was an altogether different crusade. The quest for the perfect note.

Twenties were his primary focus and became his specialty. He liked them because they avoided the scrutiny fifties and hundreds got, while still embodying plenty of purchasing power. Twenties were the economic cornerstone Everyman built a night on the town or trip to the supermarket around.

He fiddled and failed, visions of Andy Jackson dancing before his mind's eye, until he spotted some commercial papermaking equipment at auction and went in hock to the eyeballs to pick it up. A world of possibilities was suddenly open. Varying quantities of minuscule red and blue threads went into batches of cotton rag, to be pulverized and poured wet into the pulp press. He was going one step beyond.

In 1968, when he moved to New York, Roger traveled with the fifty sheets of paper he'd been unable to part with. Everything else had been dismantled and sold or destroyed. Of product, only two Jacksons remained, each with a random serial number, each capable of passing the ultraviolet-light test, each a work of art in every aspect. He realized now that his inability to part with these mementos had been suicide.

The noise of rush hour could be heard building toward that daily five-thirty P.M. crescendo as Brill sat alone in his Murray Hill study. Those two twenties stared up at him from the scrapbook in his lap. One had been repeatedly caressed; the other was as pristine as the day it came off his press. Felicity had discovered them in this scrapbook four years ago. She asked why he kept forty dollars there, and Roger proudly revealed the secret of his long-dormant enthusiasm. He'd been in love with her then.

Felicity had signed a series of contracts pledging Close Apparel backing for a French perfumer's hideously expensive new scent. It was to be the flagship for a flotilla of new cosmetics she was planning to launch. Jerry was concentrating on the creative aspects of mass-market sportswear design and had no idea that she'd pledged the corporation's liquid assets to an ambitious ad campaign, extravagant packaging, and the establishment of department store franchises. When the bills started coming in, Felicity was frantic to hide the precarious nature of her investments from her husband and partner. She remembered Roger's art school hobby and she mounted a relentless campaign to enlist his aid. Brill had never doubted his love for this willful and wonderfully persuasive woman. Eventually he gave in.

The game was something a little different for him. Bearer bonds. Felicity's mistake had been in attempting to sell the lot of them to a middleman as expert fakes, twenty-five cents on the dollar. The middleman she found was an undercover T-man posing as a buyer. Murray Chopnik swore with open admiration that had they marketed the bonds as the genuine article, the experts would have been none the wiser. Those sheets of paper, manufactured in San Francisco's China Basin in 1968, were that good.

In the ensuing nightmare years Felicity lost control of the company to Jerry anyway. Roger finally saw through the mechanics of Felicity's loving devices, and the vaginal wrench had lost its torque. There was no freedom in this truth. Murray, the ultimate opportunist, saw no reason to arrest a craftsman of such consummate skill. Not when he had him by the balls and could use him toward his own ends.

* * *

The city outside Janet Lake's penthouse windows twinkled just as they say it does in songs. Dante thought he might like to have a sofa like the butter-soft leather job he was sitting on. Opposite him, on a matching one, the lady of the house was dressed casually in faded jeans, a red cotton sweater and Topsiders. She appeared to be as in control as he'd seen her through this week of turmoil. A centered calm had returned to those remarkable eyes. She looked rested.

"What about friends?" he asked her. "Anyone you know who wouldn't mind you camping out in their guest room for a couple days?"

She sighed and shook her head. "Believe me. I've been racking my brain, but anyone like that is on the West Coast. I tend to spend my New York time working. There are a lot of social acquaintances, but none of them are close."

"What *about* the West Coast?" he suggested. "It's a thought."

Now she rolled her eyes. "With Jerry and Peter both dead, the whole sportswear thing is in chaos. I've got lawyers looking into just where I stand with Felicity. There's another fashion shoot scheduled for Friday. I'd love to get the hell out of here, but I can't."

Dante leaned forward to pick up the Coke she'd offered him. "Detective Richardson explained the manpower situation to you?"

She nodded.

"Rather than make my boss any crazier, I told him I'd take tonight's shift and find some place to stash you tomorrow. You mind me bunking here on the sofa?"

"There's a perfectly acceptable bed in the guest room."

"I'm sure there is. But the point is to protect you. Out here I can sleep with one eye on the front door."

A frown wrinkled her brow as her eyes moved first to the sofa he sat on and then back to his face.

"It doesn't seem fair that you should have to do this. I'm a pretty good judge of people's energy levels, and I'd

199

say you've been running yourself ragged with this investigation.''

He grunted. "You're right there. It's only Wednesday, and this week already feels twelve days long."

"So maybe I'm not really in any danger. The door has good locks, and I can ask the super to have the night people keep an eye out?" She asked it halfheartedly.

Joe smiled. "Take it easy, please. We fuzz aren't used to citizens being concerned with our welfare. Most taxpayers expect at least their money's worth."

"You don't seem to really mind."

He waved it off. "I could try some line about being a man with simple needs, but you'd probably gag. I do have a hungry cat who'll want feeding, and I'd like to pick up a toothbrush and clean shirt. What would you say to taking a ride?"

En route downtown, the model insisted on buying him dinner. After a few blocks, he gave up arguing. Copter was furious that Joe didn't intend to stick around. Janet seemed intrigued by the bachelor detective's Village digs. She looked around as he threw a few things together, opened a Kal Kan, and filled the kitty's water bowl. They locked up and left to look for a dining experience low-key enough to suit their combined moods.

The choice was a cozy little Italian café on West 4th Street, just a couple blocks from Dante's apartment. It wasn't crowded, and the atmosphere was tranquil. It was also cheap.

"I want you to know that I really appreciate what you're doing for me," she told him. They'd ordered a bottle of red wine, which they sipped while waiting for appetizers. She fingered the rim of her glass thoughtfully. "It gives me a whole new idea of what's involved in your line of work. I hadn't really given it much thought before now."

He smiled good-naturedly. "Any more than I've given a lot of thought to what you do. In the eyes of the world, it's all glamour and glitz. I guess I just accepted that."

As they had walked to their table, the other clientele had recognized her and watched her pass in open fascination. Even casually dressed, she was a creature of stunning beauty. In the past week Dante had lost track of that fact. To him she was just another human being trying to cope with great personal tragedy. It was the big equalizer.

Their starters came. She had a Caesar salad, while he tried the fried calamari. After a few bites, Janet set her fork down.

"So how *does* a guy like you decide to become a cop? Is it actually something you wanted to do with your life?"

"A guy like me?"

"Sure. You seem different from my image. You live in the Village. Aren't married. You have books on philosophy and psychology. You don't have a pit bull, you have a spotted cat."

Joe sipped his wine and smiled.

"My dad was a cop. I grew up around a lot of them. There were some assholes, but a lot of them I came to respect. Instead of taking all the time, they gave a lot of who they were. I'm not sure when it happened exactly, but one day I realized that I wanted to be one of them."

"Did you know you'd be good at it? I mean, even then?"

He laughed. "I guess I could take that as a sort of backhanded compliment, huh? But in truth, I still don't know that I *am* good at it. The bureaucratic bullshit is still something I have a lot of trouble with. But I'm a watcher. Always have been. It seems to pay in this business." He cut his last piece of calamari and shoveled a bite into his mouth. "I've got an idea about tomorrow I wanted to run by you."

She shrugged. "Shoot."

"Brian Brennan, the sculptor, is a buddy of mine. He's got a warehouse loft way west on 27th Street. A nice setup. Acres of room. What would you say to me stashing you there, just for the day?"

The look on her face was incredulous.

"Brian Brennan? Who lives with Diana Webster?"

"That's right. If I asked him to take you in, I know he'd go along. It isn't Park Avenue, but it's nice in a well-heeled *down*town kind of way."

With wonder in her eyes, she told him she supposed she could handle staying with his friends.

"You'll have to excuse me if this seems boorish," she said after a moment. "But why haven't you married?"

He nearly choked on a slurp of mineral water. "Jesus."

She colored slightly. "I'm sorry. I guess I can get carried away sometimes."

"Don't worry about it," he said, "everyone I know in the job is married, has a house with crabgrass in the burbs, two kids, and a dog. It's a reasonable question."

She waited as he pushed the tip of his nose with an index finger and mulled it over.

"Changing perceptions, I guess. I always thought I'd be married at this point. Maybe even more than once, the way things are these days. The women I get involved with are too headstrong to follow me down the traditional path. The last loveboat shipwrecked a couple months back."

"It's a tough world on a tender heart."

"You speaking from experience?"

She nodded. "Skye's father was my one great experiment. He could afford to give us all the security money could buy. But there wasn't any risk in that. It didn't take me long to realize that I didn't want to be someone's potted plant."

"I'm not surprised, from watching the way you handle yourself."

"I'm flattered, Detective."

Dante drained his wine and reached to refill both their glasses. "Now you're flattering me."

She shook her head; her face was suddenly serious. "Not really. I'd expect a guy like you to take a particularly cynical view of people like me. In my world it's all done with makeup and artful airbrushing. Your everyday world is so terribly real."

"Same world," he corrected. "Just different neighborhoods. If I've learned anything from this job, it's that all of us have obstacles to overcome. Don't sell yourself short."

Their entrees arrived.

TWENTY TWO

Murray Chopnik knew that shoulder rigs were for hot dogs and movie cops. Maybe not as worthless as an ankle holster, but still bad form. A soft holster clipped to the waistband at the small of the back was the preferred conveyance among law enforcement professionals not in uniform. Unless you were packing some unconventional armament. The Secret Service branch of Treasury had little choice but to carry those fully automatic jobs under their arms, in spite of the discomfort. And Murray had little choice with the noise-suppressed Beretta. With the silencer screwed on, the damn thing went twelve and a half inches in length. Right now, it had just jabbed his crazy bone, left arm, as he got out of his car on East 37th Street.

Teeth gritted against a numbing ache that shot clear to the tips of his fingers, he started up the block, moving toward Third Avenue. He would make a full circuit, checking into cars on both sides of the street for possible occupants. With the Cuban United Nations Mission located just around the corner on Lexington, there were always FBI and NYPD Intelligence Division personnel in the area. And considering his objective that night, he wanted to avoid being observed by a trained professional.

He passed Roger's building and tilted his head slightly upward. He could see that several lights in the upper duplex apartment still burned at this late hour. The lights in the lower apartment were all out. Digesting this, Murray wandered on casually to complete the circuit. Two butch-looking broads were parked in a black sedan on the corner of Lex, out of sight of his own objective. There had been no one else. In the middle of the block, moving east again, he crossed abruptly behind a hurtling yellow cab and raced up the stoop of Brill's brownstone. The goddamn Beretta muzzle jabbed him again en route. In the ribs this time.

The darkness of the tight little double-door entry area shielded the T-man as he eased a set of picks from his pocket and went to work on the latch tumblers. This was not his specialty. His picking skills were only adequate, but patience eventually paid off. The right-hand panel swung inward, enabling him to step into the small gallery area. The downstairs apartment door now lay straight ahead. The tiny elevette running up to Brill's place was on his left. He elected to forego the contraption and mount the adjacent stairs. That hamster cage on cables made one hell of a racket.

Gaining Roger's third floor landing, Murray pressed an ear to the front door and listened hard for sounds of movement. It seemed possible, from the absolute lack of any sound at all, that the photographer was upstairs in either his bedroom or study. All the better. He prayed now that the street-door lock was the only one Roger had changed since his film-producer neighbor broke his latchkey off in it. The set of keys Felicity had provided included one that supposedly fit the pickproof Medeco cylinder that secured Brill's apartment proper.

With one gloved hand gripping the knob, Chopnik inserted the key, twisted, and heard that satisfying little click of release. He turned the knob slowly and pushed the door open just a crack. From that vantage, he had a pretty good view of half the living room, the dining room, and the entrance to the kitchen beyond. Brill was nowhere to be seen.

A quick check of the entire downstairs revealed it to be uninhabited. Murray moved with the silence of fog. He strained to hear any faint sound from upstairs. Roger, an avid reader, probably had his nose in a book.

The trip upstairs took a while. This was an old, nineteenth-century house, and Roger had preserved as much of its antique charm as possible. That included the ornate oak-and-mahogany staircase. It swept grandly around on itself as it rose, and creaked like a backyard swing. By keeping tight to the inside, Murray managed the journey with little more than the occasional settling sound any old house makes.

The bedroom door was open, its interior unlit. At the opposite end of the long, railed landing, light streamed from beneath what Chopnik knew to be the study door. Bingo. He pulled the Beretta, in all its cumbersome glory, out of the shoulder rig and held it against his right thigh. A board beneath the padded Oriental runner gave a pretty good creak, kicking an extra drop of adrenaline into his bloodstream. Roger wasn't going to be able to escape at this juncture, but professional pride demanded that Murray do this quietly. If a neighbor heard a scream and came to investigate, he could be forced to kill him, too. That would be messy.

He paused before the door to collect himself. It was a damn shame, what he was about to do. The man did beautiful work, the best he'd ever seen in twenty-six years of observing topflight counterfeiting technique. But Roger had served his purpose. He was a pure liability now.

Instead of knobs, all the doors in the place had ornate brass levers. Murray applied downward pressure on the one controlling entrance to the study, and the panel gave with a barely audible click. He summoned a recollection of the room's layout and reckoned Brill's big leather-upholstered reading chair would be just left of dead ahead.

He flicked off the firing-pin block and his thumb eased the hammer back. He planted his left shoulder, and distributed his weight evenly over slightly bent knees. A controlled launch brought him square into the frame of the open doorway. His gun hand brought the weapon around to eye level, where his left met it to grip and steady it. His trigger finger was already applying pressure when what he saw brought him up short. His left hand flew from the gun to cover his mouth. His dinner barely stayed down as he faltered backward, feeling dizzy.

There was no need to kill Roger Brill. Half of his face and head were glued in bits and pieces to the back and wings of his Queen Anne-style chair. The gun, apparently a Smith & Wesson "Combat Masterpiece," dangled from one hand across his dead knees.

Murray scrambled to regain control and assess the situation. Felicity said that the man was on the edge. Murray had taken that to mean Roger had gone queasy and could queer everything. He'd never imagined suicide. . . . With effort he turned away from the mesmerizing sight of the man with the hamburger head. Murray's dazed steps took him to the swivel chair of a huge old rolltop desk. He sat.

The damning thing was right there on the blotter in front of him. It took a few minutes before he collected himself enough to focus on it. Two entire handwritten legal-pad sheets explained all the circumstances that forced him to take his own life, everything the law would need to bring the world crashing down around several sets of ears.

This concrete evidence of just how close a call it was had an immediately sobering effect on the T-man. He snatched up the note, folded it hastily, and shoved it into his jacket pocket. His imagination began to race. The gun he'd been about to use lay at his elbow on the desk, the gun that had killed Jerry Rabinowitz. The city cops called such a weapon a throwaway, an unregistered gun, not traceable in any way. Right now, Murray was thinking of it more as a "giveaway." A self-satisfied leer spread slowly across his face.

It was going to be grisly work, but wonderfully poetic. The gun was left where it was for the moment as he stood and dug for the penknife in his pocket. In addition to retrieving the slug, which more than likely lay embedded in the back of the chair, he had to make sure he did all the rest of it artistically. For starters, he pried the revolver from the dead man's fingers and pushed it into his own shoulder holster. It wasn't easy, working past all that spattered brain matter, the skull fragments, and the inordinate amount of blood. The sorry bastard was soaked with it.

He stooped to scrutinize the upholstery directly behind the spot where Roger's head must have been and tried to calculate the angle the bullet would have taken. And there it was, a tiny lateral tear hole in the leather, encrusted like everything else, in coagulated blood. Then he circled around to the back of the chair, noted an exit hole, and followed the projected line of fire.

The slug was embedded in the wall. It missed going out a window by mere inches. The entry hole was clean enough; the crumpled hunk of lead had lost a lot of steam before it burrowed in here. Murray didn't have much trouble digging it out.

The little bugger was hardly recognizable as having been a semijacketed, hollow-point projectile. The point of impact was mushroomed all the way back along what had once been the length of it. Ballistically, it could very well prove worthless, but it wasn't a one hundred fifteen grain, full-metal case SUPER-X Winchester 9mm Parabellum slug, and that's what it had to be now. He glanced quickly around the room until he found something that he thought might just do the next job.

It was a thick little ring binder emblazoned with the title, "New York Publicity Outlets." Murray set it in the desk chair with the Business Yellow Pages as a backstop. He took aim with the Beretta and cranked off a silenced 9mm round. The swivel chair rocked backward crazily as the publicity binder flipped in the air. After wading though the cordite haze, the T-man eventually found his bullet lodged up against "Costume Jewelry" on page 873 of the commercial directory. The resemblance it bore to the slug retrieved from the wall wasn't at all bad. He set back up and tried once more, just for comparison's sake. In the end he wound up still liking his first effort, and that was the slug he tapped back into the gouge the .38 had made in the plaster. Before setting the Beretta in the dead man's rigor-frozen hand, he released the clip, fed one more bullet into it, and shoved it to.

Outside of a missing suicide note and the two bullet-scarred books he now carried tucked under his arm, the place looked very much as he had found it. Treasury records would confirm that Roger had been under surveillance at one time as a suspected counterfeiter. That fair-haired cop with the wop name and his fat nigger partner could wrap up their murder investigation all nice and neat while Murray whistled all the way to Rio de Janeiro.

It was going on midnight. Janet lounged opposite Dante in her living room, Topsiders kicked off and bare feet up on the polished marble surface of the coffee table. She sipped Courvoisier from a snifter. Joe had switched to seltzer water about half an hour earlier.

She had been observing him closely all evening. He had an incredible presence that made her feel both comfortable and safe for the first time since she had learned of Peter's death. There was still a heavy sadness in her, something she knew would take a long time to shake. But tonight she believed it was something she had the strength to overcome. She wasn't alone, and she wasn't the only one who cared. This cop hadn't known her brother at all and had only met Jerry briefly, and yet she could feel the sense of outrage that seemed to fuel him.

"You're absolutely convinced it wasn't Peter's designs at all, then," she murmured, staring into her drink.

Dante yawned. "Your brother was in the wrong place

209

at the wrong time, Ms. Lake. It's one hell of a piss-poor reason to lose his life. Most reasons are."

"When are you going to stop calling me Ms. Lake, Sergeant?"

He smiled. "When you stop calling me Sergeant. The name is Joe."

"The name is Janet, Joe. You look like you're ready to fall asleep sitting up. Are you sure you won't take the guest room?"

"I'm eagerly looking forward to a night of sleep on this couch. If sleeping on it is anything like sitting on it, I might have to throw my own bed out and get one."

She pulled her feet in, planted them on the floor, and stretched languorously. It was amusing to catch the way he looked at her. Her body had that effect on a lot of men, a phenomenon she appreciated for it's economic power but also often viewed as a curse. But not right now. It had been a long time since anyone she admired had drunk her in like that. Come to think of it, quite a bit of time had passed since she'd met anyone she admired.

"Good night, Ser—Joe. I had Ellie put fresh towels in the guest room bath." She stood, picked up her glass, and carried it into the kitchen.

Minutes later, the emotions she felt as she climbed between the sheets surprised her. She had a stranger sleeping on her living room sofa, and she felt secure. It gave her hope. Maybe the entire world hadn't gone mad after all.

A phone call the previous evening had cleared the deck for Brennan to do a day of baby-sitting. Dante was up as early as Ellie the maid and had showered and dressed before Janet showed her face. He'd had some reservations about the way things might go, and was relieved to find the model good company. There'd been little evidence of the acid tongue she'd displayed the first time they met. Both of them had even opened up a little and he, for one, didn't feel like a fool for the effort. When she later embraced

Brian and Diana's Bohemian digs with unbridled enthusiasm, Joe felt like a great load had been lifted. He rolled off to throw more food at his cat and meet Jumbo at Borough Command.

The partners nearly collided, one arriving and the other just leaving the Task Force locker area.

"You get coffee?" Jumbo asked.

"On my desk."

"How'd it go last night?"

Dante beamed at him. "Never slept on a more comfortable sofa."

The big man was surprised. "She couldn't find a friend to stay with? So where is she now?"

Joe hung up his light topcoat, slammed the locker door, and led the way into the squad room.

"I've got her stashed at Brennan's."

Beasley stopped in his tracks. "Oh, good idea, Joey. That maniac specializes in paying beautiful broads to take their clothes off and lay around his studio all day."

Dante chuckled. "The more power to him, buddy. You *wouldn't* pay money to see her with her clothes off?"

Jumbo started to say something, stopped, and shook his head. Then he got a funny, far-off look in his eyes. "Dream on, hotshot. Neither you nor me could ever afford it."

By eight-thirty they'd drawn yet another stripped-down Plymouth from the motor pool and were on the road toward the Brooklyn Navy Yard. En route, Dante filled Jumbo in on what Dewey had told him late the previous afternoon.

"Sorta points the big finger in the photographer's direction, don't it?"

"Sorta does."

"So when're we gonna lean on the fucker? He was inside at Close Apparel. He knew the right shit to steal the night Peter Buckley got it."

Dante was riding shotgun today, slumped low in the seat with one knee wedged up against the dash. He nodded. "You might be right. But I still don't think he's the only guy in on this."

"So what are you thinking?"

Dante dropped his head back onto the headrest and contemplated the back of the sun visor. "I'm thinking that there are about a hundred questions I want to ask Roger Brill. But I'm also thinking that this smuggling scam is just too elaborate to have been a one-shot deal."

"You don't think they did it all in that one load."

Joe slowly shook his head. "No way. Not when the hijackers got away with a thousand sheets of blank security paper."

Jumbo's head shot around, and he fixed Dante with a wide-eyed stare. "Holy mother! Did you just say what I think you said?"

Dante grunted and dropped his eyes to stare ahead to the approach to the Williamsburg Bridge across the East River. "I'm just taking all the crazy pieces and trying to fit them into this puzzle. Brill was investigated by Treasury but never arrested. Their investigation ended just about the time that hijack happened. Agent Chopnik is the only surviving witness to the crime. It's his word that one of the other side managed to escape in a van. A van, by the way, that was never located. We saw Chopnik in the vicinity of the Rabinowitz homicide while the corpse was still twitching. And Chopnik is the same size as the janitor Jerry Rabinowitz saw. Add it up, big guy. The way I look at it right now, the bug he planted on Janet Lake was just a means of keeping tabs on our investigation."

Jumbo could barely sit still in his seat. "Jesus Christ, Joey! Are you hearin' yourself?"

Dante shut his eyes now as he nodded. "You think I want to face the fact of a dirty Fed any more than you do?"

"God Almighty," Jumbo moaned. "If you're right, the shit's gonna be all *over* the fan. I assume you've got some sorta plan?"

"To be there when the next load from Barranquilla arrives at Customs. I'm starting to see the four cartons of salesmen's samples as a sort of trial run. If it was me, I'd do a test just to make sure that my pipeline was functioning. If we play our cards right from here, the next shipment might be a way to catch these jokers with their fingers in the pie.''

The Brooklyn Navy Yard is a vast complex of decrepit World War II warehouses and decaying piers sandwiched between the strife-torn Williamsburg section of Brooklyn to the north and what the locals call ''Downtown Brooklyn'' to the south. The view across the river is nice, but that's about it for stunning visuals. Everything inside the complex is painted a peeling, baby-shit beige. Still, the location is extremely useful to companies unwilling to pay the costs of warehousing space in the higher-rent borough across the East River.

The security guard at the gate examined Jumbo's gold detective's buzzer and directed them to a building down by the water and to their left, three sections in. As they rolled toward their objective, they observed the surroundings. The place was a hive of morning activity, with semi-rigs backed up to loading bays by the dozens and forklifts scurrying to and fro. At barely nine o'clock, the business world across the river was just starting to get its first cup of coffee, but this was obviously the early bird, nuts-and-bolts end of commerce.

The reception area for the Close Apparel warehouse facility was a cramped, no-frills affair with one torn Naugahyde sofa, dated periodicals, and walls done in cheap, four-by-eight-feet sheets of imitation wood paneling. A heavily madeup young woman with masses of unruly brown hair sat behind a sliding glass window.

''Can I help you?'' It was a definite Queens accent.

''Police officers, ma'am,'' Jumbo told her. He dangled his tin before the glass. ''We'd like to talk to a Mr. George Conway.''

Conway, according to Hillary Fox, was the facility manager and, therefore, this woman's boss. A bored, nowhere demeanor changed quickly to one of flustered compliance. The woman fumbled with the receiver of her phone, misdialing once before getting through to the manager's office.

"Mr. Conway's assistant will be right down to show you the way," she told them upon hanging up. "Is that okay?"

"Just fine," Jumbo replied.

The assistant, a Close Apparel kid-on-the-way-up type, appeared just short moments later. She was tall, well groomed, and expensively dressed in a lavender wool business suit, cream-colored silk blouse, and sling-back heels.

"Gentlemen," she greeted them, extending a hand. "I'm Jill Curtis, Mr. Conway's administrative assistant. He's out on the warehouse floor dealing with an inventory problem. He asked me to escort you down."

They followed her through an electronically controlled door to the cool warehouse interior. Ms. Curtis's whole manner exuded curiosity, but she asked no questions as she led the way along an aisle stacked high on both sides with cartons on wooden pallets. It was a bit like a maze, with sudden turns here and there and wider thoroughfares crossing at intersections. Forklifts could be heard plying the depths of this cavernous place. It was at least as large as an enclosed football field.

Dante easily picked out George Conway standing in rolled-up dress shirtsleeves and tie. He was a tall, lean, and energetic looking black man who moved with animation and gestured at things as he talked. A half dozen warehouse employees focused their undivided attention on what he was saying until Jill Curtis strode into view, leading the two detectives.

Conway glanced up at their approach, said another quick few words, and turned to greet them.

"Thanks, Jill," he dismissed her. "George Conway, gentlemen."

He extended his hand. "What can I help you with?"

Joe and Jumbo both shook hands with him and introduced themselves.

"Is there someplace we can talk, out of hearing of your crew?" Dante asked him.

"My office. Just follow me."

The office was a glassed-in room located on a balcony that ran the length of the warehouse above the loading bay. From it the boss could watch what was going on across the entire floor of his operation. Outside Conway's door, in an equal-size reception-and-secretarial area, Jill Curtis could be seen doing paperwork at her desk, while a typist across from her worked at a fancy-looking, late-model computer terminal.

Conway had a refreshing openness about him. He offered coffee, which they declined, and indicated seats.

"So," he said. "Does this have something to do with all that craziness on the other side of the river?"

"Could be," Dante allowed. He twisted in his chair to get comfortable. "We're interested in when you expect your next shipment from Barranquilla."

Conway looked surprised. "Your timing's sure right," he said. "That's why the floor's such a madhouse right now. We've got an Avianca 747 loaded with summerwear scheduled to land at JFK this afternoon. Three thousand five hundred cartons, and nowhere to put them. We're jammed up with back inventory, and I didn't get authorization to rent more space until yesterday. That's corporate red tape for you."

"Let me get this straight," Dante said. "You ship the stuff airfreight? Isn't that wildly expensive?"

Conway pursed his lips and nodded. He had a long, thin face with a high forehead and deep smile lines etched on both sides of his mouth. "Yes, I suppose it is. But this is a business that makes its seasonal nut on a tight schedule. The later you wait to see what the competition is doing, the better chance you have of weeding out your own likely losers. That means last-minute production schedules . . . and last-minute shipping, too. The bigwigs figure it's worth whatever it costs. And Colombia's a whole lot closer to fly a load in from than, say, Taipei."

"How's it work, once they land a load like that at the airport?" Jumbo asked him.

Instead of answering immediately, Conway reached out and switched on a computer terminal. He tapped a few keys and scanned the screen, squinting a bit. "A day to clear Customs," he said. "Then pickup for transport here. Delivery scheduled for noon tomorrow. That's why I've got them busting hump down on the floor right now. We have a lock on a space-share with another outfit, the next building over. We're working right now to shift merchandise from overstock into that location."

"Why not put the new stuff in there?" Jumbo wondered.

"Electronic inventory control. The new garments have to come into this facility, because this is where all the computerized picking equipment is. That other shit isn't going anywhere but into discount houses at cut rates. The new gear is the company's bread and butter."

Joe pointed at the computer screen. "Can we have all that information on the new shipment? ETA. Which Customs shed it goes to. It might also be handy to know who transports it here from JFK."

Now real concern appeared on the manager's face as he asked: "What's up?"

Joe shook his head. "We're not sure there's anything up at all. Let's just say that we're trying to cover all the bases in the late innings of a tight game."

Conway obviously thought this all too cryptic, but he appeared ready to accept the careful response. He reached to tap a couple more keys, and a moment later the printer on the credenza beside his desk began to chatter away. When it stopped, he rolled his chair over and tore off the printout.

"That's everything," he said, handing it to Dante. "Flight, arrival time this afternoon, Customs location.

Your investigation isn't going to hold me up any, is it?" There was an edge of real panic in the question.

"Not if we can help it," Joe assured him. "We appreciate your cooperation, and we'll keep your pressing situation in mind."

As Conway sighed in relief, Dante folded the printout and pushed it into the breast pocket of his jacket. As he did so, his fingers touched the sketch of Treasury agent Chopnik. It gave him an idea, and he pulled it out to flatten it on the manager's desk. He placed one of his Task Force cards on top of it.

"This is off the record," he said carefully. "But if you happen to get a visit from this man, he'll most likely present the credentials of a Federal agent. They're legit. By all means, cooperate with him. If he does talk to you, we'd like to know about it."

A quizzical twinkle briefly visited Conway's eyes as he pocketed the card, studied the sketch, nodded, and handed it back.

After pulling away from the Close warehouse, Jumbo drove them three buildings down to the center-way and parked at a bank of pay phones. At one Joe dropped a quarter, called Gus Lieberman, and gave him the details of that afternoon's Barranquilla shipment to JFK.

"I'll need you to pull some strings and get Customs sweet-talked into letting us observe. Thirty-five hundred is a lot of cartons to go through in one day. It'd be nice if we had some sharp eyes on hand, to watch over their shoulders."

"And who might those sharp eyes be?" Gus asked.

"I'm calling Klein as soon as you hang up. With any luck he'll be available. Maybe he'll even have another warm body he can drag along."

The detective thought he could hear the snap of his boss's Zippo lid. Lieberman's reply came mouthed around a cigarette. Joe could almost smell the smoke.

"Consider this end taken care of. But check back with me before you head out there."

When Gus cut the connection, Dante dialed Dewey's number at Safe, Loft, and Truck.

"Dante! I was just gettin' ready to ring you, pal. My man in Frisco just came through."

"Feed me."

"Our friendly photographer was born and raised in some burg called San Leandro. That's somewhere close by in the Bay Area, I gather. After high school, he studied photography at the San Francisco Art Institute. While he was going to school there, he worked as a stat-camera operator for a commercial lithographer."

Dante felt his pulse quicken. "I'm not exactly up on the subtle nuances, but that's significant, isn't it?"

"You bet it is. This outfit was a specialty house. High-quality replication for advertising. A good stat-camera operator in a plant like that has to have an eye for clarity and critical focus. It's just the sort of eye it takes to shoot money."

"There's a big shipment from their Barranquilla plant due into JFK this afternoon."

Klein chuckled. "Be a nice neat scam, wouldn't it? Do all your setup and printing outside Treasury jurisdiction. Smuggle your handiwork up here in a totally low-risk mode. Take it off the garment shipment whenever the coast is clear."

"Like maybe this weekend," Dante mused. "The facility manager tells us that they're shut down from Friday night until Monday morning. I want to be on hand this afternoon when that stuff hits the Customs shed. What's your schedule?"

From behind him, Jumbo sounded the horn. When Joe turned, he saw the big man with the radio mike in his hand.

"How about I meet you out there with Peterson?" Dewey asked.

"Great," Dante told him. "Now I've gotta run. I'll call

218

you with the shed number and time as soon as Gus clears it with the Feds.''

Jumbo had his head out the driver's window as Joe hurried toward the car. ''That was Gus. Roger Brill's maid just found him with his head blown all over the back of his reading chair.''

The mental roller coaster Dante had been riding took a near-vertical plunge as he sprinted for the passenger side door.

''You realize what day this is?'' Jumbo asked in disgust as he stomped the accelerator to the firewall. ''It's April fuckin' Fool's Day. Sounds like the only thing I've got to be happy about is the fact that I ain't had breakfast.''

TWENTY THREE

A big black woman sat at the foot of a sweeping staircase inside Roger Brill's Murray Hill duplex apartment. Propped against the newel post at the terminus of the banister, the woman was sobbing hysterically, hands covering her face.

The uniform on the front door pointed upward. "They're in the study, Sarge. Top of the stairs and down the hall to the right. Awful fucking mess. That's the maid. She found it."

"Who's here?" Dante asked.

"Two detectives from the squad at our house. Chief Lieberman and someone else from your Task Force. Some lab guys and the ME."

As Dante started up the stairs, Jumbo jerked a thumb at the door behind them. "Nobody gets through that without checkin' with us first, right?" He had to ease his bulk sideways to get past the sobbing maid as he mounted the stairs.

Up on the landing they turned right, went to the end of a long hall, and pushed open a closed door. Everyone inside the study was off to one side, conversing with averted eyes. There wasn't much question as to why they

220

didn't want to look at the spectacle seated in that central wing chair.

"God*damn!*" Dante grunted.

"What the fuck's he got in his hand?" Jumbo wondered. "He was worried about the *noise*?"

"Mintoff and Pat Murphy are gonna think this just about wraps it," Gus said soberly. He and Dante were watching as the medical examiner's people carted Roger Brill's corpse past in a body bag. They stood on the landing, down the hall from the study, where Bernie Horvath and his team were crawling over everything inside. Jumbo was keeping an eye on developments and had emerged moments ago to report that they'd recovered the slug. It and the noise-suppressed automatic were being sealed in bags for a trip to the ballistics lab.

"He wasn't working alone, Gus. I'm convinced of that."

"And what if that gun winds up being the same one that killed Rabinowitz? They're gonna want to believe that seals it."

Dante shook his head emphatically. "Brill still doesn't match the description of the guy Rabinowitz saw leaving Close Apparel that night. I think I know who might." At Lieberman's urging, he went on to outline the way he saw the pieces fit into the puzzle.

"Chopnik?" Gus asked in disbelief.

"Why else would this sorry son of a bitch kill himself, Gus? Because he got a sudden attack of acute guilt? He saw the sky falling in on him. Two people were already dead. As a coconspirator, he's implicated in two murders."

"And you think Tony Mintoff's gonna buy that? You think he'll stick his neck out with Customs on the basis of a mad-dog Federal agent theory? Just the *thought* of running with a thing like that'll make his shit green."

Joe fixed his boss with a hard stare, straight in the eye.

"So *don't* tell him. You've got the weight. Go to Customs yourself."

"And if you wind up being wrong?"

"Then I don't see the harm done. The inspection goes quietly. We stake out the warehouse for a weekend and bury the overtime somewhere inconspicuous."

Gus gave him one of those why-do-I-put-up-with-your-crazy-bullshit looks and nodded toward the study door. "It might be nice to know where our dead friend was the evening Rabinowitz was shot."

"That occurred to me. Last we saw of him, he was off to deliver film to his lab. I suggest you send a couple of guys from the Task Force over to his studio and have them interview the staff. I would, but I'm gonna be busy at the airport, right?" Before Gus could reply, Joe broke away and stepped down the hall in search of Bernie Horvath.

The balding lab chief was standing with Jumbo next to the study's lone window as his crew appeared to be wrapping up their inquiry.

"Anything else interesting?" Dante asked them.

"Not much," Horvath told him. "Lots of ring binders full of slides. Most of *them* of pretty women. Nice library. He seemed to like hardcover best-sellers."

"That'll help a lot," the detective grumbled. "Still no suicide note?"

"Drew a blank there."

"I guess it's possible," Joe mused. "Not very thoughtful of the guy, but possible."

"It bothers me, too. There's always a note. I suppose it's possible that someone else got here first and took it."

That caught Dante's attention. "Why do you say that?"

Bernie waved away any significance Dante's question implied. "Just because I've got that kind of mind. There's no evidence of forced entry, and nothing else seems to have been disturbed. Take it with a grain of salt."

When the partners eventually emerged from the study and descended the stairs, they found Gus sitting next to the telephone in the living room.

222

"Talk to a guy named Greg Frye," he told them. "He's running the shift in your Customs sector today. He's expecting you."

Joe regarded him with clear but unspoken appreciation. "So what are you gonna tell Murphy and Mintoff about the mess upstairs?"

A small twinkle of amusement crept into the corners of the deputy chief's bloodhound eyes. He butted a half-smoked cigarette against the sole of his shoe.

"I'll hand 'em some bastardized version of the facts. A photographer of Brill's stature being dead is news, no matter how the marbles around the fact happen to roll. The PC will feed your ex-girlfriend the party line, and she'll feed it to the vultures of the Fourth Estate. You two will keep doing the job we pay you to do, and I'll hope to God you're right."

"I swear to *Christ* he pulled the trigger on himself," Chopnik hissed. "Not that it fucking much matters, except for the goddamn letter he left layin' there on his desk."

He paced the deep shag in his living room as Felicity regarded him from the recliner opposite the television.

"And you planted the gun on him? The one that killed Jerry? You think the police are going to buy that?"

Murray was beside himself with his own cleverness now. "I *know* they're gonna. It was a thing of beauty. I'm telling you that. Pure fucking inspiration."

Felicity sighed. "You can spare me the details of what a bright guy you are, Murray. I already stand in awe of your genius."

He whirled on her now. "You think I need you or your shit, sweet tits?"

A smug little smile was beamed his way. "You're stuck with me now, Tarzan. After your little act with the gun yesterday, I went home and wrote a sealed letter to my attorney. It was delivered to him just before I came here. We're partners, Murray. All the way to the end of the line.

223

If I die, the world finds out just who you are before you can get to the airport.'' She lifted a file and began working on the edge of a nicked nail. ''It would be my suggestion that you take great pains to make sure I stay in the pink of health.''

The hate-fueled surge was so strong, he could barely refrain from knocking her head off.

In the wake of a hastily wolfed-down coffee-shop lunch, Dante and Jumbo drove through Queens in surprisingly light traffic. All around them, spring still seemed determined to overcome winter. They had rolled down the windows of the maroon Fury, and a warm air mass caressed them as they traveled on the Long Island Expressway, and then on the Van Wyck to JFK airport.

Avianca flight seven was close to a half hour late. It gave the partners time to huddle with Dewey and Fred Peterson before introducing themselves to the honcho of the Customs inspection team. Joe ran through the details of the Roger Brill suicide and finished with the mad-dog Fed theory.

Greg Frye was a tough ex-Marine with tattooed forearms and crew-cut steel-gray hair. His appearance belied his actual disposition, which was genial and cooperative. He explained Customs proceedings.

''You guys are in for a bit of sitting on your hands,'' he warned. ''Generally it takes a freight crew up to three hours to unload a big bird like that. Everything's in sealed aluminum containers. We take it into the shed, bust the seal, select random cartons and open them for a look-see. Today, at Chief Lieberman's request, I guess we're going at this a bit more thoroughly.''

It was one-thirty as he spoke, and the cargo jet had only just taxied up along a distant runway. From what Frye was saying, it appeared that they might not even see the inside of their first box for another hour. If they worked at a detailed-search pace, it was going to be well after dark before they even reached the middle of the load. Dante didn't see himself breaking loose until at least eleven o'clock, and that left Janet Lake in the lurch. While they were killing time, he sought out a phone and called Brennan's place. Diana answered.

"Don't worry about her, Joe. We just aced Jane's low-impact aerobics tape, and everything's fine. We'll have dinner and you can pick her up when you're finished."

"Beasley wants to know if Brian's gotten her to take her clothes off yet."

"Tell him not to wear out his right hand dreaming about it."

When the 747 finally came to rest on the tarmac outside the international freight Customs shed, a crew from one of the domestic airlines swung into action unloading it. According to Frye, many airlines couldn't afford to maintain freight equipment, so handling arrangements were made with other airlines. Dante could understand why when he got a load of the required rigs. They were giant contraptions called jet pallet loaders or JPLs, and looked like something built for the space program. One of them motored out to the plane on huge tractor tires and began unfolding upward on a system of hydraulics. An operator standing in a little cherry-picker control basket directed this elevated platform's movement as the cargo doors of the jet came open. Apparently the deck of the plane was outfitted with conveyors designed to propel the aluminum containers out onto the JPL's deck. That deck was equipped with similar conveyors. They worked in concert with the jet's mechanism to pull the container off board. When the cargo was loaded on the JPL, the operator lowered the platform to ground level, and the rig driver then drove the thing toward the shed. The platform operator had already leapt to the ground and immediately climbed into the cage of the next loader that moved in to replace the departed one.

Inside the Customs area, the container was rolled off the rig and into a bonded holding area. A group of in-

Christopher Newman

spectors attached to Frye's team went to work on it, recording the identification numbers and breaking the seals.

"Show time," Frye told the men from NYPD.

As they moved in a group toward the inspection station, an enraged Treasury Agent Chopnik materialized through a side door and descended on the crew chief.

"Chopnik, Treasury," he snarled at Frye, flashing him the gold T-man buzzer. "What are these men doing here?"

Frye explained the situation and the request made by the New York Police Department for interagency cooperation. Chopnik spun on Dante, the only one of the cops he recognized.

"What the fuck's it take to get through to you people? The threat of a Federal court order don't cut no ice with you?"

Dante noticed that the Texas accent got heavy when the man got mad. "Anyone can make a threat," he said calmly. "As far as that court order goes, I think only a Federal judge is empowered to issue one. You know something we don't?"

The T-man's eyes blazed. "You're a fuckin' wiseass, pal. While you were out giving away parkin' tickets, I was busy protectin' four presidents of the United States. You want to fuck with me?"

"You're hardly my type, big guy."

Chopnik struggled to control himself. "I'm demanding that you and your people vacate. Your presence here interferes with a Treasury Department investigation."

Joe glanced around at Jumbo, Klein, and Peterson. "Okay," he said easily. "I'll make you a deal. These detectives and I will be glad to leave as soon as you turn over a comprehensive report on the history of your investigation to our commissioner. And don't leave out the stuff about Roger Brill. We figure that might make interesting reading."

The man's punch came out of nowhere. It was designed as a sucker shot, coming up from down low and aimed for maximum impact in the center of his target's chin. It

226

was the street fighter's ploy of dropping the best thing you had on your opponent and hoping he wouldn't be able to get up and answer it. But because he'd locked on the man's eyes, Dante saw it coming. A vicious cross-body parry sent the blow wide. It happened in an instant. Chopnik had no time to be surprised that his blow had failed to connect. A skip kick to the lower left knee doubled him up. Immediately Dante followed with a graceful, balletlike roundhouse kick to the side of the head. Chopnik collapsed like a bag of spuds.

Dante sighed, his breath coming in rough, adrenaline-fed gulps. "I feel sorry for those four presidents, buddy. That was too easy."

Frye, the customs chief, was literally wide-eyed. "I've been fiddling with Tai Kwon Do ever since the Korean conflict, and I've never seen that done better."

"I'm a little rusty," Dante told him. "But not as rusty as this guy. You never telegraph a sucker punch."

"Jesus. Is he gonna be all right?"

Joe nodded. "I pulled that roundhouse. A good shot like that would have broken the fucker's neck."

The team of Customs inspectors had stopped in the middle of what they were doing. Now they watched as the sheet-white Treasury man struggled to get to his feet from all fours. Frye glanced over at them and then back to the detectives.

"Does what he was saying change anything here?"

Dewey Klein took over for Dante. Joe's knees had begun to shake as they always did after a confrontation like this.

"We're just here to watch you do your job, Chief. To make sure that every effort is made to scrutinize this particular shipment. I don't know about you, but I'm havin' trouble seein' how that could interfere with *any*body's investigation."

Jumbo backed him up. "As far as we're concerned, this dude just tried to interfere with a NYPD homicide investigation. We got us a dozen witnesses to the fact he tried to assault a police officer.''

Frye looked past them to watch the second JPL glide across the pavement to his location. He shook his head.

''Like you say. You're only here watching us do our job. Interagency back-scratching.''

Behind him Chopnik finally managed to get to his feet, favoring his right leg. Pain and fury were mixed in his twisted expression. He moved like a drunk as he staggered toward the exit.

''I'll get even with your motherfuckin' ass, Dante!'' he rasped. With a jerk of the push bar, he was through the door and gone.

''That same guy was around here last week, doing just what you people are doing now,'' Frye told them. ''We were inspecting four cartons from the same point of origin and consigned to this same company. He wouldn't say what it was about.''

''And you didn't find anything in those boxes?'' Dante asked. The adrenaline surge had run its course, and he had recovered his equilibrium.

''Not a thing. We went over them pretty thoroughly.''

The inspection went forward. Containers were emptied of their cartons, and the cartons were then methodically gone through, one at a time. The inspectors worked with practiced efficiency, and Joe was pleased to see that it was going a little faster than he'd anticipated. By six o'clock, when Frye called a half-an-hour dinner break for his crew, they were a good two-thirds of the way through the lot. The cops were invited to join the inspectors in a nearby employee cafeteria. Dante declined but told the others to go on. Even though the place was well secured, he wanted to sit there with the shipment, watch the ongoing JPL operation, and think.

''This diet's goin' too good for me to fall off the wagon for cafeteria chow,'' Jumbo announced. ''I think I'll loiter here with Joey.''

Five minutes later the two partners were alone in the

shed together, Dante on an overturned crate and Jumbo on the concrete floor with his back to a Close Apparel container.

"How's that snake *doin'* it?" the big man asked. "I can smell slime from a long way off, and that character's got the stink all over him."

Joe shook his head in disgust. "You been watching them go through these things as closely as I have? There's absolutely nothing but clothes inside them. No false bottoms. Nothing glued under the bottom flaps. Nothing sewn into the garment linings. Fucking *zip*."

Jumbo nodded. "And we got people willing to kill for four that were similar. We ain't got a guarantee *that* inspection went as thoroughly as this one, but we know they were looked at. Tell you one thing, though. The fact that this asshole shows up here and makes that sort of fuss? There's gotta be somethin' we just ain't seein'."

TWENTY FOUR

Much to his surprise, Dante cleared JFK by nine forty-five, and was parking his Corvette in front of Brennan's building at ten-thirty. Thursday night marked the start of the weekend, and this was one of Manhattan's prime areas of street prostitution. With the recent change in the weather, the hookers were out in force. Joe waded through a host of propositions tendered by women and transvestites of varying degrees of charm and stages of undress. Inside the lobby of Brian's building, the weary detective entered the elevator car and rode it to relative safety.

The sculptor's combination living space and construction studios occupied all ten thousand square feet of the top floor. Dante stepped off into a cavernous living room decorated in monochromatic grays so as not to detract from the impressive collection of art hung on its walls. Brennan collected mostly from his peers through trades, but wasn't above the occasional purchase if he absolutely fell in love with a work.

"*There* you are," Janet said brightly, emerging from the kitchen wearing rubber gloves.

At that same moment Brennan appeared from the studio, welding mask perched atop his head. "Joe. Give me a hand here a sec, would you?"

Dante shrugged at the more attractive prospect of the two, indicating her hands. "You hire on here or something?"

"Diana had to rush off to a rehearsal. I'm almost finished. I'll be ready in a flash."

Joe followed Brian into the giant construction area. His buddy was an elfishly handsome man of forty-five, with a wiry runner's build and tireless energy. The detective often wondered if Brian ever actually slept. He could work into the wee hours and still be up for his daily five-mile river run by six-thirty.

"Thanks," Brian told him. "I've got this big fucking brace I'm welding up for a new crucible winch, and it's so big I can't move the bastard."

Together the two of them were able to hoist the chunk of six-inch I-beam into position and hold it there while Brennan tack-welded it into place.

"Thanks for keeping an eye on my witness," Joe told him as they strolled back into the front room.

Janet had dispensed with the gloves, shouldered her handbag, and was waiting for him in front of a big David Hockney canvas.

"If I'd spent any more time with my eyes on her, Diana was going to chain me out in the stairwell," Brian said. "It was my pleasure." As he spoke, he stepped up to peck Janet on the cheek. "This character's got a wild rep, blondie. Make sure he keeps his hands to himself."

In the car, as they buckled themselves in, Dante asked the model if she'd mind his stopping home to feed the cat and grab a change of clothes.

"Not at all," she replied. "Have you eaten anything tonight?"

He shook his head. "I'll grab something from my freezer and throw it into your microwave. It's a cop's life." He fired the high performance power plant and eased out

231

into the light flow of out-of-town hopefuls trolling for blow jobs.

"I heard about Roger. God, what is happening?"

"He got a case of terminally cold feet. Made a real mess of his head in the process."

She shuddered. "What does his suicide mean? I can't figure it out."

Dante took a deep breath and exhaled as he headed the Corvette east on 23rd Street. "It's hard to say exactly. He was part of whatever got your brother killed. I'm convinced of that. What actually spooked him is anyone's guess. But I've got a gut feeling we're getting close to a showdown now."

They rode in silence for a while as Joe swung south on Ninth to where it merged with Bleecker at Abingdon Square, just a couple of blocks from his place.

"It's not fair that you should run yourself ragged all day and then be forced to eat some frozen junk from a microwave," she told him as they pulled onto Perry Street. "It's only eleven, and there are plenty of restaurants still open."

As he pulled up to a hydrant just down from his building, he smiled at her. "I appreciate the concern, but I'm used to this sort of thing. You want to wait here or come in? I'll only be a minute."

She unbuckled her harness and pulled her door release. "Take it slow, Ser—*Joe.* You're going to throw a rod."

He snorted. "What would you know about throwing rods?"

"My drunken bum of a father was a long-distance trucker. Whenever he came home from a trip, he buried himself under the hood of a hot rod 302 Mustang. He raced whenever he found some sucker in a bar who would put up pink slips."

"You never cease to amaze, lady."

With a toss of her head she pushed open her door and started to climb out. "I shouldn't." She threw it back over her shoulder.

Janet insisted that her protector put his feet up, open a

beer, and call the local Chinese restaurant for a delivery. She was a lot stronger willed than she looked in a magazine spread. He sat and drank and called. The kid with the food arrived with amazing swiftness. All in all, the entire pit stop couldn't have taken any more than forty-five minutes. They emerged into the cool night at fifteen minutes before midnight.

Joe was just stepping to the passenger door of his car, key extended to unlock it, when a blue-and-white from the Sixth Precinct pulled alongside. The uniform riding shotgun had the window run down.

"Hiya, Dante. You get that trouble fixed?"

Joe had been assigned to the Sixth squad before being rerouted to the Borough Command Task Force. Most of the guys at the station knew he lived in the neighborhood, and were familiar with the metallic gray Corvette. Whenever he parked it on the street, they kept an eye out. He stopped now and peered into the dark interior of the squad car. He recognized the guy who had hailed him as Frankie Callahan, one of the Sixth Precinct's long-term fixtures.

"Hi, Frankie. What trouble is that?"

"With your car. We just talked to that character in the monkey suit the last time around. Said he thought it was your carburetor."

Dante caught Janet by the arm and backed quickly away.

"It doesn't have a fucking carburetor. Frankie. It's fuel-injected. Get on the horn and call the Bomb Squad!"

Even as he was yelling it, he was leading Janet on a mad dash up the block. Both of them were out of breath as Callahan's partner raced up the block to pull alongside again.

"What the hell's going on?" Frankie bellowed. He had the radio mike in his hand but looked bewildered.

"I'm pretty sure your guy in the monkey suit was wiring my car," Joe gasped. Bent over, hands on his knees, he gulped for air. "Jesus. The bastard said he'd get even."

"Who?"

"Get some more cars in here, for Christ's sake. Seal off both ends of the street. Right now, it doesn't matter who."

As Callahan got on the radio, Janet stared at Joe, wide-eyed. "Jesus. A *bomb*?"

"That's the hunch I've gotta play. Hell, I could be paranoid, but I know I didn't call any mechanic to work on my car."

Within minutes, both ends of the block were sealed off, and every man the precinct could spare was running up and down the street ringing doorbells and warning people to stay indoors away from windows. A unit from the Bomb Squad arrived and eased around the blockade. Dante described his fears to the commander of the unit, a short, squat lieutenant named Ceccerelli. The guy had enormous, heavily calloused hands that he gestured with as he spoke. There was grease under his short-clipped nails. He seemed to know an awful lot about explosives.

"Tricky situation here, *paisan*. These days, we got wiseguys gettin' real fancy with their triggerin' devices. A favorite is the motion sensor, just like the one that sets off your car alarm. Some guys'll wire right inta that and save theirselves a lotta hardware hassle. Then there's the remote detonator. Ignition detonator. Pressure detonator . . . triggers the device when you sit in your seat. Nice piece of machinery, that new Corvette."

Dante grimaced. "Thanks. How do you approach it, with all those options?"

Ceccerelli spoke with voice and hands. "One of my boys crawls up there on his belly, throws a line around anything solid he can find and ties it off. We tie the other end to the truck here and goose her with a little tug. If nothing happens, we go to step two."

With Janet clutching his arm, Dante watched helplessly as the lieutenant started his people through their paces. A young kid, who couldn't have been more than a year or two out of the academy, took a heavy coil of nylon rope and started along the line of parked cars toward the Corvette. He was dressed from head to toe in a special Kevlar unisuit and hood. In a good, direct blast, Joe knew that such an outfit would do little more than contain his remains in one convenient package. Guys who worked this duty had it easy enough until a call came in. Then they had to be just plain crazy.

The kid reached the car on his belly, disappeared partially beneath it for a scant few seconds, and then came away in a hurry. When he reached the lieutenant's position, he threw off the hood.

"I saw it under there, Lou. Plastique. Big fuckin' lump of it. Too high up to try and get a hand on from underneath. I couldn't see where the wires were headed."

"Nice work, Logan," the commander said. He beckoned to the driver of a specially built Bomb Squad mobile unit. When the man approached, he handed him the remainder of the coiled rope.

"Tie it off to your trailer hitch, Jerry. When I give you the high sign, just nudge her."

As the driver moved to comply, Ceccerelli lifted a bullhorn to his lips and addressed the block, telling everyone to please stay away from their windows. At the far end of the block, cops hurried for cover. When Jerry was ready, Ceccerelli raised his right hand and pointed a finger at him. The mobile bomb unit eased forward to take up the slack in the rope and then drew it tight with a gentle tug. Up the block, Dante's Corvette disintegrated in a startling, bright orange fireball. The explosion was deafening.

Janet's fingernails dug into Joe's bicep. Scraps of metal and fiber glass rained down onto the street. Dante just watched as a fire truck broke the barrier at the far end of the street. In less than a minute, they'd doused the wreck in a heavy blanket of foam.

"Jesus," he murmured. "If Frankie hadn't come along when he did, I would have put my key into that lock."

Janet realized what she was doing to his arm and eased up. He didn't seem to notice. She stared up into his face.

"That's all it would have taken, isn't it?"

235

Dante shook himself out of it and glanced down. "Probably," he agreed. "You okay?"

She swallowed hard and nodded. The corners of her eyes were suddenly moist, and a lot of the toughness she wore like armor seemed to have melted. Joe handed her a handkerchief.

"We're alive," he said matter-of-factly. "It's something to think about."

"But your car—"

He snorted derisively. "Fuck the car. I was getting tired of it anyway."

Within the hour half the brass from the job were on the scene, along with the requisite mobile units of half a dozen local news teams. An attempt to blow up a cop was big news. The next day there was going to be a lot of coverage both in newsprint and on the airwaves. Dante and Janet, meanwhile, had retreated to the refuge of a squad car after Joe had begged the duty captain from the Sixth to keep everyone but the biggies off his back.

"Let me get somebody to drive you up to your place and stick around until I can get free," he said to Janet as they sat together in the backseat.

She shook her head resolutely. "When you're ready, I'll be ready. You didn't save just your own life tonight, *Sergeant*. I'll stay right here."

God, this one could be stubborn. Joe was trying to summon the energy to go to the mat with her when a heavy fist rapped on the glass from outside. He rolled down the window; it was Gus.

"Hey, boss," Dante said. "A regular zoo out there, isn't it?"

Gus climbed into the front seat, turned to spot Janet, and shot his team leader a quizzical little glance. Dante knew it looked strange, and was wondering how he was going to explain, when Janet leaned forward and extended her hand.

"I'm Janet Lake."

"Deputy Chief Lieberman."

Gus took the beautiful woman's hand and shook it.

"Sergeant Dante was taking me home. He stopped by here to feed his cat."

Gus glanced over at Joe and rolled his eyes. "I don't think I want to know any more, miss." And to Dante, he addressed the same question already asked a dozen times in the past half hour. "You got any idea which of your many friends might want you *that* dead?"

Dante answered the question truthfully. "I'd say the smart money is on a certain disgruntled Treasury agent. I had to clobber him this afternoon."

"You had to *what*?"

Dante described the circumstances of his run-in with Chopnik. "I'm sorta surprised you haven't heard about it," he concluded.

"Not a word. You think he's this crazy?"

"Depends on what he's got to lose. What gives with the ballistics report on Brill's gun?"

"A dead match with the slug that killed Rabinowitz."

Joe nodded. "They were in it together, Gus. Brill freaked."

"I've gotta get back out there with Murphy. Rumor has it that even Tony Mintoff's decided he can't miss this one. Nothing like the promise of television exposure."

"Can you run interference for me? It's been a long day, and my fuse is getting short."

"Where are you headed?"

Dante gestured toward Janet. "Up to spend the night on the lady's couch. Who knows what sort of stunt that maniac's gonna pull next."

In another forty-five minutes, the news crews decided they'd seen enough and packed it in. Before it was over, Tony Mintoff insisted that Dante be dragged out into the glare of the klieg lights for a little song and dance with the brass. By the time Perry Street had returned to some semblance of it's customary tranquillity, it was two-fifteen. Joe was getting set to have a lingering Task Force car give them a lift up to Park Avenue when Janet stopped him.

"Tell them to go on," she told him.

"Huh?"

"Don't argue with me. Tell them you've changed your mind, you've got other plans."

He frowned at her. "Do I?"

"Yes, you do. Your own apartment and your own bed are right across the street."

When he started to open his mouth, she placed an index finger over it. "You're the detective. You figure it out."

TWENTY FIVE

The visions he'd conjured didn't come close to the reality. His pulse quickened as she swept the cotton sweater over her head and deftly unclipped the front of her bra. Her pale eyes sparkled in the dim light of his bedroom as she approached, loosening the buckle of her belt.

"I'm just as surprised as you are, fella," she murmured, a hint of amusement in her voice. "Swept off my feet by the goddamn Marlboro man. Who woulda thunk it?"

Dante peeled off his shirt and tossed it onto a chair. He could feel her eyes assessing him.

"I've never smoked, and I can't ride a horse. Make you feel any better?"

She reached out and traced her fingers across the thick muscle of his chest. There were scars. A nasty one across his shoulder, just to the right of his neck.

"A little." She touched the scar. "What does the other guy look like?"

"Dead."

Her eyes came up quickly to meet his again. "Oh. Maybe I shouldn't have—"

He cut it off, snaking an arm around her waist and pull-

239

ing her to him. Their mouths met in a hungry kiss while eager hands explored the delicious textures of new flesh. The embrace was prolonged, with an intensity that surprised them both. When they finally broke that first kiss, both were breathless.

"Well . . ." She sighed, nuzzling his neck. "I was starting to get undressed and only managed half the job. You game for another go at it?"

He chuckled, feeling the warmth in his loins. Her fingers fumbled for the button of his waistband.

"I hope you realize what a sacrifice this is for me." He placed his hands on both sides of her waist, lifted her in one quick move and let her down gently on her back. It took him another three or four seconds to slip out of his pants and join her on the bed.

It had been a night of restless sleep. After tossing through it, Murray Chopnik crawled out of bed at six-fifteen to catch the early televised news. The cold fury generated by yesterday's events still gripped him as he padded into the kitchen, set his coffee maker to work, and headed for a quick shower. Never—on the school grounds of Midland, Texas, on the ball fields, or in the bar room—had he ever been bested in a fight. And that wasn't to say he hadn't taken his licks. There'd been plenty; his *S*-bent nose attested to that. Hell, he'd been a Jew in a land populated with anti-Semite rednecks; circumstances forced him to learn quickly about taking pain and fighting back.

Murray's early education had taken him a long way, through U.S. Army Ranger training and two tours in Vietnam. He'd specialized in long-range reconnaissance and specific objective demolition. And then Secret Service training, where he'd excelled alongside washed-up college jocks and pantywaist Mormons. He'd excelled because he'd always been able to smell trouble coming from a mile out . . . up until yesterday afternoon.

Murray was fifty years old now. He wondered if maybe he hadn't lost a step. One way or the other, he was getting out, and it wouldn't really much matter. Losing a step wouldn't affect how good it was going to feel to watch some hot-bodied Brazilian *puta* suck his dick. Meanwhile he'd watched the wop cop head into his apartment with the movie star and made quick work of wiring the Corvette. Now he was going to watch that son of a bitch fry on TV.

Wes Wainwright would get him his Federal Court order, and that would clear off the dead cop's fat nigger partner. By two this afternoon the way would be clear, all the way to South America. Before he stepped into the shower, he poured four aspirin into the palm of his hand and swallowed them with a glass of water. God, his wrenched knee and neck both still hurt like the devil.

He wore a bath towel wrapped casually around his waist as he carried a steaming cup of coffee to the La-Z-Boy recliner positioned in front of the TV set. The near-scalding water from the pulse-setting on his shower head had helped to work out some of the stiffness in his neck, but he still moved with a slight limp. With thirty seconds to spare, he thumbed buttons on the remote control, eased the chair back, and sipped coffee with smug satisfaction.

The picture blinked into bright focus. NBC's program ID announced the upcoming local news segment, and then Jane Hanson, looking a little too bright and cheery for that hour, greeted him with a jolly "top-of-the-morning." Murray tickled the volume button to ensure that he got it all loud and clear.

"The New York Police Department is still trying to determine the motive behind a dramatic car bombing that occurred late last night in Greenwich Village. Detective Sergeant Joseph Dante, a resident of the quiet neighborhood, narrowly escaped being killed in a blast that destroyed his 1985 Corvette. At a press conference held at the scene, Police Commissioner Anton Mintoff had these words. . . ."

The segment cut to the scene on Perry Street, and in the background the disbelieving Murray could see the smoldering wreckage of the car. It was a nice job. The mess left by his exploding plastique was barely recognizable.

Murray wasn't listening to what that pompous little shrimp of a commissioner was saying. His mind was too busy weighing what could have happened. The goddamn device was wired to the alarm's motion sensor. Jesus, had some car thief come along and tried to boost the fucker?

"—behind this attempted murder of a police officer."

A stringer leaned forward with her microphone. "Commissioner. How is Sergeant Dante? Was he in any way injured in the blast?"

Mintoff gave it his best top-cop smile. "Fortunately, the officer miraculously escaped any injury. He contacted the Bomb Squad at eleven-forty-eight P.M., and in the course of their investigation, they triggered the device without incident. An FBI special explosives unit has been called in to conduct a thorough investigation in conjunction with our own forensics unit."

The anchor woman came back on-screen. "Several other cars were damaged in the explosion. Windows were broken in surrounding buildings. The Fire Department had the blaze under control in minutes. In other news, an apartment fire in Queens claimed . . ."

Chopnik threw the remote control at his set and missed; it hit the wall just beyond, where it shattered. Enraged, he pitched his empty coffee cup after it. Then he was on his feet, limping back and forth like a gimpy, caged lion. He'd fucked it up. It didn't seem possible, but Dante had smelled trouble and managed somehow to escape. Now Murray knew he had to strike swiftly. He had planned to have all weekend to recover the load, but the heat was building, and tonight was going to have to be the night. He'd threatened the wop cop in front of witnesses. It was time to cash his chips and clear out.

Dante rolled over and peered at the digital readout on the clock console. It was seven, and he'd overslept. Not that anyone at Borough Command was going to blame him if he was a little late. From the clock his eyes traveled over the still-slumbering form of his bedmate. A witness in a homicide investigation whom he was supposed to be protecting. It was more than a little irregular, and he was still asking himself how it had all happened. Somehow, he didn't think it was because she was turned on by exploding cars.

He pushed his thoughts aside, swung his legs out of bed, and stood as quietly as he could. Their clothes lay in disheveled heaps on the floor. Only his jacket and shirt had made it onto the chair against the wall.

"Where do you think you're going?"

He stopped in the middle of stooping to pick up his pants.

"It's damned inconvenient, but I've got this job I'm going to be late for. I tried not to wake you."

She rolled over onto her side and propped herself on one elbow. The sheet fell away from her magnificent breasts, and he wanted to drop everything and call in sick.

"But you were of course going to leave me a sensitive note saying how much you enjoyed yourself in my arms and that you'd call the first chance you got."

"Not my exact words, but yeah. I hadn't quite figured out how I was going to get you home. Thought I'd leave it until after I had a shower and made coffee."

"I'm thinking about making an offer on your body. Low-to-mid-six figures."

"You're keeping it so low because of all the wear and tear, huh?"

She rolled her eyes.

"Don't sell yourself short, buster. I suspect there are still a few good miles left in it."

Dante grabbed his robe off the back of the door and slipped into it. "Listen. If you don't cover yourself with that sheet in about two seconds, I might be forced to stick around and *see* how many miles there are."

"Promises, promises." She snuggled back under the

blankets. "Why don't you just forget about how you're going to get me home and leave me here? I'm sure I'd be safe. Maybe later we could pick up where we left off."

"You serious?"

"Once a week, whether I need to be or not . . . just to stay in shape."

"You realize I'm already in some potential hot water here. Sleeping with a witness in an ongoing investigation is . . . uh . . . frowned upon."

Her smile turned into a hard stare. "Is *that* who I am to you?"

Joe covered his face with his hands, rubbing hard as he yawned. "No, I wouldn't mind if you stayed here for a month. Go back to sleep, bright eyes. I'll give you a call from the office once I figure out where my day is headed. Just be warned that I could end up being kinda late tonight. That okay with you?"

"Don't worry about me, Joe. From what I saw of your garden last night, I think it could use some attention."

"They looked. You looked. There wasn't anything there, Joey. I realize there's something screwy as hell going on, but I wonder if you're barking up the right tree."

Gus Lieberman faced Dante and Jumbo from across his desk at Borough Command. The three of them had coffee, and Gus had another of his Carltons going.

"There *was* something there," Joe insisted. "We just didn't see it. Just like Customs never saw anything in those first four cartons."

Gus pushed back and blew smoke toward the ceiling. "What is it you want from me?"

Dante shifted in his chair to stare out at the buildings lining the other side of the street. "I want to follow that shipment from Kennedy to the warehouse and sit on it all weekend if we have to. Tonight, I want to sneak in there for a peek. On the quiet."

Gus tossed his pen onto the blotter in exasperation. "Breaking and entering? That's good, guys."

"With a warrant," Dante insisted. "What more would we need to show a judge to prove probable cause? Two murders. An attempted cop-killing. The theft of four similar cartons that kicked all this madness off. You take all that to someone like Judge Ramirez, and he'll clear us without blinking an eye."

"And if I do? What do you propose to do once you're in there?"

"Cut a few of those cartons and everything inside them to shreds. If there's anything in them, I'm going to find it."

"And how are you going to get in there? The place must have an alarm system."

Jumbo picked up the ball now and ran with it. "Dewey Klein's our resident expert in B and E, Gus. He's helpin' us escort that new load to the Navy Yard. Once we get there, we'll tell the manager that we're just followin' up on some shit. Dewey slips off and pokes around while we make small talk. After he's checked out the alarm system, he gives Joey a quick lesson in B and E, 1A."

The deputy chief smirked. "You two guys got this all figured out, right?" He shook another cigarette out and lit it, a sure sign that he was agitated. "Okay." He inhaled deeply and blew smoke out impatiently. "If I get you this warrant, you better hope to God you can bring me something with it."

Dewey Klein waited for them well outside the fence of the Customs warehousing area at Kennedy Airport. Joe and Jumbo parked behind his unmarked sedan and transferred into his backseat. Fred Peterson was there with Dewey, sitting behind the wheel. From where they were, they had a clear vantage of the inspection shed and the semitractor-trailer backed up to it.

There was concern in Klein's eyes as he regarded Dante. "Heard about your wild night. Get any sleep?"

Joe wondered which part of his wild night the man was

referring to; the job grapevine was good, but he hoped it
wasn't *that* good.

"Do I look like I did?"

"Chopnik. You're sure it was him, aren't you?"

"They taught me to add in first grade, Dewey. There's
a trail of corpses stretched out behind that guy. So how
close are they to having that truck loaded?"

Peterson lifted a pair of binoculars and peered through
them. "Maybe a pallet load left to go, Sarge. You guys
got here just in time."

Klein took a couple minutes to outline a basic hijack-
escort strategy. It involved leapfrogging back and forth in
traffic, enabling them to vary speeds and lane positions.
He and Peterson were carrying a pump .12 gauge shotgun.
Perhaps their perp would make his move on the open road.

"We'll lead, and you two follow about a hundred yards
back. Let's try to rotate out of the lead position at one
mile intervals on the beltway and every two blocks once
we hit city streets."

They waited, making small talk, until Peterson spotted
the freight handlers closing the rear doors of the rig. Joe
and Jumbo hopped out and returned to their own car.
Jumbo took the wheel, leaving Dante, the better shot, free
for any extracurricular activity. Dewey and Peterson drove
off down the access road to park a quarter mile distant.
Ten minutes more passed before the big rig thundered past.
Jumbo gave it a little room and then eased lazily into the
flow of traffic.

It was yet another warmish day, with afternoon rain in
the forecast. It was also a Friday, and traffic headed into the
city was light. As predicted, the truck swung south on the
Shore Parkway along Jamaica Bay to Flatbush Avenue.
Flatbush cut northwest across the center of Brooklyn, and
was just starting to fill with early lunch-hour traffic. Jumbo
stayed with Klein's game plan, hurrying ahead to change
places with the lead car at intervals and then slowing to
be overtaken in turn. It was a long, tedious trip and entirely uneventful. An hour after their departure from JFK

they found themselves outside the gates of the Brooklyn Navy Yard.

To avoid creating a spectacle of unseemly proportion, Jumbo stayed behind with Peterson, parked outside the perimeter of the complex, while Dante and Dewey rolled up to and through the security checkpoint.

"Nice view of the city from over here," Klein commented as they drove toward the water's edge. "It's a well-kept secret, this place."

Dante shot him a glance. "How so?"

"All the high-ticket merchandise in some of these bonded buildings. A guy who knew what was here and who had a little skill with alarm systems might be able to really make out."

Dante nodded. "I've run into people who have no idea that Manhattan's an island. Live right in the middle of it, and have never seen the Hudson River."

"I believe it. Sometimes I wonder if it ain't lucky for us cops. Places like Palm Beach and Beverly Hills, everybody knows where the high-ticket goodies are."

The Close warehouse was the last building toward the perimeter fence to the south. Dante pulled up alongside it, and they climbed out. The big transport was just backing into position against the loading bay, where a team of Conway's people had gathered on the platform.

Serious progress had been made since Joe's last visit. The entire area directly behind the loading bay was cleared. George Conway stood slightly back from the platform activity, clipboard in hand. The tall, neatly dressed black man had his tie tucked into his shirt and his sleeves rolled up.

"Looks like you met your deadline," Dante observed.

"Eight o'clock last night, Sergeant. Half my men are dead on their feet."

Joe introduced Dewey and then leaned close to ask Conway if there was somewhere they could have a few words. The manager glanced at the back of the truck. It wasn't open yet.

"Something we can talk about quickly?" he asked. "Once that stuff starts coming out of there, I've got to be sure it gets placed in its designated area."

"Five minutes, tops," Dante promised.

Conway led him toward a narrow back aisle, out of hearing of his crew. Dewey didn't join them but pretended to be nosing around idly.

Joe asked the manager about his weekend schedule again and what sort of security they had. He told him that they were concerned, considering the break-in at the Close offices, that the thief might have been after something in the shipment from South America.

"Holy smoke!" Conway muttered. "Drugs?"

Joe shrugged noncommittally. "This is *strictly* confidential."

"Absolutely," the man assured him. "The complex has a full-time security staff, and we have an alarm system. We've never been broken into."

"So this place is locked up until Monday? As of when?"

"As early this afternoon as we can get this shipment squared away. We usually quit at four."

Dante absorbed this and casually changed the subject. "Did that guy in the sketch I gave you ever pay a visit?"

Conway didn't have to think about it long. "Sure did. Chopnik. Treasury, I think it was. Big son of a gun."

"What exactly was he after?"

George thought back. "It was a security issue. Some of the outfits with bonded warehouses are claiming theft losses. That means they don't pay duty on them. I told him I'd suspect employee pilferage. We're not bonded, though, so duty payments don't concern us. Not here."

Dewey Klein came strolling along an intersecting aisle as the two men were returning to the loading platform. Joe thanked Conway on the way out, telling him that with both the Feds and NYPD doing security checks out here, there probably wasn't a thing to worry about.

Clouds were already starting to gather as the two detectives descended from the loading platform and climbed back into their unmarked sedan.

"Chopnik was here, slinging some bullshit about stock losses in some of these bonded warehouses."

"Then he probably knows the layout as well as I do."

"And?"

"If he knows anything about alarm systems, then you can't go in the easy way. That's the one he'll take." He started the car and headed it toward the front gate. "They've got movement sensors in there. Electronic beam. They're connected to big bell boxes in the outside of the building. The bells are simple enough to neutralize, but the gimmick's a dead giveaway."

"How so?"

"You squirt them full of pressurized insulation foam. Available in aerosol cans from any hardware store. Wait thirty minutes until the foam sets up, and you can walk in like you own the place. Any old pro knows the trick. I'm sure you can see the problem."

Unfortunately Dante could. If he used that method to gain access, Chopnik would show up later, discover all the bell boxes chock full of foam, and know something was afoot.

"Any other way?"

"One." Klein had a twinkle in his eye. "I broke the window lock above the commode in the men's room. I can draw you a floor plan pinpointing every beam I could spot. No guarantee I got them all, but I think I did. Once you get inside, you crawl on your belly, under the beams . . ."

TWENTY SIX

After Klein had drawn them a floor plan and before returning inside the perimeter to take up their vigil, Dante and Jumbo made a trip to a hardware store. They purchased a utility knife with plenty of sharp blades, a little flashlight with extra batteries, duct tape, and a garment seam ripper. While Jumbo drove them back through the security check at the main gate and on down toward the water of the East River, Joe got busy taping his voice-activated Dictaphone, grabbed almost as a second thought from his desk drawer, to one of two hand-held portable radios. He had no idea what he might encounter once inside the place, but he wanted Jumbo to be able to get any startling discoveries on tape.

Jumbo parked the Plymouth out of sight behind a row of empty trailers, about a hundred yards from the activity on the Close Apparel loading dock. They still had a few hours before Conway's projected quitting time rolled around. Dante went to a pay phone three buildings away and called Janet. After explaining his situation, he returned to the car, climbed into the backseat, and tried for a little sleep.

The rain that had been threatening since morning broke

a little after three. The days were starting to get longer, but now a heavy gray sky was bringing nightfall early. It was nearly dark by four-thirty, when the lights of the big transport on the dock came alive and diesel smoke belched from its twin stacks. Jumbo reached around to shake his partner.

"Joey. Looks like they're packin' it in."

Dante came slowly upright, the heels of his hands digging at his eyes as he tried to focus. "God. I feel like a sack of shit. Did I go out for long?"

"About two and a half hours."

Dante pushed the back door open and stepped out to pee. The rain was coming down hard, and he had to make it quick. As soon as he climbed into the front seat, the windows of the car started to steam up. Jumbo turned the ignition key to the accessory position and flipped on the defroster.

"He's comin' tonight," he growled. "I've gotten so's I can feel this shit."

Joe glanced over at him, feeling a lot more alert now. He'd picked up the thermos off the floor, and was pouring himself a cup of coffee.

"You, too, huh?"

"Yep. He tried to snuff you last night and fucked it up. Now it's time for him to cut and run. The fire under him is just too hot now." As he spoke, Jumbo reached up with his handkerchief and wiped a little space clear on the windshield so he could peer out. The defroster wasn't doing much, with the engine not running. "You done some thinkin' about what you'll do if he shows up while you're still in there?"

Joe sipped from his Styrofoam cup, set it on the open glove-box door, and tore open a bag of corn chips.

"I'm a big boy, Beasley. If he shows up, you just let me know over the radio, and there won't be any trouble. We've gotten too close not to catch him with his fingers in the pie. I don't intend to get in the way before he puts his whole hand into it."

Outside the warehouse Conway's crew straggled down from the loading dock and climbed into their cars to drive off. The big rig gave a lurch as the driver released its air brakes and started easing it away. Ten minutes after the truck had left, they watched the manager and his administrative assistant lock up and race to their adjacent cars under a single umbrella. In another minute both had left. Dante figured the time was ripe for a little breaking and entering. He was going to try to avoid falling headfirst into the men's room toilet in the process.

"You all set out here?"

Jumbo held up his taped-over radio-recorder contraption, depressed the transmit button to check the batteries, and gave him the thumbs-up. "Check with me as soon as you get inside. We don't want that redneck asshole throwin' no parties you don't know you're invited to."

"Wish me luck."

"Ain't a matter of luck no more, dude. We've got him where we want him."

The window Dewey had broken the lock on was impossibly narrow, and to make matters worse, there was a movement sensor in front of the door of the toilet stall. Joe nearly killed himself wedging through the window to where he could grab the stall edge to steady himself. Then he pulled the rest of his torso and hips through, locked the door so that it wouldn't swing out to trigger the beam, and scrunched down on the filthy tile floor to wriggle out snake-style.

"I'm in," he told Jumbo from just inside the main restroom door. "You copy?"

"Just jim-dandy. Keep me updated as you go."

Dewey's floor plan indicated another beam aimed directly across the rest room entrance. Dante had a tricky time wedging the door open with one foot while he belly-crawled clear. From there he took a moment to get his bearings and then set off for the far end of the place. His progress was painstakingly slow. Over some distances he was able to walk normally, but too often he was reduced to slithering. By the time he reached the area consigned to the new Barranquilla shipment, a perfectly decent pair of blue jeans and an olive drab M-65 field jacket were ready for the rag bag.

"I'm on top of it," he told Jumbo. "How's it looking out there?"

"Wet."

According to the floor plan, this was a relatively safe area. Dante wedged his minitorch up high between a couple of cartons and set to work. The box he dragged down off a stack was about two by three feet in top dimension and maybe eighteen inches in height. It had already been opened once and then resealed with Customs tape. Dante slit this tape and pulled back the flaps. The box was full of skirts in a gaily colored pastel print. The fabric felt like a cotton, with maybe a little bit of a polyester blend.

Joe began to methodically remove one garment after another. He employed the seam ripper to tear out the waistbands, hems, and linings made of a slinky white synthetic. In his haste he showed little regard for the possibility of repair. This stuff was going to wind up being a write-off. There were four dozen garments in that first box, and he destroyed them all. In the end he was left with a pile of scraps and an empty box. He flipped the box over, examined it for concealed double-wall construction, and struck out again. With the bottom tape slit, the thing started to collapse on itself. He was prepared to toss it aside and go on to the next, when he noticed something that had escaped him in Customs.

The cartons in the shipment came in two different sizes. Aside from those stacked in the area he was now working in, there were a lot more, in a slightly larger size, stacked in the area directly behind him. His pulse quickened as he rapidly checked over the floor plan for sensors and then made one complete circuit of the entire load. Of the thirty-five hundred cartons in the shipment, only two hundred or so were constructed in the dimensions of the empty skirt box. The rest were cubic in shape, roughly two and a half feet to a side.

Two hundred out of thirty-five hundred, all marked with the same designation codes and stacked in the same spot. Those old bells were starting to clang in the back of his brain.

The radio unit on his belt crackled. "How's it going in there?" Jumbo wanted to know.

"Just hang onto your hat. How's it look out there?"

"If it starts coming down much harder, I'm breakin' out the oars."

"Well, don't float away. I just might be onto something."

Joe clicked off and stood examining that stack of two hundred cartons, his hands on his hips and his brain racing at full throttle. After a moment he crouched on his heels and picked up the empty collapsed carton once again. The cardboard construction was fairly heavy-duty. Corrugated and perhaps three-sixteenths of an inch in thickness. It looked innocent enough from the outside.

With his utility knife he drew a slow, careful "X" in the face of one panel. He used the tip of the blade to pry up the heavy paper in the middle of his incision. The paper came away to reveal the usual *S*-system of corrugation beneath and nothing at all out of the ordinary. Undaunted, he tried the same thing with one of the two smaller panels.

"Bingo," he muttered to himself. "You clever bastards."

With painstaking care, he peeled back all four of the triangular flaps created by his incision. From the look of it, this wasn't money they were dealing with, but some sort of certificate. Not money in the take-it-to-the-supermarket sense, at any rate. These things were maybe eight by ten inches in dimension. He reached up for his flashlight and brought it down for a closer look.

"United States Treasury" was emblazoned across the top of each certificate in bold, elaborate script. There were eagles rampant and furled flags embellished with arrows and the usual Latin mottoes. U.S. Government Treasury bonds, payable to bearer in the amount of twenty thousand dollars each. In the stack he held in his hand, Dante discovered the serial numbers were different and sequential. He was ready to bet *real* money that the numbers were all authentic, culled from current circulation files by a certain crooked T-man.

Hurriedly now he flipped the carton over and performed similar surgery on the opposite end. Same results. Four hundred and eighty big to a box. Times two hundred . . . it boggled the mind. The recovered certificates went into his jacket's big side pockets, and he went quickly to work, cleaning up the mess he'd made.

"On my way out," he told Jumbo over the two-way.

"What'd you find in there? Anything?"

"Sort of a disappointment, big guy. Just a hundred million in Treasury bearer bonds."

"The fuck you say?"

"You heard me. Probably printed on security paper stolen from a certain Treasury armored-car heist. They look real as hell to me. I'll bring you one for your bathroom wall."

The detective dragged the pile of torn fabric along with him to a spot where he could stuff it all behind a stack of unrelated goods. The cut-up carton was disposed of by wedging it deep into a stack of cartons in the middle of the warehouse. Getting out the bathroom window was at least as much fun as it had been getting in. This time, at least, he could launch himself off the toilet.

"This is unreal, Joey." There was awe in Jumbo's voice as he fingered the two dozen bonds in his hands.

"It all adds up," Dante muttered as he sipped another cup of coffee. His clothes were in the condition of a Bowery bum's, but all vestiges of sleepiness were gone. He was keyed up, the way he always got when an investigation jelled. "Two murders and the attempted killing of a cop.

This fucker is playing for all the marbles in this one load. Once this goes down, he knows there's no turning back.''

"A hundred million bucks has gotta be plenty, don't you think?"

Dante sighed. "He wouldn't get that, but even at ten cents on the dollar, it's still a fortune. Lots of people would think ten million bucks are worth a few murders."

All around them the rain was still coming down in buckets. The complex itself was dead, with only an occasional security cart happening past. They were settling in for what could end up being a very long night. Even considering the restless nature of his nap on the car seat, Dante was grateful for having slept. It was early, barely seven o'clock, and there were still a dozen hours until daybreak.

Jumbo had just broken out the deli sandwiches they'd saved for dinner when headlights bit the darkness from down the way. They came from the direction of the main gate, moving slowly. Both men slumped quickly in the front seat on the off-chance that the driver might spot the Reliant in this downpour. Their eyes were just far enough above the dash to enable them to watch the car proceed. It pulled in next to the Close warehouse, hugged the side of the building, and came to a stop directly beneath the first alarm bell box. Jumbo lifted field glasses and peered through them into the swirling murk.

"Just got out and opened the trunk. Hard to tell if it's our T-man. Dude's got the hood up on his parka. Big enough, though." He leaned a bit farther forward as Dante wiped condensation from the windshield with a paper napkin.

"Pulling a stepladder out and setting it up on the roof of his car. Hot damn! He's goin' for that box just like Klein said he would."

"You see a can of foam?"

"Kinda hard to tell in this light. He just pulled something out of his pocket. Jesus, he's workin' like there's a fire under his fuckin' fanny."

Dante grunted. "You bet there is. I think it's time we

called in some backup. It'll take him at least a couple of hours to retrieve all that paper. There's a pay phone three buildings down. I'm not going to risk the radio. That maniac probably has a scanner. I'll sneak down and call Gus.''

Before leaving the car, Dante popped the cover off the dome light and removed the bulb. It was coming down like hell outside. He unzipped the hood from the collar of his jacket and pulled it up. Then he jumped out and made a mad dash through shadow and water to the warehouse down the way. Two phones were mounted side by side there. He dropped a quarter and punched in Lieberman's home number.

Lydia picked up and reported that his boss was in the shower. He told her to get him out, pronto. Gus came on the line less than three minutes later, and his team leader got right to the point.

''You always wanted to be C of D, right, boss?''

''Don't tell me you two hit pay dirt out there. Already?''

''How's ninety-six million in counterfeit Treasury bonds hit you? Subtract from that the four hundred and eighty thou I've already taken out of there.''

The silence of the deputy chief's pause was louder than the pounding of the rain.

''Sweet Jesus.''

''Jumbo's watching our boy break in to retrieve it as we speak,'' Joe added. ''He's running around neutralizing all the alarm-bell boxes. We're gonna need some backup to spring this trap, but I don't want the cavalry charging in here with bugles blaring. We need maybe half a dozen guys from our Task Force. Rain or no rain, they've gotta come in here on foot.''

''It's your ball game,'' Lieberman assured him. ''Where do we meet up?''

''Behind our car. You go in straight down from the main gate, to the road at the edge of the water. Go left, and you'll spot a string of a dozen semitrailers all parked in a row. We're parked between the first and second.''

"I'll need an hour."

Dante peered at his watch. "No sweat. Chopnik needs thirty minutes for the insulating foam he's using to neutralize the bell boxes. Then he'll have to be in there at least another hour to retrieve his goodies. I've got seven-oh-two. See you at eight.''

Lieberman assured him that he would, and Dante cradled it. Chopnik's car was out of sight when he returned, soaking, to the passenger seat of the K-car.

"You can just see the nose of it over there." Jumbo pointed, handing over the glasses. "Just pulled up from around back.''

Through sheets of rain, Dante could make out the front end of Chopnik's Olds Cutlass. "That means he's done them all, then.''

"I'd guess. So what's the word from the chief?''

"On his way. He thinks he'll need an hour to assemble the right elements and get them down here. That should work out just right.''

They sat back to wait out the foam and Murray Chopnik's next move. The rain showed no sign of letting up. The T-man gave it a full forty minutes before leaving his car and making a dash for the front door of the warehouse up on the loading platform. He glanced quickly back and forth before slipping something into the door knob, turning it, and stepping inside. There were no alarm bells.

Jumbo lowered the binoculars. "Too quick for him to have picked that mother. Figures the son of a bitch'd have a fuckin' key.''

"Just like the break-in on 39th and Broadway," Dante reminded him. "Clean, trouble-free access.''

"How long you wanna let him have in there?''

Joe checked the time. Gus wasn't due with reinforcements for another fifteen minutes. "I don't see why we can't hit him as soon as they get here. He won't have had time to recover everything, but red-handed is red-handed, right?''

''Whoa!'' Jumbo slouched quickly in the seat, and Dante was fast to follow. Both of them watched from cover as headlights swung around the corner from down toward the gate and headed in their direction.

''Too early for Gus,'' Joe murmured. ''And I made sure he'd come on foot.''

They watched as the car eased around into shadow opposite Chopnik's Cutlass. It was one of those big Volvo sedans. Two figures emerged, huddled under an umbrella, and hurried up the loading-platform steps.

TWENTY SEVEN

Jumbo was peering hard through the binoculars now.

"A man and a woman. Dude's wearin' a hat and a trench coat." He paused and then added, "Holy shit!"

"What, for Christ's sake?"

"It looks like the fuckin' Close broad!" Jumbo handed the glasses to Dante.

Dante was beside himself as he aimed them, his fingers easing the focus knob around until he had the pair of figures as sharp as he could get them. The woman handed the guy something out of her purse. When he took it and turned to insert it into the knob of the door, Joe could see his other hand.

"Fucker's got a gun," he hissed. "If he kills Chopnik, our entire investigation goes down the shit chute."

"But what the fuck is *she* doing here?"

Dante returned the binoculars to his partner, flipped up the hood, and tugged at the zipper of his jacket.

"I think we just found our inside man . . . only it's a woman. Christ, I'm dumb. Who was the one who *paid* for Brill's trips to Colombia?"

"What're you doing?" Jumbo demanded. "Gus is gonna be here in another five minutes."

Dante shook his head. "Those three might all be best friends, but if she just showed up with reinforcements, we might not have five minutes. I'm going back in there."

Murray Chopnik was soaking wet. It was a miserable night he'd just been mucking around in, but right now he was feeling as cozy as a napping cat. From here on, it was a cakewalk. The man on Staten Island had an Oriental consortium lined up for the goods. They were willing to pay twenty-five cents on the dollar, an excellent price that translated into twenty-four million, free and clear. A fucking fortune. His piece of it was going to make forced retirement a cozy proposition.

The money Roger had paid that Colombian shipping manager, and the corrugated-cardboard manufacturer hadn't been wasted. It was coming back in spades. Murray's American Tourister bag, lying open at his feet, already had some of the return on investment piled inside it. That poor bastard had done some gorgeous work. Printed on the real thing, it was impossible to detect that these items were forgeries.

His knife bit into the heavy brown paper covering the next neat little stash. He drew it across the surface lovingly, taking care to avoid cutting too deep. Another stack of two hundred and forty big was removed and dropped onto the growing pile in the case. He was just spinning the carton around when he heard footsteps approach. His hand went to his jacket pocket, where he gripped the butt of his Colt "Lightweight Commander," as Wes Wainwright appeared. With a smile, Murray relaxed and eased his hand back out of his pocket. Then he saw the gun in Wainwright's hand. A big, ugly Bren Ten Special.

"Getting paranoid in your old age, Wesley?" He lifted his carton knife to slit open the next panel.

"Not at all, Murray. I'm feeling better than ever, in fact."

Felicity stepped out into the open. "Hello, Murray."

Chopnik stopped in midstroke.

"What the fuck is *she* doing here?"

There was a hint of amusement in the boss T-man's eyes. "She's part of a new strategy."

Chopnik's attention focused completely on the muzzle of that big 10mm pistol. "Which new strategy is that, Wes?" he asked in a calm tone.

"Resulting from a reassessment of our collaboration and mutual goals. Your old strategy rewarded Ms. Close for services rendered by cutting her out. Unfortunately, you revealed my involvement to Mr. Brill. You explained to him why the take had to be split to compensate your boss for looking the other way. Mr. Brill mentioned that reference to Ms. Close, and she filed it away for a, er . . . rainy day. I presume you noticed how nasty the weather is."

Chopnik shifted from one foot to the other. When he spoke, his anger forced the Texas out heavily in his voice. "We been through some tough times together, Wes boy. You turnin' all that against me now, just 'cause some cunt comes to you with a sweeter deal? Fuck her. I can cut you just as good a deal as she can."

Wainwright shook his head sadly. "There's one significant difference, Murray. It lies in what I like to view as the balance of power."

"You're talkin' shit now, Wesley."

Felicity spoke for the first time. "No, he's not. He's being a realist. You see, Murray, you were going to give him forty percent of twenty-four million and disappear. Forever afterward, you'd be sitting somewhere where the law couldn't touch you, holding all the aces. If you wanted to put the touch on Wesley here, he'd be powerless to stop you."

Chopnik's eyes narrowed. "You gonna *buy* this line of bullshit?"

Wes nodded. "I already have. You see, in the new balance of power, I stay where I am at Treasury, and Felicity here stays where she is as the chairman of a fashion empire. We split fifty-fifty, and each holds the other in check.

We live happily ever after, with a little something to feather our nests in old age.''

''And how're you figurin' to explain killin' me? I was just here doin' my job, tryin' to get the drop on a couple of murderin' criminal counterfeiters.''

Wainwright glanced at Felicity and chuckled now. ''No sweat, my friend. You see, we aren't as greedy as you. We won't take the whole load out of here. We'll shoot you and leave half. Then *I* was here, just doing *my* job, trying to get the drop, as you so eloquently put it, on a murdering criminal counterfeiter.''

''Your mother was a nigger whore, Wesley!''

The smile on Wainwright's face tightened. He lifted the big Bren Ten and eased back the hammer. When the metal of another weapon tickled the hairline at the base of his skull, he froze.

''You pull that trigger, and I'm afraid I'll have to blow your brains all over the nice lady's shipment of sports-wear,'' a voice growled in his ear. ''Start bringing it back down. Real slowly.''

As the agent-in-charge started to comply, Chopnik let out a belly laugh.

''Smooth, Wesley. Who else did you lead here? The fuckin' Ringling brothers?''

Dante stepped into view from behind a pile of cartons.

''He didn't lead me here, asshole. You did. You left a wide trail of shit.'' While he spoke, Dante watched both agents like a hawk. Wainwright's weapon was down at his side now; Chopnik had to be carrying. ''I want to see one hand on top of your head, asshole. The other one digs out your shooting iron with just the thumb and index finger. I see even one other finger getting into the act, I'll shoot that hand, and we can try it with the other.''

It was going just as Joe dictated when Felicity suddenly dropped her purse and took one quick step back, a little .32 caliber Smith & Wesson revolver clutched in two out-stretched, trembling hands. It was trained roughly at Dante's chest.

"Drop it, Detective."

Dante had a sure shot at blowing Wainwright's head off and a pretty good shot at hitting either Felicity or Chopnik. The big agent had his own weapon half out of his jacket, his thumb and index finger gripping it as directed. Felicity, in her obviously agitated state, didn't look like a sure bet to hit anything, but to challenge her would be one hell of a risk.

"I *mean* it!" she shrilled.

"I'm sure," he said calmly. Inside, he was anything but calm. The strange light of Chopnik's big battery lantern made the shadows of her unsteady movement huge. Any other sudden move would be similarly magnified. And lighter caliber or not, a .32 had more than enough firepower to kill a man at this tight range. Dante had been focusing on Chopnik; now he moved his eyes to check on the woman.

Chopnik saw the cop's eyes leave him. His fingers closed around the butt of his "Lightweight Commander." He raised it and aimed with the fluidity of experience. The shot he got off caught Felicity a little too high up in the middle of her chest.

Dante saw the beginning of the big man's move out of the corner of his eye and shoved Wainwright hard in his direction. As Felicity was hit, her own gun went off in spasmodic reflex. Joe was well into a shoulder roll for cover when he felt something tear through his jacket and slice his left side like a burning hot poker. Wainwright, stumbling in Murray's direction, provided just the desired diversion. The detective came out of his roll in a sitting position, the weight of the Walther automatic ever so familiar in his hands.

Chopnik wanted desperately to clear his field of fire. Wainwright came straight into him, arms outstretched, attempting to encircle him. Murray fired once, and saw his shot hit Wes in his flailing right arm. As the agent-in-charge screamed and started to his knees, Murray caught him by the collar of his coat and went to the floor with

him, using him as a shield. When he saw that Dante still
had an angle on him, he wedged his own weapon up under
Wainwright's jaw.

"Shoot me, you fuck, and his head comes off!"

The pain in Joe's side was intense. He had no idea how
bad the wound might be, but he could feel the expanding
warmth of blood soaking his shirt.

"Why should I care, Murray?"

Chopnik could see the tiny black orifice of the Walther's
business end staring him in the face. It was a deadly, chal-
lenging eye. The tone in the wop detective's voice told him
that he really *didn't* care. It was everything or nothing,
right here and now.

Dante saw the weapon at Wainwright's chin start to
move as Chopnik let out a bellow like a charging bull
elephant and jerked the fear-frozen body of his boss to
one side. As soon as the rogue agent's thorax was exposed
and his weapon started coming up with frightening quick-
ness, Joe pumped three shots into him.

Wainwright writhed on the floor in agony while Dante
tied a tourniquet around his right arm above the shattered elbow. Jumbo, Gus, and six other Task Force detectives came pouring into the place. The two lead men
pulled up short, relief on their faces. They holstered their
guns and proceeded at a more subdued pace to view the
scene.

"Dead," Joe told Jumbo as he approached Chopnik's
crumpled corpse.

"Her, too?" Gus asked. He pointed at Felicity, who
lay facedown in a pool of blood.

"Afraid so. And our boss T-man here won't ever play
with himself right-handed again. This elbow's in little
pieces."

Wainwright's face was ashen as he looked up through
the shock-haze of his pain. "Frame," he gasped. "A
fucking frame."

Dante finished the job of tying off Wainwright's arm and

rocked back on his heels to stand. As he did so, the pain in his own side made him wince.

Gus stepped forward quickly. "Jesus, man! You're hit!"

Dante recovered, forced a smile, and shook his head. "I think I'm the lucky one in this crowd."

Paramedics showed up ten minutes later. They stripped the detective out of his jacket and went to work cleaning him up so they could get a better look at the damage.

A skinny, fuzzy-faced kid with longish red hair scrutinized the wound. Then he inverted a bottle of Betadine onto a big ball of cotton and swabbed at it. Dante winced with a quick intake of breath.

"The bullet was deflected by a rib. It's gonna sting like a slow-burning fire for at least a week," the kid told him. "You're gonna have to take it easy."

Dante glanced up at Gus and Jumbo, who were hovering over him.

"Think of it. A couple weeks medical. There *is* a pot of gold at the end of the rainbow."

Jumbo growled, sweeping a hand at the carnage around them.

"You call this a rainbow?"

As Dante pulled his filthy jacket over his shoulders for warmth against the damp chill, Wainwright was lifted onto a stretcher. The painkillers must have been taking effect. His boss-Fed arrogance was coming back at full volume.

"You bastards don't have a fucking thing on me! I came here to arrest one of my agents! Treasury business! That jackass of *yours* busted in here and blew the whole setup!"

Dante turned a questioning look on Jumbo.

"You bet your butt," the big guy assured him. He reached into his jacket to produce Dante's mini-cassette rig taped to his portable radio. "I listened to a little of it. It'll be music to the federal attorney's ears."

The redhead paramedic approached. "You fellas mind

taking this party to Bellevue Emergency? We're getting set to roll.''

"Think you could drop me at Saint Vincent's?'' Dante asked. ''It's just a couple blocks from home.''

The kid looked at Jumbo. ''Do me a favor. Make sure he doesn't *walk*.''

TWENTY EIGHT

By the time Jumbo eased to the curb in front of Dante's building on Perry Street, it was one o'clock. Gus had been called away after the trip to the emergency room. Treasury was flying some big shot up from Washington, and Mintoff wanted his own big shots to wrestle through the red tape with him.

"I've got one nearly full bottle of Black Bush in there," Joe told his buddy. "I'm aiming to put a pretty good dent in it. Wanna help?"

The big man smiled, shook his head, and patted his belly. "You realize the *calories* in that shit? The diet's *workin'*, dude. I'll take you up on it when I hit two fifty." He punched Dante lightly on the shoulder. "We'll celebrate."

Joe nodded. "Yeah, big guy. We will. I'm proud of you."

"Glad you're okay, dude. From what I could hear, it got close in there."

"Too close."

As Jumbo pulled the Plymouth away from the curb, Dante crossed the sidewalk and pushed open the low iron gate. He might be dog tired, but he knew he'd never be able to sleep after what he'd just been through. He was still thanking his lucky stars that he'd switched his portable radio to transmit and put it on top of a pile of cartons before leaping into the breach. The stuff it picked up was enough to cook Wainwright's ass in Federal stir for the rest of his life.

Inside the exterior lobby door he paused to check his mail. First of the month, and everything was bills. Life went on. The interior of his apartment was quiet, and Copter didn't even come running. The action he'd found in the bed had to be better than the prospect of greeting his beat-up patron. Joe let his mind wander over his memory of the previous night's pleasures and decided that the cat was probably right.

The raincoat he'd borrowed out of the trunk of a squad car went over the back of a dining chair. Then he crossed to the liquor cabinet and broke the seal on that bottle of Irish. The first pour, something close to a double, went down in one gulp. It soothed the inside of his throat with a thick, welcome warmth. He poured himself another, kicked off his shoes, and gingerly stripped out of his shirt and pants. The wound had taken twenty three stitches to close and still burned like hell fire.

Janet was reading in bed when he entered the room, naked and with one side heavily bandaged.

"Oh, God!" she gasped. "You're hurt!"

"Not for long," he replied, holding up his glass of whisky. "Care to join me?"

"Joe. What happened?"

He related the bulk of that night's events as quickly as he could without leaving anything out. "I killed them both," he finished. I guess I'm still riding the rough edge of that."

She had drawn up her knees and hugged them as he told it. Now, she lifted her head and nodded at his drink. "I think maybe I *will* have one of those."

When he returned with it, he sat close to her on the

edge of the bed. She took the glass and sipped a little from the healthy belt he'd poured her.

"Felicity's the part I'm having a lot of trouble with," she said softly.

Dante nodded. "She was the insider. She sent Chopnik in there that night, knowing Jerry and your brother were there."

She nodded. "I talked to my attorney today. He says that the way Jerry had Janet Lake Casuals set up, it was a wholly independent subsidiary, half owned by Jerry, with Peter and me as the other equal partners."

"And when Felicity discovered that Jerry owned the most profitable part of their enterprise . . . owned it *outright* . . . she wrote his death warrant."

"And then the bitch sent flowers to my brother's funeral."

When she downed her whiskey, Dante poured her another and one more for himself before pulling back the blanket to crawl in next to her. It hurt to move, so he moved slowly.

The next morning, he awoke to the smells of coffee brewing and bacon frying. The previous afternoon and evening's events raced through his mind as he fought the fuzziness of sleep from his head and swung his legs over the side of the bed. A sharp pain in his left side reminded him of the final outcome: Team Finest, ninety-six million, Scumbags, zero.

When he poked his head into the kitchen, he found Janet working a batch of home fries around the inside of a skillet.

"Morning, sunshine," she greeted. "How do you like your eggs?"

He got her to pause a moment and tape a piece of plastic wrap over his dressing. Then he showered. To celebrate his first day of medical leave, he decided to dispense with shaving. It was something that wouldn't sit well with his female admirers, but downtime was downtime. It had to be approached with ritual reverence. After he emerged from his ablutions, Janet sat him down to a breakfast of gargantuan proportions. Good thing, too. He was ravenous.

"I have to be in Los Angeles Monday morning," she announced over their second cup of coffee. "It's one of those television-movie-of-the-week things. They tell me they can shoot all my scenes in four days. I might have a commercial lined up for the day after that."

"And you're planning to spend the rest of the month out there, working on your tan, right?" He forced a smile. "I guess it was fun while it lasted, huh?"

She reached across the table to hold his hand.

"If you're speaking in the past tense, buster, think again. I'm not letting go of it that easily."

Her vehemence surprised him. He sighed and shook his head. "Do you think I could actually be a part of that world? *Your* world?"

She laughed. "*That* world and *my* world are two completely different things. My world is what I make it. So is yours. And mine isn't all hype and glitter, so cancel your subscriptions to *People* and *Vanity Fair*."

The coffee in his cup was gone. He reached for the pot and poured them both more.

"I'm sorry you've got to leave right now. I was enjoying myself too much, I guess."

"It's just for a week, Joe. You told me that you've got twice that much time in medical leave coming. So come with me."

"To L.A.?"

"Why not? I'm booked into the Beverly Wilshire. While I'm on the set, you can lounge around the pool. You might even be able to catch up on all the sleep you've missed the past couple of nights."

When she got rolling, she had the tenacity and enthusiasm of a terrier fighting for an old shoe. It was something he liked about her. Liked an awful lot. Just as he was starting to open his mouth to answer this full-frontal assault, the doorbell rang.

"Stay where you are, gimp. I'll get it." She tossed her napkin onto the table and rose to see who it was.

Dante's ex looked just the way he'd described her. She was a tall, raven-haired beauty with fabulous facial bones and hot, flashing brown eyes. Those eyes couldn't disguise her surprise at encountering Janet Lake on the other side of the detective's threshold.

"I'm sorry. I should have called ahead."

"It's okay," Janet assured her. "Please come in."

Dante recognized Rosa's voice. A moment later she appeared around the corner of the dining alcove. He started up out of his chair.

"Don't get up, Joe. I'm sorry I barged in on you like this."

He lowered himself gingerly. "Not a problem. Rosa Losada, Janet Lake."

The two women nodded slightly to each other. Rosa clutched her handbag against her waist and looked uneasy as all hell.

"I've been fielding media questions about the Navy Yard all night and morning. Gus said you were all right, but I thought I'd stop by and check."

"Thanks," he said sincerely. "I'm fine. Really."

"You probably haven't heard yet. Wes Wainwright grabbed a guard's gun while they were wheeling him into surgery. He put it in his mouth and blew his brains out. It happened too fast for anyone to stop him." Abruptly she turned and extended her hand to Janet. "I should go. It's nice meeting you. Joe, I'm glad you're all right."

A moment later Dante was alone with Janet again.

"It hurts more than you let on," she observed.

He forced a wan smile. "A lot of things do. I'm a tough guy, remember?"

About the Author

CHRISTOPHER NEWMAN lives in New York City. He is also the author of MIDTOWN SOUTH, SIXTH PRECINCT and MAÑANA MAN.

Also by Christopher Newman...

MANANA MAN

When Henry Bueno's old CIA friend gets knocked off by a mob hitman, Bueno goes in search of the killer. The search leads him right into an elaborate scheme masterminded by Diego Cardona—former major in the Nicaraguan secret police and buddy to a few American espionage hotshots—involving stolen guidance missile systems, political assassination and six divisions of the U.S. Marines. But the plan does not include Bueno, whose personal vendetta draws him into the devious intrigue, from South America to Silicon Valley and from Washington, D.C. to the Nicaraguan coast.